PENGUIN BOOKS

Killzone: *Ascendancy*

Killzone
Ascendancy

SAM BRADBURY

PENGUIN BOOKS

PENGUIN BOOKS

Published by the Penguin Group
Penguin Books Ltd, 80 Strand, London WC2R ORL, England
Penguin Group (USA) Inc., 375 Hudson Street, New York, New York 10014, USA
Penguin Group (Canada), 90 Eglinton Avenue East, Suite 700, Toronto, Ontario, Canada M4P 2Y3
(a division of Pearson Penguin Canada Inc.)
Penguin Ireland, 25 St Stephen's Green, Dublin 2, Ireland (a division of Penguin Books Ltd)
Penguin Group (Australia), 250 Camberwell Road,
Camberwell, Victoria 3124, Australia (a division of Pearson Australia Group Pty Ltd)
Penguin Books India Pvt Ltd, 11 Community Centre,
Panchsheel Park, New Delhi – 110 017, India
Penguin Group (NZ), 67 Apollo Drive, Rosedale, Auckland 0632, New Zealand
(a division of Pearson New Zealand Ltd)
Penguin Books (South Africa) (Pty) Ltd, 24 Sturdee Avenue,
Rosebank, Johannesburg 2196, South Africa

Penguin Books Ltd, Registered Offices: 80 Strand, London WC2R ORL, England

www.penguin.com

First published 2011
3

Typeset by Penguin Books Ltd
Printed in Great Britain by Clays Ltd, St Ives plc

A CIP catalogue record for this book is available from the British Library

ISBN: 978-0-241-95431-7

www.greenpenguin.co.uk

Killzone
Ascendancy

Prologue

It's early morning when I get the call from Bandit Recon and because I'm napping I think for a second that a bug has crawled in my ear, before I remember I'm on comms duty – me and Kowalski. I sit up on the bedroll, already shivering in the jungle's morning chill. Reach to adjust my headset.

'Base?' he says.

'Go ahead,' I reply, voice rough with sleep. *And just where in the hell is Kowalski?*

'Base, this is Bandit Two.'

It's Gedge and he's whispering. I picture him lying in the damp light camouflaged by undergrowth, looking down the sights of his sniper rifle. Barely twenty-four, he's a short, wiry kid. Grins easily, eager as a puppy, hasn't let himself get demoralized like others have. I think I can tell by his voice what he sees in his crosshairs. More than anything I want to be wrong.

I'm not: 'I have a visual on an enemy drone,' he says.

Shit.

'Is it moving towards the uplink?'

'Negative, sir, it's moving towards your position.'

Shit.

'Copy that, Bandit Two,' I reply, my voice low as I get to my feet, snatch up my M82 and cross the clearing to the comms room, stepping over sleeping grunts as I go. Around me are the sights and sounds of the jungle: the whisper of trees in the canopy and the rustle of the monstrous carnivorous sawtooth plants, the never-ending chirrup of insects and scuttle of petrusite spiders in the undergrowth. A light blanket of scarlet mist skirts the camp, bubbling luminously; clouds of fireflies dance among dangling plant fronds.

I brush through the tarp opening and into the comms room, silent apart from the hum of processors and the soft snoring of Kowalski sprawled asleep in a chair, his face bathed in the blue light of the DMS screens. His is the only seat so I park my butt on a stack of upturned ammo crates to check our perimeter readings. Clear.

But for how long?

'Status?' I ask Bandit Two.

'This thing's in sweep mode, Base,' whispers Gedge. His voice is so low now he sounds strangulated.

'Copy that,' I say. My fingers dance on another

console. I glance to check for air traffic and the screen's clear but the Higs use cloaking anyway – only the infantry show up. I check that the trip switches are intact. Now I turn my attention to the screen showing Bandit Two's position, five klicks due east, halfway between us and the uplink. His blip on the screen winks patiently and at least I'm able to confirm that his drone doesn't have back-up. The drone itself, though – cloaked.

'This ain't like any usual drone,' Gedge whispers in my ear. 'Must be a new model.'

'Speed?'

'It's still scanning right now. Wait, it's moved. Stopped. Now it's scanning again. Okay, moving. It's moving due west of my position, Base. I don't like this.'

Neither do I, kid, I think.

There's a pause.

'Permission to engage,' he says, and I catch my breath because what Gedge wants is permission to die. If he takes down the drone, they'll bomb its last known location within seconds, figuring that the drone's either found the camp or been disabled by a recon team, and that either way they bag themselves some ISA. When the smoke's cleared, they'll send infrared probes to determine a body count. Then they'll send more drones.

5

I kick Kowalski awake. 'Get Captain Narville online now.'

Moments after he's scrambled away there's a click in my headset and I toggle to Narville.

'What is it, Sev?' He's just woken up. He sounds even more exhausted than usual.

'Bandit Two has visual on a drone, sir. Wants permission to engage.'

'Christ. We need to begin immediate evac.'

'Copy that, sir, but priority is the drone. I say we let Gedge take it out while it's still outside our position.'

'Then Gedge will die,' he says, like I hadn't thought of that.

'We all die if it locates us, sir.'

'It might not.'

Narville's right. The drone might not find us. By some miracle it might sail on by. By some miracle we might be excluded from its hunt radius or outside its range.

But failing those miracles it finds us, and if it does that we're dead. The Higs will bomb and strafe the area and everything in the killzone dies. And we're shit out of miracles in the jungle.

'It's too much of a gamble, Captain,' I say. 'We need to immobilize that drone – as a matter of urgency.'

'Negative.'

'With respect, sir . . .'

'I'm not sacrificing a man, Sev.'

'The risk is too great otherwise, sir. You'll be sacrificing us all. You want that to be on you?'

There's a long pause.

'Wait,' he says, 'just . . . wait.' The pain of doubt is in his voice.

I toggle back to Gedge. 'Bandit Two, this is Base. Hold your fire.'

'Say again, Base?'

'You heard, Gedge. Order is to hold your fire.'

'Sir, the drone has now moved approximately a quarter of a klick due west. You'll have company if I don't engage soon . . .'

'I understand, Bandit Two, but those are your orders.'

'Sir, permission to track the drone?'

'Do that, Bandit Two, but stay out of sensor range.'

'Copy that.'

I stand, go to the tarp and look through to the other side of the camp, where Narville appears from within a metal lean-to. Like everyone else he sports an outgrown crop and a beard. He's pulling on a tactical vest, walking to the centre of the clearing where a bunch of grunts are huddled on bedrolls, either still sleeping or just waking up, shivering and wearily preparing for another day of survival. They're extra cold because sick soldiers get the sleeping bags, and of the twenty-seven men we have in camp eleven of them are in the sick bay suffering with fever, lung burn or combat wounds. We've got two medics left: Doc Hanley, who has a lazy eye and a tattoo of a red cross on his upper arm, and a junior MO we call Junior. Both of them appear now, to hear what Narville has to say.

'Okay, listen up, gentlemen,' he says. Soldiers pull themselves into sitting position. 'Recon reports a drone possibly heading towards our position.'

Heads drop.

'The Higs will be using zoning to try and pinpoint our location, so even if this drone fails to locate us we can expect more, and one of them will find us sooner or later. Gentlemen, we're going to have to move, at the double.'

There is no sudden scramble to evac. There is no such thing as *at the double* any more. These men are so tired they would rather die.

'Sir?' a weary grunt raises his hand, 'is Recon neutralizing the drone?'

Narville's eyes go across the clearing to where I'm standing at the door to the comms room.

'No, Recon is not neutralizing the drone. We don't want to alert the Higs,' says Narville curtly, watching me at the same time. Grunts look worried. Some shake their heads while others start reaching for body armour, rolling up their bedrolls.

'Base, this is Bandit Two,' comes Gedge's voice in my headset.

'Roger, Bandit Two.' I duck back into the comms room.

'Sir, it's still making straight for your position. My hunch is the Higs have gotten a thermal reading overnight, maybe because of the temperature drop.'

Narville comes into the comms room.

'Sev,' he says, acknowledging me.

'Captain.'

'What's the status on the drone?' he sighs.

I tell him that Gedge is moving like a wraith through the jungle tracking it, and that he sees it closing in on us. 'We need to take it down, sir.'

Narville looks at me with tired, haunted eyes. Says nothing. He can't do it, I think. He can't give the order.

So I patch him in to the comlink with Gedge. 'Bandit Two, this is Base. I have Captain Narville online. You're our eyes out there. Tell us what you see and what you advise.'

'A whole shitstorm coming down on your heads if you don't let me take it down, sir. And you better make it fast because the way it's moving you'll be in the killzone and it won't matter a damn if I take it down or not.'

'You're a brave man, soldier,' says Narville. His eyes are glistening. Shit, he's coming apart here.

'You need to give the order, sir,' I whisper to him.

'It's getting closer, sir,' chips in Gedge. 'Pretty soon there won't be a thing I can do about it. Give the order, sir. Let me take the shot.'

Narville looks at the floor and says nothing. When at last he looks up at me, his eyes are red-rimmed and swimming. 'Assume command, Sergeant Sevchenko,' he says at last, and he turns and sits heavily on the crates, his head in his hands.

I stare at him.

'Sir?' prompts Gedge on the comlink. 'Gonna have to hurry you, sir.'

My mouth works. 'Okay, Bandit Two . . .'

'Sir?'

Gedge has a wife and two kids back on Vekta. He squeezes that trigger and his wife's a widow, kids grow up without a daddy.

'I want you to hold your position,' I say suddenly. 'I'm coming to get you,' and I snatch up my M82 and a mobile tracker, ignoring Narville who's shouting at my back, '*Sev*,' as I burst out of the comms room and into the jungle.

'Say again, Base,' says Gedge in my ear.

'I said hold your position – I'm on my way.'

The phosphorescent mist on the jungle floor billows disrupted beneath my boots and vine tendrils whip my face as I hurdle tree roots.

'Negative, sir,' Gedge is saying in my ear as I run. 'I'm taking the shot.'

'You hold your fire,' I bark into the pick-up. 'That is an order, soldier.'

'Sir, permission to speak freely.'

'Permission denied.'

He speaks freely anyway. 'Sev, this is suicide. You can't make it to me in time.'

'I can draw the drone away from you,' I say. The jungle is a blur around me. I see a burster plant just in time and jump it.

I know what Rico would say right now. He'd say, *Why you doing this, Sev?* He'd say that Narville should have given the order and because he was too much of a pussy to make the call he's put it all on me. That I'm gonna die because Narville is a pussy, and that me dying like this is bullshit. *Bullshit, Sev,* he'd say.

But Rico's not here. Rico's dead. And I crash on, heading towards Gedge's position. I can do this, I think. Soon as I'm within sensor range of the drone it'll start tracking me. It'll identify me as humanoid but I'll still be moving while it does its biometric scan. And I can lead it away from camp. Away from the uplink. Away from Gedge. I can move the killzone.

'We're out of time, sir,' insists Gedge.

'Hold your fire,' I gasp.

'That's a negative, sir. I'm taking the shot.'

'Don't you fucking dare, soldier.'

'Up your ass, sir.'

I hear the gunshot.

I stop. Touch a hand to the earpiece. 'You mother-fucker,' I shout at him. 'You insubordinate asshole.'

Gedge sniggers. 'Down in one. It may be new, but it ain't tougher. Better turn your ass around, sir. Shit's about to get warm.'

I squeeze my eyes tight shut.

'You asshole, Gedge,' I say. 'What did you do that for? You got a fuckin' family. I got no one.'

That's not true. I've got Amy. But Amy doesn't know her own name, let alone mine.

'Sir, the high-speed, low-drag soldier around these parts is you,' says Gedge. 'The grunts need you more'n they need me.'

And before I can argue there's a whooshing sound that I hear clearly over the headset – except it's not the sound of a battleship, cruiser or fighter. It's a Hig dropship.

'Shit,' says Gedge. 'Looks like they sent a capture squad.'

Capture squad?

I take off again, checking his blip on the handheld. 'What's happening, Gedge?' I bark. 'Status report.'

'Enemy is dispersing. Five grunts: capture troopers and assault troopers. I think they're looking for . . . Sir, I think they're looking for me. Permission to engage.'

'Copy that,' I shout, tearing along now.

I hear shots, and not just over my headset, the firefight coming from closer than I thought so that in moments I'm almost on top of the first Hig I see. He's got his back to me, crouching with his StA-52 at his shoulder, squeezing off a couple of shots at Gedge's position. In one fluid movement I let my M82 drop to its sling, reach for my combat knife and I'm on his back before he has time to react, taking him in a knifeman's embrace with the blade at his respirator. I grunt and pull and he falls, gurgling, blood arcing from his slashed throat. Another Hig sees me and opens fire and I dive for cover, reach for the assault rifle and squeeze off a reply.

I crane round the side of a tree and see no dropship but figure there must be a clearing nearby. Then I see two Higs carrying Gedge and a covering fire opens up, ripping into the tree, showering me with splinters and forcing me to scuttle round out of sight, waiting for his clip to empty before daring a second look. They're almost out of view. I find one in my sights and take him out with a head shot.

Another returns fire and then they're gone, into the undergrowth, still carrying Gedge.

I'm on my feet after them, slamming in a fresh mag as I go, but as I come up on the clearing the dropship's already hovering above the ground and even as I'm wondering how come it bears the logo of Stahl Arms and not the Helghast military I'm having to take cover again as it engages its boosters, frying the ground below. One last attempt to take me out. That fails, assholes.

I look at the tracker. Gedge still bleeps, alive. Until the ship goes out of range and the signal winks off.

I drop to a crouch and in the moments of silence that follow put my head in my hands and wait for an air attack that never comes and more dropships that never arrive.

And it slowly dawns on me that it's over. The operation is over.

Which can't be.

Six months they've been looking for us. Six months. They get the closest they've come so far, and – what? – no back-up, no concerted attack? All they had from the engagement was a prisoner. I contemplate what they might do to Gedge – and why. Because they must know any information will be out of date just as soon as they get it out of him. It doesn't make sense.

The dropship belonging to Stahl Arms. That doesn't make any sense either.

Around me the jungle burps and chatters.

Nothing makes sense any more.

PART ONE

Six months earlier

Chapter One

I ought to have put a bullet in Rico Velasquez there and then.

He was my commander, my buddy and a war hero, but none of that mattered. Not set against the death of Garza, which had been his fault. And now him killing Scolar Visari.

The whole of Operation Archangel, a chance to put an end to the war; Jan Templar, Evelyn Batton both dead; The Red Dust – a nuclear warhead, for crying out loud – detonated over Pyrrhus City, annihilating our forces, millions dead. All for what? For Rico's fuse to blow, *again*? For one guy to fuck it all up in a moment of . . .

Madness.

That's what Visari had said when he died: 'The madness begins.' Said a whole bunch of other stuff too. Like how his death would make him a martyr. That killing him was the worst thing we could do. Fine by me, I was there to place him under arrest anyway. I hadn't fought my way through Visari Palace, through wave after wave of Helghast shock troopers and Colonel Radec just to go screwing things up. Call me Mr By-the-Book if you want, but I wanted to see Visari rot in a cell. I wanted justice – for my family and for the people of Vekta. Visari was right. For the war to end we'd needed him alive.

And he was right about the madness beginning too. As Narville and Hooper rushed past me into the chambers where Visari lay dying, I walked out onto the steps of Visari Palace that overlooked Pyrrhus, capital city of Helghan. Once it had been a maze of rundown housing and seedy factories with the only well-kept structures the military academies and statues of Visari Square. Now all was devastation. A city reduced to ruin. The Helghast didn't deserve this, I thought, looking at the horizon where a grey mushroom cloud blossomed in a roofless sky. Nobody did.

Suddenly from above was a deafening propulsion roar, the sound of ships arriving overhead, and I looked up. The sky had been cast in grey marble by the nuke blast, but now it darkened, the light blotted out by Helghast ships, hundreds of them it looked like: cruisers, dropships and fighters, lights twinkling like distant stars. Our own cruisers were hanging there, as surprised by the sudden appearance of the fleet as we were, no defences deployed, sitting ducks as the Helghast began to open fire. Right now they were going after our cruisers. How long before they came after us?

I watched balls of flame burst on the hulls of our ships, saw them billow brilliantly then fade. Heard explosions like distant thunder. One of our cruisers, miles away, cracked open and flaming sections began to descend lazily to the ground. All of it happening so far away it was like watching a movie. Like it wasn't real somehow.

But it was. And as I watched our fleet destroyed one thought ran round and round my head: that we were combat ineffective. That we were finished.

'Sev,' bellowed Rico, after a while, 'are you okay?'

'*No.*' I rounded on Rico. 'No. I am not *okay*, Rico. What the hell were you thinking? We had the guy. And you killed him. *You killed Visari.*'

'Look,' he growled, 'you haven't been in this war as long as I have. I don't expect you to understand . . .'

Below us, medics moved among the troops administering Gudkov shots to protect against the radiation. Doc Hanley approached me and Rico and beckoned us to offer up our forearms as we glared at one another. His eyes went over our shoulders to where his colleague worked to save Visari.

'I'm calling it,' I heard from behind me. 'Time of death is 21:20 hours.'

If there was any hope that Visari might have been

alive, it was snuffed out at that moment. Beside me Rico was giving me sorry-assed excuses that I only half heard above the howl of the ships, the white noise in my head and Captain Narville barking orders – 'We are mobile in five, so pack up your shit . . .' – barely acknowledging us as he descended the vast stone steps. I'd never seen him look so beat up, but as he turned to face us the reasons why were all there in the sky behind him. On the ground the convoy was already in motion. The last of our troops were piling into Intruders, APCs, HAMRs, buggies and tanks. We were oscar mike, Narville in survival mode now.

'Command's pulling the plug,' he yelled over the roar of the enemy ships overhead. 'They want us to execute an emergency exit scenario. We're pulling every soldier off this planet.'

'We're retreating?' I could hardly believe it, but that was nothing compared to Rico's reaction.

'*I ain't leaving,*' he bellowed. 'This fight isn't even half done. What is this bullshit?'

Narville rounded on Rico, eyes blazing. 'Oh no,' he roared, 'this is *not* how this is going to go down. I need you to listen and keep your trap shut. Not a single sound. Not even a "yes, sir". Is that understood?'

Rico opened his mouth to reply and was stopped by an angry upraised finger from Narville.

'Okay,' he said, 'listen up. Intel has an advanced Helghast cruiser fleet zeroing in on our position. The general wants us en route before they show their faces. The best chance we have is to cut through the Visari District and cross the Corinth River. From there it's due east to the extraction point, which is a crater the size of Kansas somewhere underneath that giant mushroom cloud. We got one shot at this. So we're doing this strictly by the numbers. It's the only place we're getting out of this hell hole.'

He gestured at a HAMR that was sitting nearby with its engine idling, looking dirty and dustblown, but low, keen and mean. Just the way we liked them. HAMRs were mobile reconnaissance vehicles. Very fast, very manoeuvrable, a favourite with all grunts. Trouble was they were in short supply.

'We don't have a lot of these babies,' confirmed Narville, 'but they're our best bet against whatever the Higs are gonna put in our way,' he said.

I'd be driving, Rico manning the turret configured with cannons, and I was just about to clamber aboard when suddenly the shriek of engines from overhead grew even louder and I jerked my head up to see a vast enemy arc cruiser breaking formation and losing altitude.

Somebody said *shit*, and it might have been me, as a massive petrusite coil on the cruiser's hull seemed to shiver malevolently then spin, strands of blue light dancing it as it charged, cannon turrets revolving, finding their target.

This was bad. This was very bad.

The cannon seemed to glow blue, then fizzed, discharging a blue bolt into a knot of troops below and those closest to impact were incinerated, but they were the lucky ones. The electrical discharge rippled outwards, burning all it touched. For a moment all we could hear was the popping of ammo cooking off and the shrieking of men being burned to death. We could smell the burning flesh and I watched as a man dropped to his knees desperately trying to beat out the flames on his legs, unaware that fire was licking at his back. In seconds he was engulfed, a human torch. He looked up at us on the steps and I swear our eyes met as the skin melted from his face and for a second he was grinning as his lips were burned away. Then, mercifully, he fell backwards, dead.

In an instant what had been a squad of soldiers was nothing but blackened corpses. The arc cruiser hovered implacably as though wanting to admire its handiwork, then it tilted slowly, the petrusite coil began to spin once more and the cannon turrets were revolving again to find another target. Fresh ISA meat to cook.

The men had been moving out quickly. Now they moved even faster, scrambling aboard APCs and buggies, engines revving.

'We need to evac *now*,' yelled Narville, 'Sev, Rico, I need you to carve us a safe corridor. Move. Move. *Move*.'

Neither of us needed telling a fourth time. Moments later we were clambering into the HAMR, Rico hating it – hating the fact that we were retreating. I was flicking switches, firing up the systems, feeling the HAMR vibrate around me.

Ahead of us stretched the convoy, a ragtag line of vehicles already moving off. The last of the men were rushing to join it, grabbing infantry handles to cling on to the outside of the vehicles while above them Intruders bobbed and dipped like metallic birds of prey. We looked like an army at least. An exhausted, depleted, retreating army – but an army all the same.

Then Narville was signalling, whirling his hand above his head and leaping into his own HAMR as the convoy moved off, great clouds of disturbed dust and ash billowing around it. We moved onto a roadway, staying close to the cliff face of Visari Palace Hill, as far away as possible from the arc cruiser's cannons and a safe distance from the sheer drop on the other side of the road.

Clear a corridor, Narville had said. Better get a move on.

'All right,' I said, 'let's do this.'

I let a buggy go by then hit the gas. Tyres spinning on the loose road, the HAMR's tail drifted out and I wrestled the wheel to bring it back in line as we came up behind the rear of the convoy.

'Hey,' warned Rico, 'don't get too close to the . . .'

The buggy ahead pulled out to overtake and I followed suit, dropping a gear, gunning the engine and wrenching the wheel to the left.

'. . . edge,' finished Rico, by now staring from the window of the HAMR and into the chasm at his side. On the other side of the gorge were buildings built into the hillside, broken windows regarding us, mocking the retreating army. Gantries overhead were a blur as they zipped past.

Dust and grit lashed the windshield. I held her steady, keeping an eye on the convoy vehicles to my right – clip one at this speed and we'd be spinning off into the void – as well as the Intruders overhead. 'Battlefield taxis' the grunts called them. They were small and the pilots were making best use of their manoeuvrability, keeping close to the convoy to use the cover of the rockface.

It meant they were close, though. Too close for comfort. And just as I had that thought there was a streak of white, a ripple of disrupted space, and a missile was hurtling towards us. Towards an Intruder, to be precise.

For a second I was the pilot and I knew exactly what was going through his head. He was going automatic. Some flip-switch in his head went to training mode and he executed an evasive move, the Intruder lurching dangerously close to the speeding convoy. The missile slammed into the cliff face on the other side of the road, drivers swerving to avoid falling rock so that I was suddenly inches away from a speeding Archer with no room on the other side either. For a second I was looking into the terrified eyes of a marine hanging from an infantry handle, then we were speeding past, the column falling back into place.

'Fire back,' I snapped at Rico.

'At what?'

'*Everything.*'

Electrics whined as the HAMR's cannon pivoted gracefully, its targeting systems scanning the buildings. Rico opened fire and the stench of cordite filled the cab, burning my lungs as he strafed the buildings with stutter fire, reducing masonry to dust. I looked fruitlessly for ear protection, the cannon deafening in the HAMR.

Now the buggy ahead of us reached the front of

the column and pulled in front of it. Doing the same, I was grateful to find the shelter of the rockface at last. For cover.

Fat lot of good it did. There was a second missile strike, only this one found its mark. A fizz, then an explosion, and suddenly the buggy ahead of us was hoisted in the air as though yanked by an invisible rope. Spinning, it rolled over us and for a split second I heard the screams of its crew and saw mangled bodies tossed around in the shell. Then it was behind us, leaving a red smear across the hull of the HAMR, and it crashed to the road, still rolling. The buggy at our twelve swerved to avoid it, a hair's breadth from sailing over the edge, and I watched it right itself when suddenly something else appeared behind it.

God knows where it had come from, a Helghast AAPC – a Bull: big and fast, its engine roaring, it came up behind the buggy, which had only just righted itself, its crew swivelling in their seats at the sudden roar from behind them. The implacable heavy armour of the Bull was the last thing they saw and they threw up their arms, screaming as it drove over the buggy and crushed them to death.

Systems hummed. The cannon swung about, our targeting systems reconfiguring. Then the ear-splitting hammer strike as Rico opened fire.

Metal clanged and . . . nothing. It did nothing. If enemy AAPCs could sneer, then . . .

And whoever was inside had decided to get their yuks with us, because instead of hitting us with the artillery rockets, or even opening fire with the LMG up top, the AAPC activated its sawblades, which roared to life with a shriek. Usually they functioned as minesweepers or were used for clearing obstacles – today they had a new objective.

Rico did a double-take, looking like he wasn't sure whether he should be impressed or petrified.

There was a firework of sparks as the Bull nudged our rear. I wrestled with the wheel. The Bull dropped back then rammed us again, the impact almost throwing me from my seat. The convoy was way behind us now. Buildings and rockface were a blur, and we were pelted with grit. I power-drifted round a corner, gaining us space, and Rico fired again – for all the good it did us. Now the AAPC had made up the ground and came up on us with a roar, nudging us, and once more I was straining to prevent the HAMR's end sliding out, the muscles in my arms screaming. There was the tortured squeal of metal on metal as the Bull's sawblades whipped at our hull. The sound of its engine was getting louder and I knew it had more to give. It was bigger than us, more powerful. We were at its mercy.

It pushed on inexorably, mashing the rear of the HAMR, forcing us into metal crash barriers at the side of the road. The barriers tore, twisting and mangling with a shriek of metal and a torrent of sparks. Rico fired again, this time taking out a section of the AAPC, which erupted into flame.

We would have cheered about that, me and Rico, if we hadn't been screaming. The shockwave from the AAPC explosion had sent the HAMR over the edge and suddenly we were careering down the hillside, tossed around inside like dice in a shaker, ahead of us a sheer drop. Below that the city.

Every sinew in my arm pleading for mercy, I tore the wheel to the right, leaning into the skid, Rico doing the same as the HAMR skidded sideways and came to a stop, a cloud of dust billowing around us. With a final clunk the HAMR settled at an angle, the two wheels on my side hanging over the cliff edge.

There was a moment of silence as we digested the fact that we hadn't plummeted the final ten metres.

I grinned at Rico. He grinned at me.

'Oh yeah,' I said.

'*Hell yeah*,' said Rico, and leaned to grab me by the shoulders, oblivious to the weight suddenly shifting in the HAMR.

Too late I tried to stop him and it tipped, for a second hanging as though we might – just *might* –

not fall. Then did, rolling over and over as we tumbled to the buildings below. I'm going to die, I knew, as the building roof rushed to meet us, and I thought of my mother, my father, my sister Amy. A summer's day on Vekta . . .

Then it went black.

And there was the sound of the breeze in the trees.

Amy blowing a bubble gum bubble. Other sounds: the electronic swish of the page from my father's reader, the soft crunch of my mother's camera as she took shots of the landscape.

Flat on my back, with my ACU twisted round me, I lay there as a world of war-damaged buildings and wounded masonry adjusted to our sudden, rude entrance. The HAMR lay on its back, mortally wounded, metal ticking as it cooled. Around us floated the debris of the nuclear strike and from somewhere far away came the rattle and pop of gunfire, of explosions, and I thought I heard screams. Standing above me was Rico, holding out a hand to pull me to my feet, and I took it gratefully, grinning at him as we stood together, staring around at the wreckage of the HAMR and both wondering how we'd escaped with our lives.

'You see anyone else?' I adjusted my webbing and

checked my gear: M32 combat knife, three M194 fragmentation grenades, M4 revolver, M82 assault rifle and – I checked mags, slammed one into the rifle and cocked it – 256 rounds of ammunition.

Rico was doing the same. He pointed towards the sound of the gunfire. 'Maybe that way.'

I nodded, frowning. The sound was of ISA under attack. Hardly begun and already the retreat was SNAFU. We were going to have to fight our way to Corinth River.

Well, it wouldn't be the first time, I thought, as we crept forward to within sight of a square where a group of ISA were under attack. Wouldn't be the last.

I got a Hig in my sights, eased off the safety, took a deep breath and squeezed the trigger . . .

Much later, we stood on a hill overlooking the city, both exhausted. Around us rained debris still – like a tickertape parade in hell.

'Who nukes their own city?' said a bewildered Rico.

I shrugged and scanned the horizon for signs of the captain.

'I don't see Narville,' I said at last. How did it get to this? What a mess.

'River's that way,' said Rico. 'That's where he said we gotta cross.'

'Yeah,' I replied, voice dripping with sarcasm, 'let's hope everybody makes it.'

'Listen, Sev,' said Rico, big bear-like shoulders dropping as he struggled to find the words, 'about Visari . . . I . . .'

'Forget it,' I said. I didn't want to hear this. I didn't want excuses. I wanted Garza back. I wanted to be able to trust Rico.

'I wanted to shoot him too,' I said, more for something to say than anything else.

'But you didn't.'

'No,' I said, 'but that's 'cause I'm not a jackass.'

Chapter Two

To understand just how big a jackass Rico was to kill Visari, you need to know the history of this whole shitstorm. And to do that we've got to go back – way back to young Tomas Sevchenko sitting in his Modern History lessons, a spotty teenage kid with two things on his mind: Girls and . . . whatever the heck the other thing was.

I didn't pay enough attention in class, of course. I liked Modern History right enough, don't get me wrong, but English was always my subject. I enjoyed reading, still do, and, anyway, Modern History came with a *major* distraction in the shape of Elisabetta Purrslip who used to sit across the aisle from me and a few rows forward. Right in my field of vision, in other words. So on the rare occasion I wasn't staring dreamily at Elisabetta's legs I was trying to goof off so she'd turn round and I could catch her eye. Either way, I wasn't paying enough attention to Mr Tovar who was telling us all about the nuclear war on Earth three hundred years ago. The near destruction of all humanity had nothing on Elisabetta Purrslip.

So, yes, not exactly an authority on that score. But this much I can tell you. Three hundred years ago on Earth: *ka-boom*. Lots of people are dead and nothing works because the generals were all so keen to press the shiny red button they forgot to ask what happens afterwards.

The answer: you've bled Earth dry, her resources are gone and you're going to have to find your minerals someplace else.

So they formed the United Colonial Nations (UCN) to investigate space colonization, while at the same time some of the bigger companies just went ahead and did it themselves, one of them being the Helghan Corporation.

Back then the Helghan Corporation was just another big conglomerate like the oil companies or fast-food chains. The difference was that it made its billions in energy and industrial refinement so was already fixed to bid for colonization rights in the Alpha Centauri solar system. Off went the Helghan Corporation ships, going where no man had gone before.

The first planet they reached, guess what they called it? Me, I would have called it something cool, but I guess they were being a bunch of kiss-asses so they called it . . .

Helghan.

Next planet they reached they were still way up the butt of the company and they called it Vekta, after the Helghan CEO, Philip Vekta.

Their sucky names were about all the planets had in common. Helghan was a shithole, or, as the books put it, 'inhospitable and with an extremely poor ecosystem', the whole rock only habitable thanks to refineries and power generators seeded by the first colonists, and the only reason *they* bothered was because of the planet's energy resources, which after all was the whole point of sailing out there in the first place.

Vekta, on the other hand, now that was an oasis. A much more human-friendly environment: agrarian, lushly forested, an agricultural paradise and a major source of food not only for those who settled there, but for those who had remained on Helghan.

Soon – we're talking nearly a hundred years, but in the turn of a school history-book page anyway – the two planets were jointly a blooming, profitable enterprise and the Helghan Protectorate was formed, so both worlds were now administered from Vekta. Life was good for the Helghans and that's when they came up with a logo: three interlinked arms to represent peace, justice and freedom.

Remember that. It'll help you enjoy the irony later.

Anyway, the people were prosperous; their morale

was high. It was good to be a Helghan then. They even established their own militia outside of the auspices of the UCN, which, I guess, was where it started to go wrong.

Because the next thing you know Helghan had set itself up as a civil administration. Then it was buying the Alpha Centauri system lock, stock and barrel.

And then they started getting greedy. At least that's what the history books said: how Helghan began levying taxes on virtually every ship in space. Traffic control, customs, search-and-rescue; any ship travelling through the Helghan system – which was every ship – had to pay.

The UCN didn't like that. The UCN had its base on Earth so it relied on traffic coming through Alpha Centauri to bring essentials. The Helghans were making that process a drag. By then the UCN had formed the interplanetary strategic alliance, the ISA, to help keep the peace, and it installed ISA troops on Helghan and Vekta, to stop the Helghans going tonto with the taxes.

The Helghans didn't like that, which meant there was a whole bunch of not-liking-that being passed around, and of course the war on Earth was ancient history by now so maybe they just decided it was time for another one.

So when the UCN told Helghan to stop being such

ball-breakers with the taxes the Helghans told the UCN to shove it.

And that was just for starters. Next Helghan tried to get rid of all ISA forces from Vekta and Helghan, which was a dumb move any way you looked at it. Helghans had the numbers, but they didn't have the training and experience and they didn't have the high-end weaponry of the ISA marines, nor the tactical expertise. The marines weren't leaving without a fight and they served the Helghans a cold glass of shut-the-fuck-up until reinforcements arrived.

That was the first extrasolar war. Result: the Helghans getting their asses handed to them by the ISA. Didn't stop there either. The UCN shut down the entire Helghan administration. All civil servants and executives of the corporation were arrested. Now things weren't looking so rosy for the Helghans, especially as the UCN decided it needed to keep a closer eye on them. And how better to keep a closer eye on them than to colonize their beloved Vekta?

Suddenly Vekta wasn't such a nice place to live. A paradise no longer, it had been colonized by the enemy and the original inhabitants weren't happy. Many of them took up arms as terrorists and in return ISA forces made life hard for all Helghans on Vekta. So hard that in 2204, that's more than a hundred and fifty years ago, in case you stopped taking count, the

Helghans decided they could take it no longer. There was a mass exodus of Helghans from Vekta to the planet Helghan. Vekta now belonged to the UCN.

Now, like I say, Helghan: not exactly five-star accommodation. Nobody wanted to live there, which is why they'd all settled on Vekta. That was the Eden. That was the paradise. Helghan on the other hand was an iceberg: a harsh, cold and isolated storage facility, rich in minerals, sure, but barely any green to be seen. Add to that the fact that the Helghans had started the first extrasolar war. They were like the bullies who had got what's coming to them and nobody gave a rat's ass if life was tough on their grey, poisonous and stormy planet. Tough shit for being such monumental ball-breakers in the first place. Matter of fact the UCN even declared the Helghan administration a sovereign nation and gave them their planet. It was like they were saying, 'We want nothing to do with you. Have your toxic planet – go. You're welcome to it.'

Christ, it must have been tough for the Helghans. Millions of them died. If the climate didn't get them, starvation did. Their world was one of oppression and refugee camps, of masks and protective suits to guard against the increased gravity, electric storms and toxic atmosphere. Going outside meant wearing a respiration mask, but even that didn't help with life expectancies. Few made it past their thirties, lung burn the most common way to die.

You know what they did, though? They adapted. The heads of the refugee camps came together to cooperate in rebuilding their civilization and they began making the most of their planet's vast resources. They became a planet of miners, breaking their backs to extract minerals for trade, even though the UCN weren't willing to pay a fair price for them – talk about holding a grudge – and even went so far as to impose trade sanctions to keep prices down. Didn't stop the Helghans. They kept on working. Kept on adapting.

A few pages of the book later and it's 2305 and the third generation of indigenous Helghans were born. This lot had an advantage over their ancestors: they'd adapted to suit their environment. They'd grown lungs that were more efficient, bodies that were more resist-ant to the heavier gravity of their planet.

If you wanted to be kind, you'd say they'd evolved. If you wanted to be cruel, they'd mutated.

One of those born part of that third-generation was Scolar Visari. Yup, *that* Scolar Visari. The one whose destiny lay with a bullet from Rico's assault rifle. Visari apparently showed great potential as a kid. I've seen pictures of him that age, staring out of the pages of textbooks, and he doesn't look like any kid I've ever seen, whatever his great promise. He looks like a little demon kid if you ask me. But he grew to be a man of his time, because just as Helghan seemed to have got off its knees, so began a food shortage. The population blamed their empty bellies on the greed of Vekta and guess who was able to exploit that?

Scolar Visari was by now a noted orator, a rabble-rouser, and he was pushing all the right buttons, saying what the Helghans wanted to hear. Like how the Helghan people had advanced beyond mere human to become 'extra-human'. And how wearing a mask, always a symbol of the lower, working classes on Helghan, actually represented the strength and fortitude of the Helghan people, and should be celebrated. It was Visari who coined the word 'Helghast' to describe this new race of extra-human people.

Visari was going to lead them out of the darkness.

Chapter Three

We still had the odd terrorist attack on Vekta when I was growing up there. And, no, you didn't miss it. I just forgot to mention that I was born somewhere in all of that – in 2334, to be precise, around about the time of the food shortage on Helghan.

Be great to tell you I had a tough childhood. It would seem fitting somehow. Like Rico, who was born in the Vekta City slums, living by his fists and his wits, eventually joining the army aged eighteen. A lifer.

But I'd be talking out my cornhole. We lived in the nice part of Vekta City. My father was a draughtsman. By day he sat in a room in front of wall-mounted screens, designing transport systems. My mother was – well, she was my mother. And she was my younger sister's mother too. And when she wasn't being our mother she was a painter, the old-fashioned way, with brushes and an easel. Oftentimes we'd drive out of the city on a weekend. When we reached the checkpoints, ISA troops would stop us, make Dad open the trunk for inspection and then stare in through the passenger window at my mother for way longer than was needed – it was only years later that I realized my Mom was a stone-cold fox. Then the troops would look in on me and my sister sitting in the back seat: me, wide-eyed, like, cool, *real* soldiers, with *real* guns; Amy blowing bubble gum bubbles at them. She always thought soldiers were assholes. Jerks with rifles. I often think about that.

Years later I got to talking to Rico about those checkpoints we saw as kids. Turned out he'd never seen them growing up. Never left Vekta City until his teens.

Anyway. We'd drive: me, Mom, Dad and bubble-blowing Amy. Until Vekta City and the checkpoints were behind us. Until the refineries and giant comms towers were distant smudges on the horizon. To where it was just countryside, hardly anything man-made in sight. Usually we'd stop and have something to eat, and Mom would take pictures: of us sometimes, but mainly of *things*, like the trees, flowers, streams, wildlife. So she could take them home and use them for her painting.

I took it for granted then, that beautiful country-side just a short drive away. But I was a kid, with a head full of superheroes and war stories. I would have preferred being at home with a book or a controller in my hand. The thought all of that landscape was – makes me laugh to think it – but it was *boring* to me back then.

Of course now I yearn to see it again. Now I'd give anything to be back there, even for just a second. With Mom, Dad and Amy there too. Anything.

It was after one of those trips to the country that I arrived at school the following Monday, me in my senior year now, with Mr Tovar and Modern History the first lesson of the day. Mr Tovar was as happy as a dog with two dicks.

'Do you remember Scolar Visari, class?' he beamed, and we all mumbled and nodded our heads. 'He's staged a military coup on Helghan.'

We all groaned and yawned and at least one of us watched Elisabetta tuck a lock of hair behind her ear. We were thinking SFW. So fuckin' what?

Of course we should have taken it more seriously and listened. But what did it matter to a bunch of seventeen-year-olds that some guy on a mouldy planet had staged a military coup? So fuckin' what that he had taken on the title of 'Autarch' and announced plans to begin building the Helghast army as well as devising a new Helghast alphabet and even a new language. And remember the old logo? Peace, justice and freedom? He was going to get rid of that too, and replace it with three arrows representing duty, obedience and loyalty.

But so fuckin' what?

Things get serious when you leave school. All of a sudden you've got the rest of your life to worry about. It's how you manage that move, that's what it's all about.

Me? How did I handle it? I joined the ISA.

Why? Maybe I secretly believed all the recruitment baloney. Maybe I had my head too full of movies and videogames and instead of playing at being a grunt I wanted to be one for real – wanted to know how it felt to actually hold a real assault rifle. Maybe I wanted adventure, excitement and the violent jolt of combat adrenalin.

Or maybe I just wanted to worry my parents, or annoy them. God knows why, they'd been nothing but great to me, but I guess that's what kids do, and, hey, it worked because they were worried and they were annoyed.

Either way, I signed up.

Chapter Four

I didn't last long in the forces.

If I tried to put my finger on why, then I suppose it was the huge chasm between what I was expecting from the ISA and what I got.

What was I expecting? Duh. Action, of course. Sunrise on day one: Private Tomas 'Sev' Sevchenko running around popping caps in the ass of any motherfucker who dared take up arms against the colonies. In this case that meant the Helghast. They being the ones who, so said intel at least, were preparing for a large-scale invasion.

Trouble was the Helghast were in no hurry to get their shit together, and maybe wouldn't even bother at all. When I first joined the ISA, Vekta was at DEFCON 2, which meant we believed invasion to be imminent. New recruits – that's me – were training to repel a possible invasion, and, without wanting to sound like some kind of war junkie, that gives your training an edge: because any moment now you might be called upon to defend your home.

But what happens when that action takes its sweet

time arriving? You find yourself training. Then more training. Then training for more training. You find yourself on constant manoeuvres. And when you're not on manoeuvres you're waiting to go on manoeuvres. And then the threat level gets reduced from DEFCON 2 to three – no enemy activity reported – and the devil finds work for idle hands to do. Nothing too naughty. Years later I was to meet Rico and I'd discover what 'getting into trouble with your superiors' really meant. Me? We're talking minor acts of disobedience. Well, they call it insubordination in the army, but again, compared to the likes of Mr Velasquez, my crimes were strictly small-time: giving a commanding officer a bit of lip, flipping off a medical officer, generally behaving like a smart-ass. I did take an Exo for a joyride, that's true. And I was almost court-martialled for failing a breathalyser while on sentry duty, but that was about it. I was a bored kid and I was discovering that the army just wasn't for me. So, after a year or so of that, the ISA and I decided to part ways by mutual consent. I returned to my parents' house, tail wedged well and truly between my legs, much to the derision of Amy and the delight of my mother and father. What can I say? I was still trying to find my place in life. I guess I still am.

For a while I kicked around doing nothing until

my father got me training to be a draughtsman like him. I showed a natural aptitude for it. According to him I did anyway, my hands flitting across the screens, grids and patterns appearing beneath my fingertips. I wore an open-necked shirt and sensible shoes. I was creating work for a portfolio, so said my father, and when we were done he was going to introduce me to agencies in the city. He loved the idea of all that. His eyes would go all misty and twinkly like he was on the verge of tears. I grew a beard and Mom said it made me look older.

At the time I thought all that was preferable to the army, but only just. I was still looking for something else – something else was out there for me surely. Then the alert status went up, back to DEFCON 2 – not maximum readiness, but near as damn it.

As an ex-military guy, I was following the news more carefully than most, and still talking to a buddy in the service, Dante Garza. The ISA was mobilizing, he said. He was pleased about that. More than a few times I'd stood at checkpoints with Garza, checking out the honeys passing through, getting dudes to open their trunks, winking at the kids. And Garza was looking for action too. Only difference was he'd hung around. According to him, intel suggested that a Helghast invasion of Vekta was imminent. Sure, we'd heard all that before. Even Mom, Dad and Amy hardly turned a hair. But watching the footage of ISA troops mustering, I sensed something different. Like the threat was more real at this time. Then I started getting messages. Guys I'd served with who had also got frustrated and left, telling me they were going to rejoin.

'It's real, Sev,' said one of Garza's messages. His excitement was palpable. 'It's happening.'

The next morning I awoke, looked out of my bedroom window at a city just rubbing the sleep from its eyes and decided. The world that I knew was under threat. So I went to my cupboard, stood on my little tippee-toes and reached to the top shelf for my uniform.

I'd kept in shape by running, kickboxing, afternoons spent at the range, so the uniform still fitted. My parents and Amy were sitting at the breakfast bar when I walked in wearing my uniform. The television was on, a beautiful reporter with glossy red lips saying how the Helghast had imposed a complete media blackout. For the first time my parents looked worried and when they turned from the screen to see me in my uniform I think they knew.

It was real. It was happening.

I reported to my local garrison. They put me in a company of other guys who'd answered the call of duty. Rusty guys like me. We began training to get us back into shape and for a few days I began to worry that I'd rejoined only to do yet more training and manoeuvres. Was the whole cycle going to start again? Was I going to find myself returning home with my tail between my legs? Amy laughing, Mom and Dad grateful? Back to the LCD screens and dreaming of something else?

No, as it turned out. And what an asshole I was to ever wish for different.

The Helghast had collaborators within our operation, so that when their cruisers entered our atmosphere and the order was given to fire on them, the systems malfunctioned. Their cruisers were able to deploy Overlord dropships and ground troops began the first wave of the attack. First blood to them.

Our infantry had been mobilized the moment our screens picked up the invasion, but we were still caught with our pants round our ankles. Visari sent his youngest and most inexperienced troops against ISA forces, wave after wave of them, cannon fodder. They kept us busy while shock troopers – his more experienced and skilled infantry – secured other areas of the city. In a matter of hours the whole of Vekta City was a war zone, pockets of ISA resistance fighting wherever possible, some civilians taking up arms, most simply fleeing as the Helghast advanced with a ruthless, deadly efficiency.

And they came with the anger and bitterness of the ages flowing through their veins. They came with Visari's speeches ringing in their ears, his words reminding them that we the humans had stolen from them, had oppressed them – that Vekta was their home planet and that it had been unjustly taken from them. They were brutal in exercising that anger. Fighting with the ISA in the northern part of the city, word reached us that civilians were being ruthlessly slaughtered. I thought of Mom, Dad and Amy, and fought on. I was seeing action for the first time, using live ammunition on live targets. Shit had got real all of a sudden. When a bullet smacked into the grunt by my side and his jaw disappeared, then the next one sheared off the top of his skull and a fine spray of blood and brain matter landed on my face – that's when it got real. That moment I very badly wanted to be back training or on manoeuvres, or scoping out the honeys at checkpoints, or growing a beard in front of a screen. I was fighting for the survival of my planet and my family, but mainly I was fighting for my own.

Growing up and then joining the ISA I had the idea that the army was a portal to adventure, and that battle was a time of heroism and comradeship. I believed all that recruitment baloney, remember? Sure I pretended to be cynical like everybody else.

But underneath it all we loved that stuff about being all that you could be. Wouldn't have been there otherwise. Me I thought that the army was the ultimate finger to the world – a kiss-off to wage slaves like my dad who sat in front of screens all day, sipping lukewarm coffee from plastic cups, kissing the wife in the morning, again at night, breeding rugrats and watching a life that had once seemed so full of promise reduced to numbers on a bedside clock.

Not for me, I thought. The army was my escape, battle its greatest statement. That's where I would be truly free.

Bullshit.

It was all bullshit.

Battle's not about heroism and comradeship; it's about survival. Battle's not about doing your duty; it's staying sane and staying alive – doing *whatever you have to do* to stay alive. You kill enemy troops not in search of glory or in defence of your planet, but because you want to leave the battle zone in an APC and not in a bodybag. There is no poetry or romance in war; it's brutal and ugly and terrifying and it turns men into animals – shrieking, screaming and stampeding animals destroying everything in their path.

Eventually I'd change my thinking on that – and I'd realize that changing your thinking is what marks the difference between a rookie and a combat vet –

but right then that's what I believed. That war was just survival.

I guess you know how that war turned out. The Helghast were beaten. Only just. They took one of our nuclear weapons, Red Dust, during their retreat. But they were defeated all the same, and in years to come kids in Modern History will be reading about Jan Templar, whose actions stopped Vekta being overrun. They'll be told he was a hero and I guess he was – there has to be at least one, right?

It was only later, after the fighting had stopped, that I found out what happened to my family.

My father had tried to protect Mom and Amy, so the Helghast used a bolt gun to nail him to the door. And as he hung there, crucified, they killed my mother. Amy they left alive, but catatonic. These days she sits in a chair in a psychiatric hospital, rocking back and forth, with lunchtime rusk drying on her chin.

During the invasion over 100,000 men, women and children were slaughtered by the Helghast. Excuse me if I don't break it down into figures for shootings, burnings and beheadings. Let's just say we had never known such savagery on Vekta, and after the invasion our world was consumed with rage and grief and paranoia and thoughts of vengeance. On Helghan Visari licked his wounds and called our civilian casualties collateral damage in order to divert attention away from what they really were, which was war crimes, while on Vekta the talk was of reprisals, and the ever-present rumour of the ISA retaliation.

The rumour was on point. We were planning retaliation and it was called Operation Archangel. It was during preparations for the operation that Templar brought me into Special Forces. His idea was to put together an organization of small squads, four or five men each. Hand-picked – there would be no more traitors in our ranks if we could help it – they were chosen for their skill, courage, initiative and resourcefulness. How the hell I ended up there I'll never know, but Templar saw something in me and I was attached to Alpha where I ended up second-in-command to Rico. Thanks to his personal experience of being betrayed by two officers, Rico was a bit of a firework to put it mildly, but Templar trusted him and in return Rico trusted Templar.

So that was us: Rico in command; me, second-in-command, then Shawn Natko and my old buddy Dante Garza. We were being assembled for the biggest military operation our worlds had ever known. Objective: to bring Visari to justice. To end the war.

The night before the operation was due to start I visited Amy in the psych hospital, to maybe say goodbye. A duty nurse stopped me and I read her name badge: E. Purrslip.

'You're Amy's older brother?' she asked. Life had got to her. The psych hospital had got to her. She was pale and drawn and there was no longer light in her eyes.

'That's right,' I said.

'Tomas Sevchenko?'

'Yes, ma'am,' I said, puffing out my chest. Did she recognize me? I wondered.

She gave me an appraising look. 'Well, you should button up your coat, Mr Sevchenko,' she said at last. 'Amy's likely to have an episode if she sees your uniform. She becomes hysterical when she sees soldiers and uniforms.'

And with that she went, pumps squeaking on the corridor floor, and I looked down at myself, ashamed. What was I thinking, coming here in uniform? Jesus.

In the end I just gazed at Amy through the doors of the recreation room, then left. The next day I went to war.

We dropped in Pyrrhus. Our aim was to try to capture the city and, though we met fierce resistance the moment we landed, things were proceeding according to plan – until the Helghast switched the lights on: electric arc towers powered by a rare element called petrusite.

Let me tell you about petrusite. Volatile as all hell, it takes its charge from the air, condensing it into a high-voltage and very powerful force that the Higs had mainly been using as an energy source. On our team was a scientist, Evelyn Batton. She realized that the Helghast were harnessing the power of petrusite and using massive amounts of it against us – defensively, in the case of the arc towers; offensively in the case of arc cannons. During the operation Evelyn was captured along with Natko and my old buddy Garza, and, attempting a rescue, Rico and I came up on Colonel Radec interrogating them. Just as I was trying to work out a way to outflank them, things got heated and Rico rushed in, like an asshole. Garza was killed in the firefight.

Shit was getting bad then and we attempted to regroup at our cruiser, New Sun, but we were boarded by the enemy, and Radec mounted an assault on the bridge. He wanted the codes for Red Dust and he got them. Killing Evelyn and wounding Templar first, he managed to download them from a console then left the stricken New Sun. But he made a mistake, Radec did. He left Templar alive. We can only guess at what happened next, but it seems certain that it was Templar who sent the New Sun crashing into the Tharsis Refinery, destroying the Helghast petrusite grid.

With the defence grid deactivated, we had the smell of victory in our nostrils. But it was then that Radec detonated the bomb. Most of our forces went with it as did thousands of Helghast, but I guess to Radec and Visari they were dispensable, more collateral damage and a small price to pay for liquidating the invading ISA force.

There was still one more chance, which was why Rico and I decided to mount an attack on Visari Palace and hopefully end this thing once and for all by taking Scolar Visari captive.

Well, you already know how that turned out. And I guess with the fact that Rico was responsible not only for Visari's death but also indirectly responsible for Garza's, you can understand why I considered putting a bullet in him.

I guess, with Rico being Rico, you can guess why I never had any intention of going through with it.

I didn't know it then, but pretty soon it wouldn't matter what the hell I'd decided.

Chapter Five

We had to fight our way back to Narville. Every inch of the way. Find cover. Squeeze the trigger. Short, controlled bursts. It was exhausting, brutal and hand-to-hand at times. The Higs were throwing everything they had at us. Someone up top thought that by throwing everything at us their sheer numbers would overwhelm us, but that guy whoever he was had to be a politician or a despot, not a soldier, because that's not how war works and it stopped working that way centuries ago. I'd take one trained, committed and disciplined soldier over a hundred rookies any time. Any time.

Plus, we were determined. And the closer we got the more determined we became. And we were redlining determination now because we were closer to the river, and that meant we were closer to the crater and therefore to the extraction point and why not go the whole nine yards – we were closer to getting back home.

But it also made us closer to the epicentre of the blast and Red Dust was living up to its name. The air was thick with it. It coated us with grime and clogged our nostrils and seared our lungs. We were tired. Weighed down with body armour, ammo and our rifles, it's a miracle we stayed as alert as we did. But we did. Which was why Rico and I saw the Helghast before they saw us.

We came up on them through the wreckage of a once-proud building, steel tendrils poking from its carcass. On the other side of the wall, huge shards of tortured metal thrust from the ground like knife blades, glowing red. Still searing hot either from the blast or some other ordnance – something that had opened a crater in the earth.

And it looked as though the Helghast wanted a piece of whatever was in that crater, because here on the other side was an Overlord dropship. We saw it at the same time and instantly crouched, at once becoming part of the rusty landscape, both silently wondering if we'd been spotted. I shifted, brought my rifle forward and looked down the sights at what was below. Flicked the safety off. Not far from the dropship were three of the enemy: what looked like a scientist, as well as two hazmat troopers, and they hadn't heard us or they'd have been making for cover right now rather than continuing to do what they were doing, which was . . .

Bad.

The petrusite kind of bad. In the centre of the pit was a lake of it – and it was green. Green light danced and sparkled across its surface. A pool of colour within the rubble of the blasted city that would have been beautiful if we didn't know exactly what petrusite could do. And that was the regular petrusite. This particular stuff – this was different to what we'd encountered before. It was more alive somehow. More active. Certainly the Helghast were taking no chances. The two hazmat troopers were wearing radiation suits, as was the scientist. Irradiated petrusite? Rico and I shared a look, maybe coming to the same conclusion at the same time. We watched as one of the canisters was offered to the reservoir, dipped in and filled. In response the amorphous green glow became even more energetic, frantic almost. As though it resented being disturbed and was fighting back like a dog resisting on a lead, gnashing its teeth and snapping its jaws. Then suddenly the tendrils of energy entwined round both canister and tongs, rearing up before the scientist had a chance to react and for a moment it looked as though he might be pulled, screaming, into the river of dancing petrusite, until one of the troopers moved forward to steady him. Their relief palpable, they withdrew the canister, which automatically sealed, and the three of them began to make their way back to the dropship. Their backs were to us now and I levelled the rifle at them, Rico doing the same.

'Let's get down there,' he said.

'That's not our objective, Rico. We've got to stick to Narville's orders this time.'

He didn't argue – there's a first time for everything. Then I saw that he was regarding his gloved hand. On it liquid seemed to shimmer.

'What the hell is this stuff?' he said, eyebrows knitted close together.

I said nothing, instead watching as the dropship took off and taking note of the logo on the side – the logo of Jorhan Stahl's Stahl Arms.

I knew about Stahl Arms. The corporation that made the StA-52 assault rifles used by the Hig grunts. But what kind of weapons were they making now?

From not far away came the crackle of gunfire and we scrambled to our feet, nodded at each other to go.

Time to rejoin the battle. Time to find Narville, cross the river and get off this rock.

Chapter Six

It felt like an age, but we found him, and Christ knows how, but we arrived in one piece. Trouble was we were the only ones at all glad about that. When we finally hooked up with Narville, he looked us over like we were a pair of cockroaches and I had the feeling it was more than just our lack of regulation military headgear that had put the stick up his ass. Just the sight of Rico and me riled him. Like he blamed us for getting him into this mess.

'Sevchenko,' he shouted over the noise of engines, 'glad you could join us.' To Rico he nodded, barely acknowledging him.

We started walking, past the wounded laid out on the road. One grunt screaming; looked like a tank had crushed his legs. Probably one of ours, poor bastard. No amount of blood plasma was going to help him. Two medics knelt over him, shaking their heads hopelessly. By their side Doc Hanley was using a defib on an infrantryman whose helmet was shattered, the white bone of his skull exposed. I looked away.

Around us towered the remains of buildings, raining debris. Everywhere lay bodies and piles of rubble. Once-ornate railings had been twisted into grotesque shapes and Helghast flags still fluttered, blackened and tattered. I took a look at what was left of the convoy. We were not far from the bridge now and I could see it stretching over a river that steamed, as though shrouded in fog. The roadway was a jumble of broken-down and burnt-out vehicles, of ruptured concrete and shapeless metal, like some giant had slammed his fist down onto it.

And waiting to cross it were our tanks. Archers. They were light and fast – and shit-hot at dealing with enemy infantry. Not so effective with anything over thirty tons, though. And looking down the line there weren't too many of them into the bargain.

'Is this everybody?' I asked, trying to keep the disbelief from my voice.

Narville looked over the top of his map. If he had looked pale and drawn back at the palace, well he was a picture of health then compared to the way he looked now. The battle from there to here had added years to him.

'The damn convoy's scattered all down the river,' he said, unable to hide the note of resignation. 'We're pushing through so we can secure the crater for the evac.' He indicated the tanks.

I looked at Rico just as he was looking at me. We had this habit of doing that, like we had some kind of psychic link. He'd be thinking what I was thinking, which was that we should wait for the rest of the column to join us. Sure, I could see what was on Narville's mind. After all, we had three cruisers engaged in a battle over the crater and though they were heavily armed and the Helghast no longer had the element of surprise, the Higs had the numbers. Our cruisers couldn't hold out for too much longer.

But even so.

Hanging back, I whispered to Rico, 'I'm not sure this is a good idea. The thinner we spread our numbers the easier it is for the Helghast to pick us off.'

'Yeah, good point,' replied Rico from the side of his mouth.

But the difference between Rico and me is that I keep this shit to myself. Rico on the other hand . . .

'Sir, with all due respect, I'd like to suggest –' he called to Narville, who immediately wheeled round to confront him.

'No. I think I made it very clear that I don't want to hear a single word out of your mouth,' he yelled.

That shut Rico up.

'Sev,' roared Narville, 'take Velasquez and his mouth out of my face. I need to have you on point. We're going to use the Exo to clear the road.'

And that's the thing about the military. You got any uncertainties or doubts, you keep them to yourself. You just secure that shit. And then you carry on with the task of babysitting a big mech to clear a bridge strewn with barricades and enemy infantry.

'Yes, sir,' I said.

As we began to walk away, Narville bawled at us, 'Pick up your feet. The closer we get to that crater, the closer we get to home.'

Rico would be thinking the same as me: that we had a long way to go yet.

We reached the Exo. Inside it was Dorweiler and he had to be hotter than all hell in there. Exoskeletons are one-man, two-legged mobile battle suits. They're heavily armoured and heavily armed: a chain gun, steel claws and missile battery. They're also highly mobile, so perfect for operations like this one, with debris and wreckage to negotiate and clear. Big as the Exo was, though, there wasn't much room for the pilot, and inside it, squished into the central cavity like meat rations in a tin, was Dorweiler. Partial to the odd cheeseburger or three, Dorweiler hated Exo detail, but got it because he was one of the best. Not everybody can handle piloting the battle suit at the same time as managing chain guns and a semi-automatic missile battery. Dorweiler was one of those who could, and since they weren't about to redesign the

Exoskeleton around either his stature or his diet that meant he had to suffer.

He was moaning from inside the cabin as Rico and I arrived and rapped on the side of the suit to let him know we were there. In response there was a muffled greeting that might have been a cuss. Or maybe just confirmation that we were ready to roll. We were going to take the bridge.

With a great clang, the sound of metal complaining and gears engaging, the Exo started up and took its first steps forward towards the bridge. Overhead were Helghast cruisers, blue petrusite beams pulsing and crackling, aimed at what I didn't know, but at least it wasn't us. Fighters roared overhead, and dropships too, and now I saw that from the dropships came lines, and more Helghast infantry were descending onto the highway in front of us, scurrying for cover, most heading for a barricade about halfway across the bridge.

The Exo took its first steps. Straight away the Higs on the bridge opened fire, the range making the barrage ineffective – for now. Dorweiler returned fire from the Exo, sending missiles into a building on the opposite shore. Fire bloomed briefly before the building seemed to disintegrate, falling in a cloud of dust and debris. Rico and I moved up behind the Exo. Enemy infantry opened fire from behind a barricade halfway across and it sent us scurrying to take cover. That barrier, I thought. That was going to be tough to break.

From somewhere came an RPG round exploding into the road nearby and lashing us with grit and stones, turning everything into razor-sharp shrapnel. I shouldered the assault rifle and squeezed off a few rounds at the barricade. Smoke drifted across the road, blinding me for a moment. There was another explosion to my right and I was sent to my knees, my ears ringing, feeling warmth on my cheek.

I felt to check the ear was still there. It's an automatic reaction in the field. When you get an explosion nearby, a frag grenade or an RPG – one that knocks you off your feet, sends you deaf or blind for a moment – your next thought is of the guys who get arms and legs torn off, who say the first they knew of it was either seeing their leg across the other side of the road or feeling for it and finding nothing there but a mushy stump. The body's good like that. It gives you a few moments' grace before it tells you that you've lost one of your limbs. Only then does the pain start. So you take the hit and you feel to make sure all your bits are still there.

They were. Just blood, a minor laceration, nothing to worry about, no ear missing. I got to my feet. The

Exo was raking fire across the barricade, Helghast there throwing up their arms as they died. It was about to crash through when from the other side leapt a troop transport – least that's what I think it was. This thing was like a mechanized bug, with four heavily articulated and armoured legs. It looked like they usually came with a full complement of three Hig troops ready to deploy from the spine – I guess they could penetrate deep and quickly that way – but this one was without cargo, which was how come it was light enough to bound over the barricade and come at the Exo before Dorweiler could use missiles on it.

In an instant the Exo and the carrier were locked in combat. I thought of Dorweiler, sweating. Chain guns must have been jammed or reloading because he engaged the claws, and for a moment the two were going hand to hand, looking more like fighting men than mechs.

'Hold her, steady, Dorweiler,' I muttered, dropping to one knee and rattling off a clip at the bot, the bullets spanging harmlessly off its armour. Another bang, another RPG blast, a shower of concrete and debris. By my side a trooper went down clutching his neck, a jagged disc of metal jutting from it. It had severed his carotid artery, and a mist of red spray haloed him as he sank, dead before he hit the deck.

Squinting through the smoke I could see the telltale red glow of the Helghast infantry finding their cover and crouching. Our infantry was moving up the flank. The rattling of assault rifles was like static against the great ringing of metal that came from the struggling bots.

Rico and I concentrated our fire on the Helghast carrier, hoping to at least give Dorweiler the edge. Maybe it worked, because with a great screech the Exo slammed a foot into the bot. Then he activated its boosters, shooting the Exo into the air and landing on top of the carrier, finally disabling it. I pictured Dorweiler grinning in the pilot seat. We'd be hearing about that one for a while. And now – cool as you like – Dorweiler kicked the carcass of the troop transport at the barricade, shoving a hole into it.

He stormed through the busted barricade, announcing his entry with a series of missile blasts. The chain gun was operational again and he raked it across a building to our left, turning everything to rubble, Helghast infantry screaming and exploding in a shower of red. Now the enemy were retreating up the bridge, taking cover and returning fire but losing formation and unable to muster a counter-attack in the face of the Exo's firepower.

But Dorweiler must have taken damage during the fight with the troop transport. His armour was breached, perhaps. An RPG round rocked the Exo and the next thing we heard over the comlink was Dorweiler. 'This is Exo One. I've sustained heavy damage. Resuming forward progress.'

But as he did I could see the rear of the battle suit on fire. I began to run.

'I see flames, Dorweiler,' I said into my pick-up. 'Do you copy?'

'Negative.'

Trying to catch up with it. Christ, he didn't know.

'Get out of there, Dorweiler,' I screamed. 'You've got flames. Get out of there *now*.'

'This is Exo One,' he said, trying to maintain radio protocol. 'Critical systems failure.'

Narville's scream came over the comlink. He'd seen the flames too. 'Dorweiler, bail out.'

'I can't. It's stuck.'

A sudden blast of thick warmth as the Exoskeleton went up. In the cabin Dorweiler burned alive. His scream in my headset became a crackle.

'The Exo is down,' said Narville flatly. 'Armour Five. Sevchenko and Velasquez are alone out there. Get your ass in gear.'

'I'm on it, Captain,' replied Armour Five from an Archer.

Rico and I moved up, Narville yelling at his troops for cover fire. Most of the Helghast were in disarray after the Exo offensive, but those who weren't retreating had dug in. They needed picking off and clearing to allow the Archers through.

Rico and me. We're good at picking off and clearing. Real good at that. Any Helghast who stayed behind paid for their bravery.

I found cover and opened fire on a building to my left, almost a whole mag, seeing a Helghast fall in a welter of blood. Another was thrown back with the flesh of his face turned to mash.

From behind me I heard the rumble of an Archer and it crashed through the final barricade. Its cannon spoke, wiping up the last of the Helghast on the other side. They were mostly gone now, and what was left of their force had retreated so they could regroup someplace else. At least we'd given ourselves a breather.

'The area is secure,' shouted Rico in my headset. 'We are green.'

Our infantry was mopping up as we rejoined Narville, who had bad news. Was there any other kind? Our last three cruisers – the ships we were relying on to get us off this rock – were tracking twelve Helghast battleships on their way.

They didn't have long, I thought. We had to get the rest of the convoy together and make it to the extraction point. Narville had other ideas. He wanted us to push through to the extraction point without waiting for the rest of the column.

'We can't afford any more hold-ups,' he snapped before I could protest. 'Sevchenko, we need a route to that crater now, or none of us are leaving. You've got the HAMRs. When you see Helghast armour, you punch right into it. We'll ram us a route back home.'

He turned. 'As long as everyone follows orders, we'll be fine,' he said, as though he was telling himself, not us.

Watching him go, I realized I knew pretty much zip about Captain Jason Narville. I knew that he'd been on secondment to Earth when the Higs attacked Vekta, and that he was one of those who didn't make it back in time to help repel the invasion. Even though we'd kicked ass it had hit Narville hard that he wasn't around to do it, but, hey, we all have baggage. Mine is that I should have been with my family the day the Higs came calling. Should have died with them or died protecting them.

And you tried not to let the baggage get in the way in case it made you scared or angry or careless or any other shit that stopped you being a good soldier.

So what of Narville? I'd heard the grunts talking. Seen them standing around in groups muttering about how Narville was spazzing. In other words:

making decisions with his heart and not his head. Me, I knew that he'd been in charge of the operation to take Visari Square when we'd invaded, and that he'd done a great job, so I'd been giving him the benefit of the doubt. Up to now that was. Now I wasn't so sure.

But, like I say, that's the military. So Rico and I trotted to the HAMRs, ready to do the captain's bidding: take out any Hig armour, punch our way through to the extraction point. Should be a gas.

Chapter Seven

Some distance away, high above Pyrrhus in Visari Palace, was the grand senate hall where the Helghast leaders met. At either end of the long, echoing chamber were huge double doors. The wall on one side was hung with paintings and wall hangings celebrating the glory of Helghast; on the opposite wall were ornate windows stretching floor to ceiling, their light casting the room in a grey hue. The floor was an expanse of bronzed marble, polished to a high shine, and moments ago it had rung with the sound of the senators' boots as they entered the great chamber and took their seats around a long rectangular table at one end.

These were the evolved Helghast, the leaders. As a badge of their status, they wore no respiration masks. And, though the planet was ablaze and their people dying, they perched on high in the guarded and reinforced room. The Helghast watchwords of 'duty, obedience and loyalty' applied to all of the people – but less so to some than to others.

The senators were not unduly concerned about

events preceding their meeting. It was true that they had spent much of the last few hours installed in heavily fortified panic facilities below ground at Visari Palace, emerging only when the ISA had ended their occupation (wrestling with guilt, some of them, knowing that they had remained hidden, leaving their Autarch to face the hostiles alone). It was true that prior to re-establishing supremacy, the ISA had bested their fleet in order to occupy their planet's orbit. And, yes, it was true that the ISA had deployed multiple battle groups against them, and that the invasion had resulted in untold devastation as well as military and civilian casualties, and that their petrusite defences, while impressive, and certainly effective in the short term, had ultimately failed to keep the ISA troops at bay. It was true also that a nuclear warhead had been detonated in their capital city in order to annihilate the enemy forces, and that their Autarch Scolar Visari had been shot and killed by the ISA scum.

And yet while any single one of these events might have severely unnerved any other set of senators – *Vektan* senators, for example – for the Helghast overlords they represented nothing more than a mere pause for thought. Old, fat and corrupt they may have been. Diseased both literally and figuratively they certainly were. But they were tough men, accustomed to war. As accustomed to it as they were to its associated power struggles, and ironically enough it was these they feared more than any ISA bullet.

With the ascent of Scolar Visari, Helghan had reconfigured itself into a society that glorified combat and exalted military victory above all things, no price being too high to pay in order to secure Helghast dominance, no sacrifice too great. Or so preached the leaders, at least. During their own planet's invasion of Vekta they had seen near-certain victory metamorphose into defeat. Now they were seeing their imminent defeat become victory. Yet on occasion these momentous events had paled in comparison to the internal fight for dominance, a battle that soon would be fought afresh, with new combatants.

Visari had been head of the Visari Corporation, which was one of the planet's primary weapons manufacturers. It was the Visari Corporation that had developed and built the VC1 Flame Thrower, VC9 Rocket Launcher, VC21 Boltgun, VC25 Cannon and VC32 Sniper Rifle. The high-end, high-tech weapons used by the empire's elite troops. The Visari Corporation was also responsible for originating possibly the empire's most devastating weapon, the VC5 Arc Gun. Obscenely powerful, it was powered by petrusite. Activate it and a bolt of petrusite would lock on to the nearest available target, resulting in destruction that while not instant, was total.

In competition, Jorhan Stahl's Stahl Arms produced a greater number of weapons, among them the assault rifles and pistols used by the infantry, those Helghast the leaders so unthinkingly sent to die. For this reason Stahl Arms was the planet's largest weapons manufacturer, even though it lacked both the figurehead of an autarch or the technological superiority.

In the last few hours, though, things had begun to change. And so it was that the senators turned their attention to a section of the table that rose with a hum, clicked, then became translucent before a recognizable image appeared – an image of the ISA forces, parts of the convoy now crossing the Corinth River, making its way to the extraction point.

Although it was an operation happening just a short flight away it might as well have been on a different planet for all the impact it made on the room. The chamber's toughened windows were sealed against all pollutants, and that included noise, and the senators watched in silence. Each of the men kept his counsel. Their expressions were blank, thoughts unreadable.

Now the image expanded, opening out to take in more of Pyrrhus and allowing them to see the ISA forces in greater detail. And it became evident that even though much of the column was able to cross the river, plenty of vehicles and troops remained behind and were scattered throughout the city, fighting their way through to join their comrades.

This information the senators received with the same attitude of studied dispassion, and then, as the image flicked off, they turned their attention to the end of the table where Admiral Orlock rose from his chair.

He was a huge and imposing man, built as though hewn from rock. Bald but for an intimidating, bushy moustache, his eyes were cruel black pinpricks. Before the military his youth was spent fighting in the slums of Pyrrhus and down his left cheek ran a large scar, the relic of a knife fight decades ago from which only one man had emerged alive. Unlike many of the senators with a background in the forces, Orlock preferred not to wear his medals, but all knew of his military glories. They knew that he was as ruthless and unsparing with his own men as he was with the enemy. They had all heard the stories of his brutality in battle. To know him was to fear him as an adversary.

And now he stood with the crest of the Helghast army behind him, and his two guards clicked to attention, the sound echoing around the cavernous room. The scar gave the landscape of his face a parched and arid look; his mouth was thin and dry and when he spoke it was with a pugnacious rasp.

'As the senators can see,' he said, slowly and deliberately, pacing the length of the table, 'the ISA forces are in disarray.'

He stopped and was now standing behind a large, sumptuously upholstered chair – so lavish it was almost a throne – and he laid his hands across its high leather back. This was Scolar Visari's chair, the assassinated Helghast leader, and if there were those who might have said that Orlock placed his hands on the back of the autarch's chair in a somewhat proprietorial manner, then they would have been correct. However, a new Helghast leader had yet to be appointed. Those discussions were yet to come. First there was the matter of reprisals, of avenging the death of Visari and punishing the ISA for invading Helghan. This, it seemed, was a task to which Admiral Orlock had appointed himself, and it was clear from his satisfied demeanour that he considered things to be going well in this regard.

He cast his gaze around the room in order to verify that those assembled were suitably impressed by the progress made so far.

'In less than three hours my soldiers will overwhelm them,' he continued, his voice like stones flung at the wall. 'None of Visari's killers will survive.'

At this the senate bowed their heads respectfully, and there was a small outbreak of applause. Just as it was fading came a lone voice of dissent.

'Am I missing something?' said Jorhan Stahl, who had been sitting regarding Admiral Orlock with rather less reverence than the majority of those assembled. 'What about the tank group on the left?'

The room went the kind of quiet rooms do when an unwelcome opinion is rudely offered: a kind of shocked, humming quiet as the senators turned to look at the far end of the table where Stahl sat, languidly smoking a cigarette. Two of his capture troopers stood behind him, alert and ready to come to their master's defence. He was the only one of them apart from Orlock to come with a personal bodyguard. That fact alone made it clear how seriously he intended to contest the autarchy.

With a sigh Orlock turned his attention to Stahl. 'I'm thrilled that the private sector is taking an interest in state affairs,' he rasped. 'Again.'

He raised an ironic eyebrow at the other senators.

Stahl looked unconcerned. He lacked the military bearing of Orlock; he was smaller and his features were grey and sharp. But the watchfulness of his eyes spoke of intelligence and cunning within, and there was a knowing, disingenuous tone to his voice that tended to unnerve those around him.

'The ISA tank group on the left,' he said, gesturing at the frozen image on the monitor, his eyes never leaving Orlock. 'Are you ignoring it on purpose? Or is this all part of some strategy beyond our understanding?' He smiled thinly.

Orlock affected amusement, playing to the room somewhat as he replied, 'You build weapons, Stahl. I decide how to use them.'

Now Stahl stood from his chair, stubbing out his cigarette and striding across the room towards Orlock, his capture troopers in tow. 'Am I the only person who sees a problem with this kind of archaic thinking?' he said, voice scarred by smoke. 'If the Helghast are going to rule, we need to adapt, like we did when we first arrived on Helghan. This *so-called* strategy won't work. Overwhelming numbers alone are not enough.'

There was a muted but nonetheless all-too-audible sharp intake of breath and Admiral Orlock bristled, his two guards coming forward also, alive to the sudden threat. The senators, cowards and sycophants to a man, cringed in anticipation of violence, and Senator Gunsteling attempted to intercede, either hoping to prevent hostilities occurring, or to increase his standing in the eyes of Admiral Orlock who, on present evidence at least, looked most likely to be the next autarch.

'Let's not presume to tell the admiral how to do his job, shall we, Chairman?' he said with a wheedling tone.

Stahl ignored him. 'Why not bargain with the ISA?' he suggested sweetly. 'Lure them towards us. Promise them . . . whatever. And when they're close . . . all in one place . . . then we kill them.'

'Chairman Stahl,' snapped Senator Gunsteling, finding a little resolve from somewhere, 'that is quite enough. Return to your seat.'

Stahl treated his order with the contempt it deserved. By now he had moved to the middle of the room and was standing face to face with Admiral Orlock, Visari's chair between them. Now it was Stahl's turn to lay a proprietorial hand on the back of the luxurious seat. Orlock regarded the hand for a moment, as though it was not a hand, but a turd. Then his eyes went up to look directly at Stahl and there was steel in his voice as he said, 'Visari may have tolerated you, Stahl. But I am not Visari.'

'Yes. That much is abundantly clear,' said Stahl with the ghost of a smile. Again the room seemed to pulsate with shock, but neither Orlock nor Stahl were aware of anything now outside of each other. And Stahl leaned forward, so close that only the admiral could hear him, and said, 'Does it hurt? Knowing that, no matter what you do, you will never emerge from Visari's shadow? Is that why you let him die?'

His blood up, Orlock yanked the chair from

between them and it skidded away as the admiral squared up to Stahl, his eyes blazing. Stahl, though by far the smaller of the two men, did not flinch, and for a moment they stood eyeball to eyeball. Both sets of bodyguards tensed, ready to raise their weapons.

'The Helghast will never bargain with the ISA. There will be no quarter,' hissed Orlock.

He jabbed at a button on the console in order to address the ground troops and at last this chamber on high was linked to the conflict below. Orlock's voice was relayed to the comlink of every Helghast soldier in the city as he said, 'Attention, all troops. This is the admiral. Double your efforts. I want the ISA dead within the hour.'

He released the button and glared challengingly at Stahl, who backed away as though to concede his point. The guards relaxed, as did the senators, and Stahl returned to his seat, outwardly deferential to the admiral, while inwardly most pleased with the outcome.

For Jorhan Stahl had plans. Big plans.

First, however, he wanted any faith the senators had in Admiral Orlock severely shaken and, as such, the confrontation had been a success – by letting himself be provoked Orlock had played right into his hands. Stahl hid a smile as he took his seat and turned his attention to the monitor.

Now to enjoy seeing the destruction of the ISA forces, he thought, as the room watched red blips showing the Helghast moving rapidly towards the shoreline of the Corinth River.

Chapter Eight

We were over the river, on the shoreline, racing towards the crater, and the Higs were pummelling us, especially the four HAMRs leading the way. Our job was to punch a hole in their defences for the rest of the convoy to blow through: Rico and his HC, Solowka, were in HAMR Four; yours truly in the turret of HAMR Two, with my HC, Gomez, in the driver's seat. Gomez was only happy when he was driving – and driving made him very happy. He'd learned to drive on his family's land in the Vektan countryside and, shit, did they train those farm boys right because Gomez could *really* drive that thing.

We bounced along the shoreline, skeletal buildings and girders reaching from the dirt like the fingers of a corpse. Above us in a rusty, mottled sky were Helghast ships making their way to join the onslaught of our cruisers. The howl of them was deafening. The thump of automatic gunfire was deafening. The roar of the HAMR engines was deafening. My world was forged from mechanical noise.

Bullets spanged into the hull of the HAMR and I

spun the turret, opening fire on Hig infantry in a building to my left. Bastards had occupied all of the higher ground and were raining gunfire on us. From another building tracer fire split the sky. Shells spattered into mud and concrete and rattled off the HAMR's armour.

Let them come. I wanted to be off this planet so bad I could taste it.

'*Oh baby*,' shouted Gomez, so loud I wasn't sure if I heard him over the comlink or from the driver's seat below. 'There's our cruiser. Is that the Dauntless or the Compulsion?'

I swivelled in the turret, straining against the harness to see our ships. We had three cruisers in position – the Compulsion, Dauntless and Arcturus – but I saw nothing ... nothing but a skyline of jagged buildings, like a row of broken teeth. Maybe Gomez was mistaken.

Suddenly: '*It's the Compulsion*,' shouted Rico from HAMR Four, and even over the static-soaked line I could hear the joy in his voice. I twisted as Gomez crested a busted-up bit of the highway and suddenly there it was. In the middle of a sky riven by war hung our ships, three giant sentinels barely withstanding the barrage of the Helghast missiles. Explosive blasts marbled the sky, the sound of them dull in the distance.

'All units,' called Rico, 'we've spotted our evac. Stick together. Get everybody to the extraction site. We'll plough the road.'

'Copy that,' I replied.

We were close now. Christ, we were close, and the enemy must have known that too. Their best bet was to send armour after us, but maybe they were clean out of tanks and APCs because there was no armour we could see.

'Sev, at your six. You got armour.'

Shit. Spoke too soon. The turret whined as I spun to get visual on a line of AAPCs at our rear. My cannons spat, barrels glowing with the heat. The first carrier careered off the track in a shower of sparks and fire, but behind it was another one and it returned fire, forcing me to crouch in the turret as hot sparks rained down around me, screaming at Gomez to speed up.

'Gimme a fucking break,' he shrieked in reply, just as the second tank rammed us.

'*Evasive*, Gomez,' I yelled back, 'execute evasive . . .'

He did and I lurched in the harness as the HAMR slid in a storm of dirt. If an AAPC could look surprised then that's how the Hig carrier looked as suddenly we were side by side with it and it was firing at nothing. The cannon jumped in my hands as I emptied into the carrier, which rolled and exploded. Gomez whoop-whooped his approval and pulled us back on to the track, wheels spinning, picking up speed again. I looked behind and could see some of our convoy but not all, just as confirmation came over the comlink.

'Enemy keeps reinforcing.'

'We've got massive Hig build-up here.'

'Command, we're going to have to find another way through.'

Trying to shake off the feeling that things were falling apart, that the whole evac was FUBAR, I warned Gomez about incoming RPGs then reduced a crumbling building to dust with the cannon, seeing screaming Higs fall. Ahead of us, Rico was mopping up the last of the armour, but judging by the sound of what was coming over the comlink they'd closed in behind us, scattering even more of the column. This wasn't over yet. Christ, not by any means.

And so much for punching a hole. When the HAMRs eventually pulled over, what came through in our wake was a skinny procession of APCs, buggies and Archers. Only a fraction of the convoy, and a demoralized fraction at that: inside the APCs troops stared out of the windows with wide, haunted eyes, and what I saw on their faces was disbelief. They couldn't understand how we could go from being a conquering force one moment to a tattered, retreating army the next. We, the ISA, the biggest bad-asses in the galaxy. There's no training for that. Defeat has no protocols. It was beyond their capacity to grasp.

Over the comlink we started getting reports that the Higs had fallen back to establish a perimeter, that they had set up mobile arc cannons and armour. There was no end to it. They wanted us dead as badly as we wanted to get out.

Then: 'Alpha Squad, do you read?' I heard in my headset.

'Copy that, this is Sevchenko, Alpha Squad.'

'This is PFT Gutman,' he said. 'We're pinned down here and attempting to disable an arc cannon. Request back-up.'

'Give me your location, PFT Gutman,' I said, and indicated to Rico, raising Gomez at the same time. The dilapidated fragment of convoy trundled on towards the extraction point as our two HAMRs turned and we began negotiating the rubble towards Gutman's signal. Elsewhere the rest of the convoy was finding other ways through; like all of us, fighting every inch of the way.

Sure, the Higs wanted us dead badly.

But we wanted to get out more badly than that.

Chapter Nine

We were close to the pinned-down squad when an enemy arc cruiser opened fire on one of our Intruders – one so close to me that I saw the pilot's eyes widen a second before he burned to death and the Intruder exploded in a ball of flame, raining shrapnel on me in the gunner's turret of the HAMR. I shrank down in the harness as the burning dropship flailed in the air then sank with a whine of stricken engines, finally hitting the ground.

Right in our path.

'Gomez,' I shouted, '*stop.*'

'Copy that,' replied Gomez, wrestling with the wheel and swerving at the very last second. Beside us, Rico's HAMR also skidded to a halt.

We found ourselves below the level of a highway; from it came the sound of a firefight: Gutman and his men. I was unclipping my harness at the same time as Rico, the pair of us jumping down from our HAMRs, assault rifles ready. Gutman and his men were close.

'Gomez, remain here,' I said, slamming a clip into my M82.

'No fucking way, sir.' He grinned a big insolent farm-boy's grin at me. 'I'm coming with you.' He pulled out his sidearm and cocked it to show he meant business.

'Listen, I need you here monitoring comms and ready for evac,' I sighed. 'Solowka's staying too. Keep each other company.'

Gomez pulled a face. 'Alpha Squad business only, eh?'

'Yeah, and business is booming.'

He frowned, but holstered his pistol. 'You make it back in one piece, please, sir.'

I looked from the turret towards the extraction point where our cruisers battled on. 'Sure,' I said, and climbed down from the vehicle.

Private Gutman and his men were taking cover from hostile gunfire, most of it coming from a gantry at their twelve. They had a second Intruder in support, but as we ran over to the group a beam of petrusite fizzed into the air from the far side of the gantry. It found the Intruder and blew it into fragments, raining white-hot shrapnel down on us as we took cover, huge chunks of the dropship thunking down into the road, followed by cooking chunks of flesh.

How many? I wondered. How many had been on the ship? When do we get to stop dying?

Further up the road was another ISA group and this lot was beckoning madly to Gutman's group to join them. Everywhere there were bodies of dead ISA. The two groups were pinned down, the men terrified, and for a second I felt a spasm of irritation: what the fuck did these guys think they were doing? Why the hell didn't the first group move up and join the second? Use cover. Set up a grid. Lean and peek. Judging by the bodies in the street they'd been trying to run the distance between them, but it was a dumb tactic. It was getting them killed.

'What the hell are you doing? Come forward,' yelled the trooper from down the street. Bullets smacked into the concrete and another beam of petrusite divided the sky as though to ward off any further advance. These guys didn't need telling twice.

'No way, man. No way,' Gutman was calling as Rico and I scuttled over, keeping low and squeezing off a few rounds at the hidden Helghast troops. Gutman looked us over, boggle-eyed, sweat gleaming on his brow. Seeing we were friendlies he relaxed a little. Then on realizing we were Alpha Squad he decided we were in charge right now. Never was a soldier so pleased to be demoted.

'What are you doing?' I snapped at him. 'You gotta keep moving.'

'Captain Narville said we need to take out the arc

cannon,' he managed between gasping, frightened breaths, 'but the machine guns are tearing us apart.' He gestured up at the gantry. 'We just don't have enough men. The convoy's too scattered.'

Rico and I shared a glance. That psychic connection again.

'See?' said Rico to me, in a near-whisper. 'We told Narville this was going to happen.'

I nodded. Looked around and saw a side door.

'Okay,' I told him, 'I'm going to get to higher ground and take out the machine guns. You think you can get these guys to move forward?'

Rico gave me a withering look. Of course he could. And as if to prove the point he leapt up, already opening fire and urging the terrified men on, providing cover as I went left, first through the door and out of harm's way. The last I saw was Rico yelling at the soldiers, and I grinned: they were in good hands now.

Another Intruder went down. I could hear Rico over the comlink, cursing, ordering the men to form up on him, at the same time shouting at me to clean up the machine gunners on the gantry.

Okay, Rico. One thing at a time. Making my way up I met Helghast on the stairs, exchanged fire, took them out, made my way up a floor and surprised some more guards. Two snipers were startled and tried to turn their rifles on me, but were too slow; the first I took down with a headshot, the second I shot in the stomach and he lay writhing for a moment.

I tried not to think about them, especially the writhing one, who died in agony. I tried not to think that their ancestors once lived on Earth, just as mine did, and that somewhere within all that fanaticism was a human being, with the same hopes and fears as me. I tried not to think of all that as I watched the dying sniper gurgle and spasm on the floor. Instead I thought of my mom, my dad and Amy. And then took his sniper rifle.

It was a VC32. I checked the ammo was armour-piercing and took up position. Over the other side of a courtyard were more snipers and I steadied my breathing, the VC32 snug in my shoulder. I adjusted the scope to find the first Hig sniper who was behind cover in a building opposite, oblivious to me. I positioned the crosshairs on his head, tried not to think of him as human, squeezed the trigger. His head exploded.

I worked my way to the gantry where I cleared up a couple of machine gunners. By the time I got there, Rico and the ISA group had advanced, but were still pinned down.

Below was the arc cannon – an APC with a modified turret. The cannon itself was revolving slowly, moving to coordinates, and the thick, contoured barrel seemed to shimmer, as though barely able to contain the death within. It was still shimmering as Rico's grunts moved up, killed the crew and laid demo charges. Thumbs up; the guys retreated for the fireworks, getting as far away as possible.

It exploded with a heat that seared the skin, a wall of fire rising as high as my position. There was a moment's silence after the explosion. None of us had seen one of these things go up before. We didn't know the stability of petrusite; there might be secondary explosions, some unforeseen reaction. But there was nothing. The APC burned. A thick column of black, oily smoke rose up to join the nuclear haze above, and the grunts were giving it *Aroohah*, and slapping each other high-fives.

Whoop it up, guys, I thought. Enjoy it while it lasts. But it was just one arc nest, and the news over the comlink was bad. The convoy was scattered in different positions around the crater, trying to break through the Higs' perimeter. In my headset I could hear group commanders calling in, trying to raise Narville and calling for Intruder support to airlift them over the Hig defences or just to provide reinforcements or back-up. Cutting through all of them came a woman's voice.

'Assistance . . . I repeat. Echo Echo Two Three Mayday. This is Jammer, over. Can anyone hear us?'

She sounded close to panicking, just holding it

together. Rico shot a glance at me and replied. 'My name is Sergeant Velasquez. I hear you. Over.'

'Oh, thank God,' replied Jammer. 'We're in quadrant four-four-one. We have been cut off and need assistance.'

'All right, stay calm, Jammer,' replied Rico. 'Send me your exact coordinates and we'll come get you.'

We did our psychic thing. We were going to get her. She was hardly the only ISA trooper needing help, but she was nearby, and, shit – Alpha Squad never left a man behind and we sure as hell never left a woman behind. We were just about to leave the group and return to our HAMRs when Narville cut in.

'That's a *negative*,' he barked over the comlink. 'Jammer, hang tight. Intruders are on their way.'

Rico frowned. I knew that look. That was a look that said Rico wasn't in the mood for trusting a word Narville said. Couldn't blame him. I was beginning to have some fairly major doubts about the captain myself. Nobody ever said getting off this rock was going to be easy but, damn, if you wanted to be kind you'd say our retreat had not proceeded according to plan, and if you wanted to be honest you'd say there'd been one almighty screw-up. And now we were paying the price: us, the likes of Gutman and now this Jammer. The whole thing left a bad taste in my mouth and I was way to the south of hothead than

Rico. I laid a hand on his shoulder to calm him down as Narville gave us our orders: 'Stick to the plan and clear the path to the extraction point,' he barked over the comlink. '*Now.*'

I gave Rico a secure-that-shit look before turning to address our group, opening my mouth to speak when suddenly the ground quaked, there was a great roar and we were about to get our first look at a MAWLR.

Chapter Ten

What was left of the buildings thumped to the ground around us. Again the tremor and this time we turned to see a shape appear behind a set of burnt-out sky-scrapers to our left – more an impression of a shape really.

Metal shone dully. I saw heavy armour and malevolent-looking gun turrets as the thing rose, dwarfing the buildings around it, leaving us open-mouthed in shock. We were looking at a gigantic mech, like nothing I'd ever seen before.

MAWLR – Mounted Artillery Walker/Long Range – one of those Hig master weapons talked about in hushed tones by grunts. It was a spider-mech, its legs ten-times-larger versions of those on the troop transport, fully articulated and all-terrain. Scaled shielding covered them, as well as the vast command centre and multiple gun turrets at its head, an ugly bulbous facility built for one purpose. Death. It towered over us now, hydraulics screeching, pro-pulsion units roaring. It seemed to pause as though looking about in order to orientate itself to the metrics of the battlefield, but if its targeting systems had tracked us then they obviously decided we were too small fry to bother with. For the MAWLR there was metal more attractive and it came in the form of the ISA cruiser Compulsion, hovering above the extraction point.

From our position on the ground we heard the whine – the whine of the vast mech's petrusite cannon as it reconfigured to target the Compulsion.

And opened fire.

The petrusite beam hit the Compulsion, but not full on. I watched as the cruiser seemed to shudder in the sky. Behind it were the other two cruisers, the Arcturus and the Dauntless, both of them hanging still – sitting targets for the MAWLR. They were already under fire from Helghast fighters and battleships and only just standing firm. They had moments left. Below them the first exhausted, ragged remnants of our army were gathering, ready for Intruders to carry them to safety. I felt my world lurch. So close to home – suddenly it all seemed so far away.

Over the comlink came the voice of Captain Mandaloniz. 'Dispersive armour is holding. All cruisers, this is the Compulsion. Lock weapons on the MAWLR and fire.'

The sky went orange, purple and red as the combined firepower of the remaining ISA cruisers opened up on the MAWLR. This was one heavily armoured Mech, though, and the cruisers were firing from long range. Not only that but they had Helghast airborne divisions to cope with too. The salvo sent the MAWLR crashing to its left to avoid a rain of missiles from above. The ground shook as ordnance detonated around us.

Now came the voice of Captain Mandaloniz again. 'Captain Narville,' he announced, the strain audible in his voice, 'we can't hold this position much longer. If you're going to get here, you better make it fast.'

At the same time, Rico and I made a move towards the HAMRs. Just as the MAWLR took a step away from us and crushed them – easy as a grunt stamping rations tins.

There was a moment of shock, then I was shouting into the pick-up, '*Gomez*, can you hear me?'

Thinking: *You made him stay, Sev. If he's dead, it's on you.*

I'd needed him alive and driving. Thought he'd be safer there.

Maybe he'd left his position.

But there was no answer. Not from Gomez nor from Solowka. Just dead air and the sight of the two crushed HAMRs, wheels at odd, dislocated angles, turrets bent, like a pair of crushed and discarded tin cans. More wreckage in a city full of wreckage. I tried not to think about Gomez, who loved driving because it made him happy, and his ma and pa, home on the farm.

'We gonna need new transport,' I said flatly, after a pause. One of the ISA group dropped his eyes and pointed back behind us. 'We saw a couple of Exos back that way,' he shrugged.

Perfect. 'Come on,' I said to Rico, indicating to the men at the same time. 'You guys get to your evac posts, now.'

The fleet was under fire both from the air and from the ground now. Our forces were scattered and confused, desperately trying to make their way to the crater any way they could, hammering on the Helghast defences, who hammered back with tanks, infantry, RPGs and, worst of all, the arc cannons that were shredding our Intruders. We were fucked, unless . . .

Unless Rico and I could use those Exos to clear a path for the whole convoy to use. A safe corridor. That was what we needed.

Okay. We were Alpha Squad. We could do this. We took off, sprinting in the direction we'd been shown.

'Captain Narville,' I called as I ran, 'find us a highway we can use.'

'Higs are plugging all the gaps right now,' he came back.

'Find us one that's not so plugged and relay the coordinates to the convoy. We'll clear a route through with the Exos.'

'Copy that.'

Moments later the coordinates came back. We had our corridor. A main artery through what had once been a busy Pyrrhus suburb. It was all on us now: me and Rico. We were getting these boys out. Never leave a man behind.

The Higs were everywhere now, and as we came upon a battle site we could see they'd taken down Zulu Squad. Not without cost, though, and among the wreckage and bodies of ISA were smouldering Helghast hovertanks and Bulls, bodies hanging out of them. The area had a quiet, ghostly feel that prickled my skin. In the middle of the highway stood the two Exos like a pair of dormant guards.

Inside one was an ISA corpse, a ragged black hole where his left eye had been. Rico snatched his ID tags before pulling the corpse from the cabin in order to clamber inside himself. The other Exo, mine, looked as though it had suffered greater damage, but, following Rico's lead, I climbed in, trying to remember the last time I'd piloted one of these things. Back on the Maelstra Barrens it was. I was no hotshot then and wouldn't be now. We left that kind of thing to Dorweiler.

I clipped my feet into waldo stirrups, then looking at the console in front of me jammed my finger at the right-looking switches. Red and green dashboard lights winked on. Motors engaged and the hydraulics sighed. Powering up, the mech began to hum, louder now. I took hold of the two joysticks and moved the twist grip gingerly. The Exo rose a little with a movement that was far more graceful than I remembered.

Dorweiler once told me that the trick to piloting a mech was to imagine its metallic limbs as extensions of your own. I pictured him in the mess hall with a mug of beer in one hand and a burger in the other, grinning at me with bits of meat and bread between his teeth. 'Just slip your arms and legs in and forget all about them. Then they ain't your arms and legs any more – what's your arms and legs is the Exoskeleton; them's your limbs now. Get that right you can make thirty tons feel like it ain't nothing.'

We'd see.

It was still warm I realized, but no matter. No time to think of the dead. There would be time later for them. For now I was following Rico as he powered his own Exo up and set off, jabbering coordinates over the comlink once more. I felt resolved. Once more I thought we could do this. We could really do this.

Chapter Eleven

Moments after getting the Exo moving I was feeling right at home. At Rico's suggestion I checked the weapons systems, which, despite the Exo being so beat up were in good working order, and we took off, going fast.

Over the comlink came Rico. 'Power levels normal. Switching to auxiliary systems.'

We came to the top of a low hill overlooking the smoking and blackened remains of what had once been a residential area. It was bisected by one main highway – and that was our route to the crater – but even as we watched we could see Hig armour moving to block it. And they had themselves an arc cannon or two into the bargain. Narville was right: they really were plugging the gaps. As we pounded down the hill towards the highway, ISA buggies and APCs were arriving, gunfire raining down on them from buildings to left and right.

'We're spread pretty thin, Command,' came an anguished cry from one of the ground troops.

'Okay,' replied Rico, 'let's get back on track. Follow us in.'

Into the maze of broken-down buildings we went. ISA tanks began appearing to our right, supporting us, and straight away we were taking heavy fire. From the rubble of the city came the screech of an RPG round which exploded with a sharp report and a blinding orange flash, rocking the whole of the Exo. I felt perspiration make its way down the back of my neck, a weird ticklish feeling – a feeling that was out of place on the battlefield somehow. I found myself wanting to scratch, but worried about letting go of the twin joysticks, and suddenly the humour of the situation was almost too much for me: piloting an unfamiliar mech across a nuclear city while facing an enemy barrage. What's bothering Sergeant Tomas 'Sev' Sevchenko the most? The droplet of sweat tickling his neck.

A crackle of static in my headset. Rico. 'Two arc cannons ahead.'

Jesus.

'Incoming armour. Locking on.'

We were on the road now, buildings either side of us, a valley of bullets. And there on the road were Helghast tanks, lying in wait for the column, expecting Archers and APCs but getting us instead. Nice to know we still had a few tricks up our sleeve. Our targeting systems adjusted. On the screen in front of me a grid shifted as the Exo found her prey. I squeezed the trigger and sent a couple of missiles into a tank ahead of me. The Hig in the turret screamed as the tank was ripped apart from beneath him and his torso flung to the ground where it lay flapping, entrails hanging like ribbons from his open stomach.

Another tank. My missiles spoke again and the chain gun rattled. Around me were the burnt remnants of buildings and structures, like huge splinters driven into the earth, and from them poured enemy infantry, disappearing in a hail of bullets and red vapour as the barrel of my chain gun glowed red and the Exo pounded forward. Inside the cockpit it was a nightmarish cacophony of battle – the *thump-thump* of the weapons, the shriek of the engines, the whine of the motors. It was as though all of the last few hours were nothing but a build-up to this moment – that things had reached a pitch: we the ISA desperate and greedy for home; the Helghast desperate to stop us. Each time we seemed to have burst through their defences they reacted with even greater outrage, throwing even more men and vehicles at us. Each time we inflicted upon them defeat they came back at us more viciously, as though they held us responsible not just for the death of Visari but for the nuke too.

Now came the arc cannons, positioned across the highway. I saw the evil bulbous turrets move, trying to find us, and shouted to Rico. We both deployed multiple missiles at range, before the arc cannons got their fix, and the APCs burst open, the explosion rocking the cabins of the Exos even from a distance.

'Arc cannons are down,' announced Rico. 'The road is clear.'

'Appreciated, Command,' said an AC over the comlink.

Then came a bang and a flash. A sound like the air was ripping and an RPG round exploded onto the hull of an Archer next to me. An ISA hanging on to the infantry handle dissolved into a spray of blood and bone. Still they were coming at us, positioned on a bridge now and raining fire upon us: a hail of bullets that splattered into the concrete and mud around. I sent a missile to the bridge. Helghast burned and died and we moved on, clearing the route, destroying everything in our path, staying alive – though Christ knows how. If not for the Exo's arm and superior firepower we would have died in the valley for sure. Behind every barricade was a machine-gun nest or grenadier, so it seemed anyway. So it felt like.

Home, I kept thinking. Home.

Until at last the final Helghast tank was turned into a ball of flame, the remains of their infantry had been mowed down or was retreating and Rico was urging the convoy to break through.

'Get your asses in gear,' he was screaming. Where the fuck was the rest of the convoy? Suddenly the comlink had gone quiet.

Then in my headset came the anguished response, 'Convoy is breaking up, Command. We're in serious shit out here.'

What? Serious shit? How come . . .

'Sir, there's a –'

He was cut off moments before I heard it for myself. A great clanging of metal that sent my Exo's tracking systems wild. Still pounding forward, I twisted in the Exo to see the MAWLR on our six and bearing down on us. I twisted back to face front and pulled on the twist-grip, speeding up, Rico doing the same ahead of me. There was the whine of a warning klaxon as the sensors picked up enemy targeting systems attempting to lock on and now I drew level with Rico and could see that he too was jabbing at buttons on the console in front of him. He looked up, caught my eye, the nearest I've ever seen him to looking terrified.

Pounding after us came the MAWLR, the earth shaking. We were leading it towards the extraction zone, I realized. Two klicks north, out of sight, with only the raging air battle above to betray its position.

'Got to lead it away from our boys, Rico,' I yelled.

'Copy that,' he said, and we both turned, hoping the MAWLR would follow.

Be careful what you wish for, eh? It came after us. Now we were coming up on some open space and I was sweating freely now, leaning on the sticks, but terrified of the Exo losing its footing. Hit a hole at this speed and I was going down. Dorweiler, God rest his soul, he had natural padding. Not me, and whoever had designed this thing had gone easy on the luxurious upholstery. I was going down. And it was going to hurt. Just another day in the ISA.

Behind us, the MAWLR opened fire. Either it had got impatient or thought it had a lock. Whatever.

The world went white. A blinding flash. I felt a wave of something burst in the air, a shudder that went through me and that rocked the cabin of the mech so hard it could no longer maintain balance. The Exo spun and so did I, cracking my head on one of the uprights. Things went grey, then brown, then the ground was rushing up to meet me, the wind-shield spider-cracking, me thrown around inside the cabin as we hit the ground with a great screech of agonized metal and a cloud of billowing dirt.

In the sudden calm that followed, as the hydraulics sighed and died and the Exo's limbs relaxed into extinction, I lay there for a second wondering if I was dead. But then I couldn't be dead because death surely wouldn't be as full of suck as this was right now. Death wouldn't feel like lying in the crumpled remains of a combat Exoskeleton wondering if a gigantic mech was preparing a second bolt of petrusite to finish you off. Death had to be better than that.

I groaned. Around me smoke settled and then parted like drapes. I gasped at the heavy Helghast air, started patting myself down, checking everything was there: hands, arms, feet, legs, ears, nose. Rico must have had a softer landing than I had. Either that or he was made of some kind of indestructible metal. But he came sprinting round the steaming skeleton of the Exo to collect me. We looked about for the MAWLR and saw it on the horizon. It had turned, was heading back towards the crater – the extraction point – to where our troops were now headed. Things were coming apart. I had a moment of simply not knowing what to do, then over the comlink came the voice of Jammer again.

'Captain Narville, this is Jammer.' She sounded close to breaking point now. 'Do you read?'

We both flinched as from above us came a great explosion and we were showered by a fine drizzle of debris. Still the battle raged in the skies. Our cruisers being overrun.

Over my headset Jammer was breaking up. 'Captain Narville, we can't stay here. Where are those Intruders?'

We heard Narville reply. 'This is Narville. If they didn't make it . . . there's no one else I can send. For what it's worth, I'm sorry, Jammer.'

'I'll go,' said Rico suddenly.

I looked at him sharply.

'Velasquez, stick to your orders,' barked Narville over the comlink.

Like I'm always saying, Rico had a shorter fuse than most people. Hell, he had a shorter fuse than most grunts, who have a shorter fuse than most. So far we'd stood by, done things the military way, let Captain Narville make stupid-ass mistakes, let him allow the convoy to be broken up so the Helghast could pick us off. We'd only got this far thanks to me, to Rico, to the likes of Dorweiler and Gomez and Solowka. Good men who died following stupid commands.

'Fuck your orders,' exploded Rico. 'I didn't come here to run from Helghast. I don't leave people behind. Hang on, Jammer. I'm coming.'

'*Velasquez*,' snapped Narville, but Rico wasn't listening. He'd yanked out his headset so he couldn't hear the captain any more. And he looked at me as though daring me to stop him. I knew better than to try, instead saying, 'I'm with you, Rico.'

'This one's on me, buddy. Besides, you gotta tell Narville to wait, okay?'

I nodded.

'I'll meet you at the extraction point,' said Rico simply. And that was it. He sprinted away and I watched him go, wondering if I'd ever see him again.

Chapter Twelve

Okay, no time to get all misty-eyed – I had to make it to the extraction zone, hope that as much of the convoy as possible had made it through the corridor.

With the air full of thunder, I jumped into a trench and started to make my way back towards the crater, stopping every now and then to crouch as stray missiles exploded on the ground above me, showering me with mud and concrete chips. The noise now was intense, the ferocity of the battle even greater, if that was possible. And when I surprised Helghast troops in the trench they came at me as though they wanted to die – like dying was better than letting me leave alive.

'Don't let them escape. Kill them all,' I heard. Nice of the guy to let me know he was coming. I crouched, tucked the assault rifle into my shoulder and squeezed off a burst that took out his stomach as he came over the lip of the trench. He plunged, screaming, alive enough to shout for back-up, and I put another bullet in his head, changed the clip just as a second infantryman came running. I took him down. He joined his comrade twitching on the floor of the trench and I stayed on one knee for a moment or so, in case they had any pals. No. Good.

I kept going, hunched over, taking heart from their recklessness. Their desperation was making them easy to kill. The assault infantry usually find cover before opening fire – or so we were taught at the academy. Not these, though. They were rushing headlong into battle, more intent on screaming obscenities at me than on killing me. I took down another and he fell, his assault rifle by his outstretched arm. I snatched his ammo, and was about to go through his tactical vest for frag grenades, when something stopped me.

Fluttering to the dirt of the trench floor beside me was a picture and I bent my head to look at it, half expecting to see the ugly mug of Scolar Visari staring back at me. But it wasn't. It was a Helghast woman. A fellow soldier, by the looks of things. She stood, wearing the uniform of an elite shock trooper, smiling, with her SMG in the crook of one arm and her combat helmet under the other. Looking at her I realized she looked almost pretty; the pictures of Helghast women I'd seen at home made it seem as though they were all in the final stages of radiation poisoning. They had ghostly white skin and white scalps shone through oily, bedraggled hair. Some of the more lurid illustrations even showed them toothless or with rotting teeth.

This one, though. Like I say, almost pretty. Her skin was paler than that of the women I was used to seeing, but otherwise she looked just like any other human. There was even something cute about her smile. I glanced at the dead assault infantryman with new eyes. Were they brother and sister? Husband and wife? For a second I considered ripping off his respirator and helmet as though seeing his face might give me a clue, but just then a commando came screaming over the top of the trench, waving an LS13 like he was doing some kind of dance. I twisted and pumped three bullets into his head then rolled to avoid the body as he fell, blood and brain matter spilling from the jagged hole. Deciding I liked the look of his shotgun for this kind of work, I took it, chambered a round and straight away found myself confronted with two more assault infantry. I dropped them both, continued dashing up the trench, the crater much closer now, the noise of the battle practically deafening – so loud it seemed to drown out all thoughts. So loud that I almost didn't hear the voice in my headset: a stranded ISA calling to Narville.

'We can't get to the crater,' said the grunt. 'There are Helghast everywhere.'

'Don't give up, son.' Narville sounded close to breaking himself. 'We'll hold this position as long as we can . . .'

I threw a couple of my frag grenades to take out a pair of advancing assault infantry, ducking away from the blast. At first I thought the screams I heard were the two dying Higs, but realized they came from my headset. It was the same ISA guy as before. 'We have incoming Helghast, all directions, repeat all –' he screamed, before the link went dead.

Then came another grunt: 'We're tracking multiple APCs coming in your direction.'

Another shouting, 'Push forward, push forward.'

I shoved more shells into the shotgun, kept running. All I could hear over the comlink was my own men being cut to pieces. Then at last I was emerging from the trench and into the crater.

Into a scene straight out of a nightmare.

The sky was almost black with craft. In the middle were our three cruisers: the Compulsion, Arcturus and the Dauntless. All three of the once-majestic ships showed signs of extensive damage. Fire bloomed along their holds. Flaming debris spiralled away from them. Around them buzzed Helghast ships: their fighters, which attacked in groups of three, making fast, damaging sorties on the cruisers; larger battleships firing missile batteries, gradually depleting the cruisers' shields; and the leech pods, which pierced the hulls of the cruisers and stuck there like metal ticks. Inside each leech pod were up to six Hig soldiers and the crews of each cruiser would have to reach them and neutralize them before they could deploy.

As I watched, the barrage only seemed to intensify and the cruisers appeared to tremble in the black and orange sky. Below them, the crater. This had been the epicentre of the Red Dust blast and everything within a mile radius was rubble and wreckage. Everything, that is, apart from one building, black and gutted but still standing, right in the centre of the crater. It had been two buildings once, connected by a series of gantries so that it looked like – and here's irony for you – a huge letter H silhouetted against the nightmarish sky.

It was here that our troops had been assembling. Here from where the Intruders were taking off, transferring their precious cargo from the bomb-bleached planet to the relative safety of the cruisers above. It was a mad dash, a disorganized retreat. Enemy sniper fire was picking off troops caught between taking cover, returning fire and clamouring to board one of the Intruders. At the perimeter I could see the red eyes of the Helghast. They were getting closer. Just assault infantry as far as I could see, and, while our boys were holding them back, if they got an LMG set up, we were sitting ducks.

I had to get over there now and, trying to work out a route from my position at the edge of the crater to the husk of the building, I suddenly heard a great rush of metal from behind me and spun to see a MAWLR rising from a position at my rear. There to my left was another.

I knew what these guys could do. I saw the petrusite cannon on the first begin to spin, winding up, charging, and it fired, the blue electrical bolt lighting the sky, but passing – miraculously – between two of the cruisers, coming closest to the Arcturus, which was highest, rising – *surely* – to safety.

And it did – the cruiser got lucky. Chalk one up for the good guys. I scrambled out to the lip of the trench and used the cover of the MAWLRs to dash across the crater, scrambling over piles of rubble and towards the AO where four Intruders were picking up the last of our boys. They were doing it by the numbers, some providing covering fire as others clambered aboard, grabbing hold of straps or clinging onto the rail. All had hope in their desperate eyes.

There was no sign of Rico, but Narville was standing on the deck of an Intruder that hung a few feet off the ground, being buffeted by explosions, hanging on for grim life as around him the last of the ground troops were scrambling onto the cargo beds of the dropships.

'Goddamn, this isn't a drill,' he shouted, flinching

as a fresh hail of bullets spanged off his Intruder. 'Get to your transports. *Move.*'

He saw me. 'Sevchenko,' he said, and gave me a thumbs-up. 'Good job clearing that corridor.'

'Rico more than me, sir,' I hollered. 'Is he here?'

'No, he is not here, Sergeant, and we're not waiting for him.'

I felt a surge of anger. 'You mean you won't.'

'I mean I can't, Sev,' he insisted, and I saw that this had nothing to do with how he felt about Rico and all to do with getting his men to safety.

With a rushing sound one of the Intruders began to rise. Heavy with troops, some hanging off, some dangling dangerously off the sides, it took a moment to regain its balance and I found myself holding my breath, willing the little battlefield taxi to take the extra weight. It did. A muted cheer went up.

I scanned the AO for Rico.

Come on, Rico. Come on.

The second dropship began its ascent, just as loaded with men. A grunt lost his grip and with a scream plummeted to the waste ground beneath, breaking his back on the stone and lying with his limbs splayed out at odd angles. Above him the Intruder listed at the sudden weight imbalance, then righted itself.

Come on, Rico. Come on, Rico.

A third Intruder went up in a hail of tracer fire.

'*Sevchenko, give me your hand,*' commanded Narville.

I hesitated. 'Where the hell is Rico?' I shouted over the roar of engines and tumult of battle. Narville opened his mouth just as a second petrusite blast ripped into the dark skies, exploding on the shields of the Dauntless.

I heard Captain Mandaloniz over the comlink, calling from the Compulsion, 'Damage report.'

'The Dauntless reports minor damage. And the Arcturus has safely reached orbit.'

Despite myself I grinned at Narville to hear the news.

'Thank God,' said Mandaloniz over the comlink, 'looks like we're going home.'

He had spoken too soon. From the left came the MAWLR, pounding across the wasteland like a giant prehistoric bird towards us. I looked at it, then back to Narville who stood with his hand outstretched, appealing to me to come aboard. Desperately, I scanned once again for Rico. No sign.

Come on, Rico. Come on.

The MAWLR stopped, towering over the AO. Motors engaged as the main turret rotated to target the ISA cruisers above us. Then it opened fire, and with a sound like metal ripping, the blue petrusite bolt split the sky and hit the Dauntless. A direct hit. It fired a second time.

Above us the Dauntless was enveloped in blue-tinged flame, the petrusite seeming to swarm all over it. Suddenly it listed violently.

My headset spat static and Captain Donaggio from the Dauntless came online. He sounded panicked. 'Dauntless to Compulsion, we have been hit. Do you copy?'

I looked upwards at the cruiser, picturing him on the bridge. He'd be regaining his balance after the lurch, unaware that blue death danced around the outside of his ship.

'Copy that, Dauntless,' confirmed Mandaloniz on the Compulsion. He was seeing what we were seeing, the Dauntless besieged by petrusite, and he knew what we knew. That right now the Dauntless was shutting down.

'We have systems reporting major shield damage,' said Donaggio, 'but I'm being given conflicting readings. Compulsion, do you have visual, because I'm getting reports of a hull breach here? What's my status? Repeat, what's my status?'

They were dead, was their status – just didn't know it yet.

'Uh, status is critical, Dauntless,' replied Mandaloniz, hopelessness in his voice. 'Advise immediate evac.'

'*Immediate evac?*' replied Donaggio disbelievingly

because you didn't 'immediate evac' a cruiser. Sure, it was *possible* to evac, and there were procedures for doing it. But immediate?

'Say again, Compulsion. Did you just advise immediate evac?'

'Affirmative, Dauntless.'

Donaggio understood now. Perhaps as the last of the lights on his console winked out.

'Copy that, Compulsion,' he said. 'Dauntless out. Tell them we tr—'

Then he was cut off as the ship's systems imploded and, crippled, it began losing altitude, dropping slowly, like a vast stalactite. I thought of the crew. The ISA troops they had already rescued. All of them, moments away from death.

Over the comlink came Mandaloniz, yelling at Narville to move. At the perimeter I saw Helghast retreating, needing to get as far away from the crash site as possible. I saw Narville look away from the site of the descending cruiser and to me. He was imploring me. 'Sev, get aboard now.' One eye on the Dauntless. 'Get aboard now, soldier. That is an order.'

I took another look around the AO, still desperately scanning for Rico. 'No. Not without Rico.'

Behind us there was an explosion that ripped through the Dauntless and part of the ship sheared off, as though cleaved in two. Narville's eyes were wide as he said, 'I'm sorry, Sev.' And he yanked me aboard so hard that I was sprawling to the deck before I had a chance to resist.

No. No one gets left behind.

With a roar of boosters the Intruder began to rise. I scrambled to my feet to confront Narville, only to see the Dauntless as she began to break apart like a bottle smashing in slow motion. Arcing from her were giant chunks of flaming shrapnel, the pieces spinning out of control and liable to go anywhere – likely to plough into us, vulnerable in our tiny battle-field taxi.

Then . . .

Christ knows how I heard him, but I did.

'*Hey.*'

It was Rico.

I threw myself to the side and leaned over the railing to see him below us, dust and dirt and our Intruder's propellant fumes swirling around him, shielding his eyes with one hand and waving his rifle with the other. With him was a girl – Jammer, I guessed – who stood supporting an injured grunt, his arm round her shoulder. With them, another six or so ISA guys. All of them were looking up at us with wide, beseeching eyes.

'*There*,' I shouted. 'It's Rico.'

Narville saw. Then looming over us was the main

body of the Dauntless about to impact the AO and I was desperately waving to Rico to find cover. He saw too, and just had time to realize the moment was lost before he was urging Jammer and the ISA guys to disperse. Glancing up at me, our eyes met one final time and then he was gone – lost in the eddying dust. The Intruder rocked as with an almighty shockwave the Dauntless finally exploded into the crater. Huge shards of red-hot flaming metal were racing up and past us, narrowly missing us, the air suddenly full of debris and shrapnel. Our Intruder was bounced around and though it was small enough to avoid the larger hunks of metal the Compulsion wasn't so fortunate. A colossal fragment of the Dauntless collided with it and a series of mini explosions bloomed along its length.

That's okay, I thought. They had protocols to deal with that; sections of the cruiser could go offline and the ship would remain operational. We powered towards it still.

Then an even larger piece of shrapnel sliced into it and suddenly the entire cruiser was ripped open like a tin can, venting atmosphere and bodies into space.

And we had nowhere to go. I lurched to the other side of the Intruder, shoving grunts out of my way and craning over the side to stare at the ground beneath, and desperately looking for any sign of Rico. All that was below us was the furnace of the

Dauntless, flaming debris and shrapnel everywhere, like a series of sentry posts. Then the air seemed to shake as a massive section of the Compulsion stabbed into the ground and split, and we were rocked by yet another explosion as Narville came over the comlink, unable to hide the resignation, the sheer defeat in his voice: 'This is Captain Narville contacting all surviving personnel. Retreat to emergency fallback locations. I repeat, emergency protocol Five-Nine-Echo is in effect.'

He looked at me. 'God help us,' he said.

PART TWO

Chapter Thirteen

It was six months after the ISA's aborted invasion of Helghan, and Pyrrhus City had been transformed. Though it remained uninhabited and its buildings razed, the Helghast machine had swung into action, reshaping the city from a bomb site into something more. Something that was no longer a city. The people would still gather here when Orlock called a rally. They would come in their tens of thousands to hear him outline his plans for the Helghast future. But they would not live here. It was being developed for another purpose.

Jorhan Stahl gazed upon it now from the windows of Visari Palace, the dark monolithic structure that cast a shadow both literal and metaphorical over the site. He looked towards the crater where most of the activity was focused, where huge structures reached from the ground way, way up into the roof of the sky. They would be finished soon, and Orlock would call his rally, and the people would form in lines to hear him and cheer him on, and once again the Helghast nation would rise.

And Jorhan Stahl would be there. For he had a few plans of his own and was feeling quietly triumphant with their progress so far. Indeed, as he made his way towards the senate rooms of the Imperial Palace, his capture troopers at his heel, the temptation to break into a grin and sneer openly at the other senators, in particular the hapless Admiral Orlock, was so great it was almost overwhelming. So inviting in fact that he found he had to make an almost physical effort to prevent himself from doing so.

Yet how sweet it would be to surrender to the urge. After so many years of having these old and withered men look upon him with disdain, how precious the moment would be when they discovered that the tables had been turned and their time was over. That they were obsolete and that from now on it would be he who looked upon them with disdain. That from now on they would have to acquiesce to his will.

Because the truth was that the senators – most of them at least, enough to form a majority – were men who held their positions not because they deserved them, or had earned the obedience and respect of the Helghast people, but because of their loyalty to the autarch, Scolar Visari.

The *now-deceased* autarch, Scolar Visari, that was, who had rewarded his confederates, not only by appointing them to the senate but by making the appointment hereditary, effectively establishing a system of birthright and patrimony to be preserved in perpetuity. All would bow to Visari's chosen few – forever.

This was unacceptable to Jorhan Stahl. Just as it had been unacceptable to his father before him.

Prior to establishing Stahl Arms, Khage Stahl had worked among the canyon mines of the Maelstra Barrens, maintaining pipelines used to transport the vast reserves of petrusite from the Tharsis refinery. And he had seen for himself how the petrusite that was at first used as a power source was developed and weaponized by none other than Scolar Visari. The very same Scolar Visari who had told the people that the Vektans profited from their suffering, when in fact there was not a single Vektan who profited from Helghast suffering as much as Scolar Visari did himself. The very same Scolar Visari who spoke grandly of returning power to the people while in secret bestowing power upon his associates.

Khage Stahl had tried to wrangle ultimate power himself, but had been foiled by Visari's associates, Orlock among them. He had remained contemptuous of the man's hypocrisy until the day he died. A contempt that was hereditary.

So, no, it was not at all acceptable to Jorhan Stahl

that Scolar Visari or his associates should be his masters. Thus, the ISA invasion had afforded him an opportunity he had grasped with both hands. Or at the very least, was *in the process* of grasping with both hands, for there was still some way to go yet. Which was why, as he took his seat along with the rest of the senate, he resisted the temptation to grin and sneer.

Not that matters had gone according to plan, certainly not at first. Six months ago, the senators had enjoyed the benefits of their hermetically sealed environment in order to view the action below. Watching the Arcturus escape, there had been much pursing of lips, and one or two disgruntled mutterings. The senators had watched Admiral Orlock carefully. In turn the Admiral had showed no emotion, simply standing with his hands clasped behind his back, watching events below. The next development was one that had pleased the assembled dignitaries greatly. And they'd allowed themselves a smattering of applause when the flaming wreckage of the Dauntless had sliced into the body of the Compulsion, sending the cruiser hurtling towards the ground, enveloped by fire; next breaking into laughter as the three ISA Intruders, bound for the sanctuary of the Dauntless, were suddenly forced to make their escape.

Stahl of course had watched the proceedings with a rising sense of trepidation, realizing that there were a number of outcomes that might prove unfavourable to him – not conducive to his plans. His tactics rather depended on Admiral Orlock being made to look foolish and incompetent. The MAWLR was after all a product of Scolar Visari's development labs; if it succeeded in destroying all three of the ISA's cruisers it would be seen as a vindication of the dead autarch's policies, not to mention his industrial and business acumen. It would be a victory for Visari and thus also for his fawning disciples. When the Arcturus had left, Stahl had felt a little warm thrill in the pit of his stomach – the exquisite sensation of a well-laid scheme coming to fruition; a sweet, luxuriant tingle; a reminder of his own great skills as a tactician.

However, the thrill had been short-lived. Next, Visari's MAWLR had destroyed the Dauntless, and it might as well have destroyed the Compulsion too, for that ship was annihilated in the same action. The MAWLR, then, quite a success – a success for Visari, by proxy Admiral Orlock; a defeat for Jorhan Stahl.

Nevertheless, there was a handful of ISA troops who had escaped. This despite the fact that the skies had been full of Helghast fighters and battleships, and the ground crawling with infantry, including commandos and elite shock troopers. The escapees had been allowed to somehow evaporate, like mist, their tiny Intruders able to avoid an onslaught of missile batteries and AA fire, even blasts from petrusite cannons. They had gone to ground. Two groups of them, as far as they knew. But as for where they were the senate was clueless.

There had followed six months of cluelessness during which Stahl had basked in that same delightful sensation of his own cleverness. Six months of meetings during which he had been able to remind Admiral Orlock of the failure of his tactics. What tremendous sport – the only drawback being that he could not allow himself to gloat as fully as he would wish. There would, however, be time for that.

And so now they gathered, as usual: Stahl with his capture troopers and Orlock with his personal bodyguard, and Stahl gazed across the great meeting table at Orlock with flinty eyes, ready to bait the old warhorse once again.

'It's been six months since Visari was murdered and where is the ISA?' he announced airily. 'Why haven't you found them yet?'

Senator Gunsteling, who Stahl despised above all other senators, being the oldest and most decrepit of Visari's lickspittles, replied in a wheedling tone, 'But they've proved to be more tenacious than expected.'

Stahl allowed himself a smile. This was so easy.

There were senators here he had to bribe. But quite honestly he sometimes wondered why he bothered when those who remained loyal to Orlock were so hapless in their defence of him.

'Which was my exact point six months ago,' he said, and turned his gaze on Orlock. 'If you had just listened to me, offered them whatever they wanted, we could have killed them and been done with it. But, no, you had to do it your way. You had to pound them until they scattered.'

'The ISA will be dealt with in due time,' rasped Orlock.

'When?' Stahl was playing to the room now. 'Hours you said, not months. The people of Helghan want results, not empty promises from you, Orlock.'

Inside Stahl was gleeful. No, Orlock had not managed to locate the ISA forces – he on the other hand knew exactly where they were; indeed, had taken several of their number prisoner.

'Once again you've somehow managed to distract us from the real topic at hand. Why haven't you delivered your weapon prototypes to the military?'

Now we get to it, thought Stahl. The weapons.

It was no secret that Stahl Arms had collected irradiated petrusite from close to the Red Dust blast and had been experimenting with it in order to create super-weapons. The military were keen to lay their hands on the prototypes, and at each meeting of the senate Stahl had assured members that matters were in hand.

Of course, he had no intention whatsoever of handing anything to the military. It was quite frankly an insult to his intelligence that the senate thought he would meekly hand over his weapon prototypes – in other words, relinquish control of the most powerful weapons on the planet to his enemies. Yet they seemed to believe this and at every meeting Orlock would repeat his requests for updates into the development of the weapons and Stahl would smile and inform him that prototypes were being built 'as we speak' and that he would soon be in a position to show to the senate his development team's schematics and models.

The designs, he informed them with a smile, were going to blow them away.

It seemed that Orlock assumed that Stahl would indeed do this at some point and it suited Stahl's purpose to let the admiral continue believing this – except during those moments when he wished to rile the admiral.

One of those moments being imminent.

Now, in fact, and he smiled sweetly as he said, 'Let me see … Why haven't I delivered prototypes? Because, Admiral, this is irradiated petrusite far beyond anything you've used before. I refuse to place weapons of this magnitude in the hands of an incompetent.'

Incendiary words, he knew, and they had the desired effect. Orlock stood, shaking with rage, while around them the other senators burst into excited chatter, some shouting, the bodyguards tense, eyeing one another.

'That's going too far, Stahl,' yelled Senator Gunsteling, obedient lap dog that he was. 'The admiral has been instrumental in the negotiations with the Vektan government.'

'Too little, too late,' smirked Stahl.

Opposite him sat Senator Kuisma, whose predilection for young boys and his recklessness in pursuit of them had left him open to blackmail. Stahl had been more than happy to oblige, compiling several hours of footage of Kuisma in action. And he looked at him now, giving him an imperceptible nod, his cue to speak.

'Given the admiral's continued failure to eradicate the ISA from our home, I motion for the Helghast military to be placed in the direct control of someone who will use it more effectively: Chairman Stahl,' said Kuisma obediently.

Stahl nodded gratefully at Kuisma, as though this commendation came as a surprise to him, just as the rest of the table erupted into a rage, chief among them Orlock, who spluttered, 'He is an industrialist.'

'With a sizeable private army and the technology to back it up,' countered Kuisma.

If only they knew quite how sizeable, thought Stahl, who had spent the intervening months building his forces.

'Is there a second?' asked Senator Gunsteling.

There was silence.

'Motion denied,' said Senator Gunsteling. The relief in the room was palpable.

Stahl stood, disgusted. He pointed to Orlock. 'As long as this man remains in sole charge of the military, I refused to commit my resources to your cause.'

His capture troopers fell in behind him as he went to leave the room, doing so in full expectation of being persuaded to stay.

He was not disappointed, hearing one of the senators mutter, 'We need him.' And there was a moment of silence at his back before Senator Gunsteling, with an accompanying snort of disgust from Admiral Orlock, said, 'Just a moment, Chairman.'

Stahl stopped. And still with his back to the men he rearranged his expression so that as he turned he projected an air of hurt into the room.

'Will you give us time to consider?' asked Senator Gunsteling.

'What?' snapped Admiral Orlock.

'In two days' time,' said Stahl, assuming a haughty air, 'I'll be making a live broadcast to the Helghast nation.'

'About what?' questioned Senator Gunsteling.

'Something that will make your decision much easier,' said Stahl enigmatically. And with that he turned on his heel and left, his shoes ringing on the polished floor, the huge double doors of the cavernous Senate Room clunking shut behind him, so that he was forced to imagine the shocked faces of the senators he left in his wake.

Chapter Fourteen

Six months we'd been hiding in the jungle. Six months of hell in a hostile, alien place where every tree and every mutant, luminescent plant hid a potential deadly poison, and every living thing was a mortal enemy; where the heat sapped our souls and the dense air burned our lungs.

On the bright side, we were now the alliance's most experienced jungle troops. On the not-so-bright side, we'd learned everything the hard way. Like PFT Oakley, who discovered that you should never reach for one of the countless vines and creepers that hang from the dark canopy of the jungle because they might shatter into sharp, lacerating fibres. He found that out when he ripped open most of his left arm, then picked up an infection in the wound. He wouldn't be grabbing any more creepers any time soon. Not with both hands anyway – Doc Hanley had been forced to amputate.

Infection: there was something else we got to learn about the hard way. Poisons were everywhere and could be absorbed in the most unexpected ways.

Like certain fungi – if you brushed up against them, two days later your skin would start to change colour, take on a greenish-grey tinge. Two days after that the MO would be frowning at your readings. Two days after that you'd be screaming and begging for mercy. One of our guys put a bullet in himself just to ease the pain.

Then there were the insects. Grotesque crawling things with wings that rustled, which would settle on your skin then pulse blackly as they began a meal of your blood; or the swarms of culicidae, long-legged and with sharp, flesh-piercing probosces. Each of us was stung hundreds of times a day – stung or feasted upon – knowing that each bite might bring death to our bloodstream. Death from what the Doc didn't quite know, but the symptoms were similar to malaria or yellow fever, so he said, though neither he nor Junior had first-hand experience of either malaria or yellow fever. We didn't have that back on Vekta. We didn't have several billion flying insects capable of transmitting these diseases on Vekta. We had trees and meadows and picnics with Mom and Dad. Not small, slithering, poisonous creatures that only came at night, things out of a nightmare: spiders, frogs and snakes with their big bug eyes, skins gleaming green and gold, ruthless, indiscriminate survival experts.

And we had no experience of the parasites that attached themselves to our skins as we slept. On Vekta the water was clean and you didn't die from dehydration even though you were surrounded by pools and streams. If we took a bath in a stream or waterfall pool, we could expect to get out, dry ourselves off, relax and open a beer. Not here – not in this venomous, poisonous place. I saw a grunt come running from a river, screaming, covered in pulsing leeches, all over. And I do mean *all over*. He screamed loudest when they pulled the bloodsuckers from his dick. Nobody bothered taking baths after that.

We were used to an enemy we could see and shoot, an enemy that had an ideology; that was who we'd been trained to face. Here in the jungle we were so far out of our comfort zone it wasn't even funny. Dehydration, malnutrition, exhaustion – all of it was gradually defeating us. And the heat was killing us. Jesus, it sucked the energy from you, right from the moment you woke up until last thing at night, when the temperature would suddenly and violently drop so that while a mere hour or so ago your clothes had been dripping with perspiration now they froze to the skin. Men shivered with fever, then groaned with the heat, then trembled through the freezing nights.

After a while it got to you that you rarely saw proper daylight. It was as though you were stuck in perpetual evening, surrounded by the moans of your feverish comrades, with the ticking, buzzing, humming, scratching, shuffling, scuttling and slithering sounds of the jungle all around you.

Like I say: hell.

So how come we were there? Why put a bunch of grunts into hostile, unfamiliar territory, limiting their chances of survival, gradually whittling down their numbers? Why do all that?

First, because the jungle was a good hiding place. In the six months since the failed evac, the Helghast had been looking for us, and thanks to the canopy it was almost impossible to find us using ground infantry, while the foliage jumbled their tracking systems. Even if they knew we were here, they couldn't find us.

Just as importantly, though, the jungle was where the uplink was based.

All those months ago we'd set up our first base in the vicinity of the grounded cruiser, Valiant, which had been shot down during the first wave of the Helghast fight-back. Bandit Recon had made forays, hoping to find it, and had done, discovering that most of the Valiant's comms equipment was still operational. Bandit was able to establish an uplink capable of relaying a signal from the camp and boosting it to Earth. We got happy that day and, minutes after Earth came online, Narville had entered the makeshift comms room to speak to them, the hopeful cheers of his men ringing in his ears. Some had even begun to pack their things. Grunts were talking brightly about evac being in a matter of days, and how we'd need to oscar mike to an evac zone, and as soon as we were there the ISA cruisers would appear in our orbit and the next thing we'd see would be Intruders dropping to rescue us, our comrades inside smiling and waving and drawling, 'Hey, what the fuck took you so long?'

Didn't play out like that, though.

Narville had emerged a defeated man. First of all there was to be no immediate evac. Negotiations were taking place between the UCN and the Helghast senate. Sure, we were still at war. But a major military operation – a rescue attempt, for example – might be seen as an escalation in hostilities, and jeopardize the negotiations.

As Narville spoke, his voice flat and emotionless, his chin set, the soldiers' heads had begun to drop. They began to murmur, 'This is bullshit. *Bullshit.*'

However, said Narville, quietening them with a hand, Earth would be prepared to mount a covert operation to effect a rescue. And their heads went up a little. We should hang tight, he said, while Earth set the wheels in motion. The operation would require careful planning and preparation. We can't expect miracles, gentlemen.

No, there are no miracles in the jungle. Because that was three months ago. Three months of survival and three months of living for the uplink like it was our God.

We stayed close to our God – when we had to move base, we stayed within comms distance of the uplink. And we protected our God. We kept Bandit Recon out there to guard it night and day.

And each day it looked more hopeless, until I was beginning to think that we should move base – only right out of the jungle now, because it was killing us – one by one. We could leave a squad by the uplink, I was insisting whenever Narville would listen – which was never. Told to stay as close to the uplink as possible, he was damn sure going to obey that order.

Then we lost Gedge and there was still no sign of an evac date. I was beginning to wonder whether Earth really had our best interests at heart, and that just maybe, to them, we were expendable, and I was still wondering that right up until the morning that Kowalski came running over to me, more animated than usual.

Like most of us, he was bearded, his hair unkempt, but, unlike most of us, it suited him – gave him the look of an old-time trapper. The rest of us just looked like guys in need of hair clippers. We'd come into the jungle looking like grunts; we were going to leave it looking like prehistoric men.

If we ever left it.

Kowalski leaned in towards me, lowering his voice. 'Sir, Bandit Recon missed their last check-in. That was two hours ago.'

'What about the signal?'

'There isn't one, sir.'

'The uplink's down?'

'Looks that way, sir.'

My stomach did a flip. 'We'd better go see Narville,' I sighed.

We found Narville across camp. 'Sergeant, tell me something good,' he said. 'What's the news on our evacuation transport from Earth?' He was doing his best to sound as though he had his act together. Like that shit with Gedge had never happened.

'Bandit Recon is gone, sir,' I told him. 'We've lost the radio uplink to Earth Command.'

His head dropped. 'Tell me it's not the Helghast.'

Kowalski butted in. 'If it is, they're using a new kind of comms signal. We're not picking up anything. Not them . . . not Earth . . .'

'And they're gonna find us,' I interrupted. 'It's only a matter of time. We've got to keep moving.'

Narville shook his head. 'Listen. We stay put until Earth Fleet arrives. Like you said, it's only a matter of time. Until then, get that radio uplink working.'

Kowalski moved off and Narville took hold of my arm. 'You know what's at stake here, Sevchenko,' he said. He looked me in the eye for what was probably the first time since Gedge had been taken. 'That uplink's our only hope of getting out of here alive.'

'Yes, sir,' I said. 'I know.'

I grabbed Kowalski and we pulled on tactical vests and body armour, slipped M32 combat knives into sheaths and packed grenades into packs; we adjusted knee and elbow pads, secured M4 revolvers and silencers, checked our M82s, checked them again and packed maximum ammo. We looked at each other: groovy.

We moved out, going fast but as silently as possible – out of the clearing and into the jungle, which danced and shone around us, assaulting us with new sights, sounds and smells. The Higs were out there. They had to be. And the way it looked they'd neutralized Bandit Recon.

Again, though: there was no Helghast air support. No blanket bombing. No tracer fire ripping up the jungle.

'It's too quiet,' said Kowalski, echoing my thoughts as we moved through the vegetation scanning for petrusite spiders, burster plants. Anything that crawled or slithered or looked like it might snap. And of course . . .

Higs.

We saw them before they saw us, most likely a small recon patrol. There would be a troop transport around here somewhere, probably one of the new spiders we'd seen back in Pyrrhus – what seemed like a lifetime ago. This was just the kind of terrain they were built for . . .

And what do you know? They weren't Helghast military. Sure looked like them at first glance, but no – they were Stahl's men. Dead men, soon to be. We picked them off. But did it up close and personal, with knives and death grips. Then we saw it: the troop transport, sitting in the middle of a clearing, and there, on the other side of the LZ was the rest of the squad. We crept into their area, taking more of them out with silenced shots. One was a capture trooper, on his uniform the logo of Stahl Arms. It was capture troopers I'd seen taking Gedge. I felt a worm of disquiet in my stomach.

We left the Hig troop transport crew dead and moved on, getting closer to the uplink, when suddenly we were stopped by a noise at our twelve. Then we saw one of our guys – Bandit Four – running across a small, craggy clearing. On him in an instant was a capture trooper, who took him down and disabled him, then picked up his unconscious body and slung it over his shoulder. Other Higs were arriving. Now I saw more troop transports, and I laid a suppressing hand on Kowalski's M82 when he brought it to his shoulder.

'*No*,' I whispered. I didn't want Bandit Four taken any more than he did, but we had to get the uplink back – and we couldn't afford to give away our position with the numbers against us.

We watched as Bandit Four was heaved into a nearby dropship, and the air was full of engine noise as the ship took off.

We looked at each other, frowning, then carried on, making our way through the jungle as quickly as before until, about one and a half klicks later, we came up on the ridge above the wreck of the Valiant – a chunk of her, at least, what had once been the comms centre. There in the ship's gashed-open belly was the radio uplink, somehow more shiny than the twisted and burnt metal that surrounded it. Also among the wreckage was the odd bit of evidence that Bandit Recon had made their camp there: a bed roll, one or two billycans. But there was no sign of the troops themselves. The place was quiet.

We were about to climb down when suddenly there was the roar of dropships and we flung ourselves out of sight as the air above the wreck filled with Overlords – three of them, all bearing the logo of Stahl Arms. Infantry lines unfurled. Down them came Hig grunts.

I keyed my headset and toggled to base. 'Captain Narville, this is Sevchenko. Come in,' I said into the pick-up.

The headset clicked. On came Narville. 'Speak to me, soldier. Do you have a visual on the uplink?'

'Yeah, I see it all right. But, sir, there's a massive military build-up here. They're obviously not here for a downed cruiser. You need to evacuate the camp immediately.'

'Sergeant, please don't make me repeat myself. It's beyond necessary that I have that uplink. Is that clear?'

'Yes, sir. Can do.' My heart sank. Fucking Narville. Couldn't see the threat when it was right there in front of his face. I turned to Kowalski. 'Okay, I'll deal with the uplink. You get back to base. Try to convince Narville to get everybody out of there.'

I watched him go, then crept forward, closer to the wreck of the Valiant. The Hig troops had begun to disperse outwards, creating a perimeter, and they weren't paying as close attention to their LZ as they should have been, so I was able to climb down into the crater unobserved and found cover between some rocks – where what I saw made me catch my breath.

There, standing among the broken metal shards of the Valiant, were three Hig soldiers, obviously enjoying themselves – having the time of their lives at the expense of an ISA guy kneeling hurt at their feet.

Poor kid. It was Bandit Six, I was sure of it. He knelt as though trying to catch his breath, his head hung, ropes of blood and snot trailing from his mouth and nose. The men were yelling at him, tormenting him. One of them held a weapon, a huge thing that I'd never seen before, with some of the same characteristics as the VC5 Arc Rifle but much bigger, more evil-looking, and he was shouting something at Bandit Six. Then grabbed him by the scruff of the neck and dragged him to his feet.

'I said *get up*,' he growled.

Bandit Six was looking at him, barely able to focus, his head lolling with pain. He was thrown to the deck, snivelling as he was kicked.

'You'd better go. Run,' jeered the first Hig.

The second chuckled and hefted the arc rifle. The effort of doing so meant he had to lean back slightly as Bandit Six got to his feet and with a cry of despair began to run. Right towards where I was hidden.

Our eyes met for a moment and I saw the recognition register on his face. Then the rifleman opened fire. It didn't matter that he was off balance and barely aiming the rifle. The petrusite found its target, knocking Bandit Six to the ground, where the lethal energy swarmed over him. He screamed. Looking up, he saw me again and his hand was outstretched, trying to find mine. I reached forward and suddenly he was hoisted away from me. A second bolt from the petrusite had taken him and was lifting him, his entire body now engulfed by swirling, glowing energy. Screaming, his eyes bugged. Blood began seeping from his ears and nostrils and mouth. His skin appeared to ripple, twist and distend as though in zero-gravity training. Or as though his entire body was being incinerated from the inside to the out. Finally his eyeballs burst and thick purple fluid gushed from his nose until at last he simply exploded, blood, flesh and other matter showering me in my hiding place.

'I love this thing,' cried the Helghast soldier, holding the arc rifle like it was a prize catch.

I touched my finger to my face and looked at Bandit Six's blood. I'm not a vengeful guy, believe it or not. I knew that most enemy grunts were just like ISA grunts. They were guys doing a job, and they had families – wives, kids, girlfriends – just like anyone else. Being a fanatic, it doesn't stop you loving what's yours. But these three – these three had lost their humanity. I watched them take off in a dropship, leaving a small squad behind them, then took a hold on myself. First job was to get that uplink working and I was in no mood to pussy about.

I moved into the crash site and took them out one by one: assault infantry and capture troopers. I kept my temper in check. Kept it together. Tried not to be vengeful and cruel, emotional or careless. Stayed cold and professional. Until the crash site was clear once again and – for the time being, at least – was under ISA control. Now I moved to the uplink, hit keys on the console display and felt a surge of relief as the screen glowed a comforting blue. Numbers spun, readings flicked on and off. A link blinked into life and Earth came online. I patched in Narville, and pictured him standing in the comms room, hunched over the uplink console. Over my headset came a voice from Earth, sounding distant amid the interference.

'Earth verify – uplink lima – verify command code . . .'

Narville came on. 'Blue Command, this is Captain Narville. Verify delta echo two three kilo.'

In return there was static.

'Blue Command,' said Narville, just the hint of

concern in his voice. To get this far then lose the link again – that would be the ultimate bitch. 'Do you read?'

'Go ahead, Captain Narville,' said General Bradshaw. It was a voice I knew well.

'General, thank God. The Higs are knocking at our door. Can the fleet still find us if we have to move?'

There was a long pause.

'General?' said Narville.

In a sombre voice the general said, 'Captain, listen to me. As of last night, the Vektan colonial government has capitulated. All hostilities are to be ceased immediately.'

My stomach lurched and when he recovered his voice Narville sounded as shocked as I felt. 'What are you talking about?' he managed.

'The war is over, Captain,' said the general matter-of-factly. 'You and your men will have to surrender to the Helghast forces so we can negotiate your release as prisoners of war.'

'Forgive me, General, but are you out of your mind? This is the Helghast we're talking about. You have no idea what they do to their prisoners.'

Surrender? I couldn't believe what I was hearing. I went cold.

'Those are your orders, Captain,' continued the

general. 'Stand down and surrender. The Helghast have agreed to abide by the rules of war – you will be treated humanely.'

I thought of Bandit Six. I'd seen the humane way the Helghast treated their prisoners. Were Gedge and Bandit Four being treated humanely? Somehow I doubted it.

That moment the screen flashed a warning. The signal had been intercepted. '*Captain*,' I yelled, 'they've picked up our signal. You need to stop this transmission right now.'

Christ they were fast. No sooner were the words out of my mouth than I saw dropships in the air above me. They were heading west – heading towards the camp.

'Sir, get the hell out of there,' I called, 'but don't surrender. Tell me you're not going to surrender.'

'Copy that, Sev,' said Narville.

Suddenly bullets raked across my position and I was sent scuttling for cover. Not for long, though. I'd had enough of this shit. We'd been betrayed by Earth; we were being left to rot or die at the hands of the Helghast torture masters. I was mad now.

I tossed a frag and felt nothing but grim satisfaction as two Higs died screaming, perforated by shrapnel. I put my head down and started running back towards base. Any troops I came across along the way – they died. Until I found myself coming upon one of ours, a grunt lying on the deck.

Shit, it was Kowalski. He was drenched in blood, trying to speak. I knelt to him, took his hand and shushed him as he breathed his last breath in short shallow gasps, and when he died I put my hand to his eyelids and closed them.

Another guy dead. Another visitor to my bad dreams.

This is bullshit. That's what Rico would say if he was here now. *This is bullshit.* He'd be right.

I got to my feet, called into my headset, 'Captain, this is Sevchenko. Do you read me?' He came online. In the background I could hear gunfire, screaming and explosions. They'd found us. At last, after all those months of searching, they had found us – and by the sounds of things were annihilating us.

'Captain Narville,' I called, 'do you read?'

'Little busy right now, Sergeant,' he replied.

'Okay. Okay. Hold on. I'm on my way.'

'Negative,' he snapped, 'we're evacuating, the base is overrun. Proceed to the rendezvous.'

No way. No way was I doing that.

'I'm sorry, sir. Not a chance.'

I had to reach them. Had to be with my men.

I stood. 'Double-time it, Sev,' I said to myself, and set off, coming closer to the base now, starting to see our grunts making their way away from it, some kind of evac in place at least. I saw Doc Hanley, his arm round a wounded soldier, helping him away from the clearing. Behind him came Junior, doing the same. Others were helping sick and wounded men. They pointed me back along the path in the direction of the camp from where I could hear staccato gunfire and the *thump-thump* of mortar rounds landing, more screaming. Now came more of our ISA guys.

'Narville's back at the base, holding it while we evac,' screamed one at me, just as an enemy dropship roared overhead.

I stopped. In one direction went our boys, moving to the rendezvous point. In the other direction lay Narville. And who knows why the captain had decided to make a final stand. Rico would say it was because he was a pussy who'd finally found some guts from somewhere. But I thought different. Narville wanted to make amends. He wanted to be the captain who stayed behind and died so his men could escape, rather than the captain who failed them, and I could see that. I could understand that.

Maybe I should have left him to it, but something stopped me. Something in me wouldn't let him die like that, and I dashed down into the base, now thick with smoke, in the middle of it Narville, who almost put a bullet in me before he recognized me – then acknowledged me with a curt nod. I took my place beside him and we kept up a covering fire as the last of our grunts scrambled up the path and away from the base. And then – they just kept on coming, the Helghast. Jesus, it felt like there were a thousand of them. We took out as many as we could. We must have dropped at least ten each, but they had the numbers and it was just a matter of time before they took us.

We kept firing. Kept dropping them, standing back to back now. The only cover we had was the smoke of the battle and I guess Narville thought the same way I did: that it was better to go out like this than surrender and die slowly in captivity. That this would be a good death.

I dropped a Hig to my left then turned – too late to catch a capture trooper right in my face, his knives slashing at my assault rifle, which dropped from my fingers.

This is it, I thought, going down. This is death.

Sucks to die on Amy like this, I thought, as blackness embraced me . . .

I'm all she's got.

You know how you feel when you wake up after a moment like that? It isn't relief. Because just for a moment there you were dead and the pain was over. The fighting was over. There was no more killing, no more disgust and shame and guilt. Just peace.

Then a capture trooper kicks you into consciousness.

'Open your eyes,' he commanded. I blinked. Over me stood a Hig dressed in a hazmat suit. In his hand he held a small biometric scanner with a luminous green screen that he ran over my face. It bleeped affirmative.

'This is him,' said the capture trooper. 'Report to Chairman Stahl that we have positive ID on both Narville and Sevchenko. Mission is accomplished.'

From my position on the ground I looked to my right and saw a dropship. In the hold sat Narville, his hands secured behind his back, and our eyes met, but his were dead, expressionless. This wasn't how he wanted it to be. He'd seen himself going out in a blaze of glory, not like this, not at the hands of some Helghast sadist somewhere. Now I was pulled roughly to my feet, my hands secured with a tie and shoved towards the dropships.

'Fuck off,' I shouted at one of my captors.

'I said *get in there*,' he rasped.

'And I said *fuck off*,' I retorted, sounding tough and defiant. Sounding more tough and defiant than I felt. As my two guards climbed in with me the dropship began to take off, and my mind was racing.

Think, Sev, think.

How the hell was I going to get out of this one?

Chapter Fifteen

Funny. It was the first time I'd ever been inside a Helghast Overlord. A prisoner in one, for the love of Mary. And you know what I was thinking?

I was thinking: Well howdy-doody, this is one kick-ass dropship.

My hands were in restraints and I'd been shoved into a rack normally used for seating nervous but combat-ready Hig grunts. They'd be clicked into harnesses and preparing to use the ship's rappelling system. That's right: rappelling system. You know how we dispersed from Intruders? We jumped off them. And harness? We got a handrail.

My two guards thought it would be a gas not to strap me in so I was thrown about the cabin as we sped low across the Helghast mountains, dipping and banking in a convoy of four. I soaked it up, but I did a lot of shouting, like every tumble I took was killing me, while they stood hanging onto straps, jeering, kicking me and occasionally reaching to deposit me back in the rack ready for the next time I was pitched face-first from my seat.

Laugh it up, guys, I thought. Laugh it up. I needed them thinking I was softened up and weak, because not securing me into the harness was their first mistake – and I didn't want them correcting it.

Then the climate changed. The temperature dropped and what I saw from the window was no longer the lush green of foliage, it was white and aqua-blue, and it rippled and shone.

We were flying over the Frozen Shores now. The Helghan Arctic. And the turbulence in the cabin ceased so at last I could sit, careful to look groggy but defiant, staring at my two guards in the rack opposite. They watched me implacably from behind their respirators, red goggle eyes glowing, their assault rifles on their laps.

Okay, I thought, what did I know about the HGH Overlord? That they're armed with twin-mounted VnS-10 Scylla machine guns and missile pods. And that they're heavily armoured. The window had to be a weak spot, but otherwise Overlords were like aerial tanks, about as far removed from Intruders as you could possibly imagine.

The Helghast had the tech edge on us, that much was clear, I thought, then reminded myself that it came at a cost we weren't willing to pay – living in service to the state and to the military. Visari was right when he told his people they were no longer human; he'd turned them into machines.

You can try to hide your humanity, I thought, thinking of the sweethearts' picture I'd seen. But you can't wipe it out. Somewhere in every Helghast lived that human. And that, I suddenly realized, was a fact I could use to my advantage.

I stared out of the window at the blur of the water as we rushed across an endless sea. The ship weaved between two icebergs, but I stayed on my seat. Then I returned my attention to my two guards.

'You know what he said when he died?' I said. 'Scolar Visari? You know what he told us?'

They looked at me. I wished I could see their eyes. It's easier to give someone the needle when you can see his eyes.

'He said he'd made slaves of the Helghast people. Called you the spineless masses. How do you like that, huh? He was laughing at you guys, played you for assholes.'

'He brought glory to the Helghast,' said one of them flatly, the guy on the left, who was more psycho than his pal, had been that bit more generous with the kicks and punches. He leaned forward now. 'It was the tyranny of the UCN that made us slaves. The autarch ended that, and *you* do not desecrate his memory with bullshit and lies.'

The combat knife he had at his belt wasn't secured. That was good intel.

He sure was a fan of Scolar Visari. That was also good intel.

'Hey, I wouldn't lie to you,' I said breezily. 'Maybe you should just wake up and smell the coffee on this one. I mean, he was one cowardly son of a bitch . . .'

Opposite me psycho grunt bristled. I didn't need to see his eyes any more. 'Oh man, *such* a pussy. You know what he did – what he did right before we delivered bullets to his gut? Pissed his pants. We had to shoot him just to save him from the shame. My buddy Rico said we should kill him before he shit himself and stank the whole place up.'

Psycho rose to his feet and straight away his buddy was holding him back.

'Whoa . . . whoa. Relax, man,' I jeered.

'You touch him and Stahl's gonna kill us both,' warned the second grunt.

'Whoo,' I goaded, 'that sounds bad.'

'You shut your mouth,' spat Grunt Two.

Psycho relaxed a little and Grunt Two let him go. I waited for a beat before saying, 'Look, all I said was that Visari died crying like a little bitch. If you can't handle the facts –'

Psycho charged me and threw a punch and, even though I turned into it, it caught me on the temple hard. I saw stars, but slipped beneath his flailing arms and reached with my bound hand to his leg and the unsecured combat knife there, snatched it out of the sheath and plunged it deep into his thigh. Praying I'd hit the femoral artery. Needing to hit the femoral artery.

I missed. He howled in pain and surprise and staggered back, but if I'd been on target we'd already be knee-deep in blood and I'd be one on one with Grunt Two. Instead Psycho pulled out the knife and leapt towards me, and there was no way Grunt Two was going to pull him back from this one. I closed my eyes and waited for the blade.

Then came a sound like a hammer strike on the side of the ship, which lurched violently as I opened my eyes to see Psycho standing with a harpoon protruding through his chest. A harpoon that had, thanks to some pretty fucking precision marksmanship, penetrated the window, then impaled the grunt.

Me and Grunt Two stared at the harpoon sticking out of Psycho's chest.

Psycho looked at the harpoon sticking out of his chest.

Then with a loud snick the harpoon opened into a grappling hook and Psycho was yanked back, hitting the door of the ship, pinned by the hook, wriggling.

He screamed and struggled. But only for a moment. Then the hook pulled through him, the door was torn off and both were sucked out, the Hig trailing blood and intestines.

The ship listed, the cabin suddenly a vortex. The roar of decompression was deafening and Grunt Two was sent off balance, his assault rifle skittering across the floor. He snatched it up before I could get to it and lurched to the open door – just as an Intruder swung into view.

An Intruder with a ghost standing on the deck. A ghost who was holding a minigun.

'*Rico*,' I shouted.

'Get down,' yelled Rico, and he opened up on Grunt Two who dropped screaming in a hail of bullets. The next thing I knew Rico had tossed aside the minigun and leapt from his Intruder and into the Overlord, landing in a crouch on the deck. He was real, he was alive and he was kicking butt and taking names. He had the beginnings of a bitchin' 'fro and some old guy wanted his beard back, but otherwise I was happy to report that Mr Rico Velasquez was here and he was as bad-ass as ever.

Shame his aim hadn't improved. The burst from the minigun must've snicked a turbine because suddenly the dropship was spinning. From the door I saw another Overlord in trouble, losing altitude with smoke pouring from it, clipping a third dropship as it fell and sending that one spinning out of control too. Seconds ago we had been a convoy of four. Now just one remained as the other three went down.

Which would have been just peachy if me and Rico hadn't been aboard one of them. With a single movement he sliced my cuffs then was dragging me up and to the door as the spinning dropship fell away from us and suddenly we were launched into space, air rushing around us. I saw the white-crested sea below me. I had time to think that it isn't the fall that kills you, it's the landing, when the Intruder slid into position below me. I thumped onto its deck with a back-breaking crunch, and blacked out.

Not for long. I came to with Rico kneeling over me. Which meant I was alive too. In the sky around us, I saw two more Intruders, troops on each of them – the squad Rico had rescued. I caught sight of the pilot on Raider Two and saw a woman's face. That had to be Jammer. No sign of Narville, though, which meant he'd either been in one of the Over-lords that had crashed or . . .

'We've lost Narville's dropship, sir,' I heard from the other Intruder.

'Damn it,' cursed Rico. 'Listen up, people. Pack it in. We are oscar mike back to base. Return to base.'

'Wait,' I said, 'you can't leave Narville.'

Rico gave me a look that said different.

'We've gotta go after him,' I pressed. 'No one gets left behind.'

'Sev,' he said. 'We barely got you. We don't have the firepower to –'

'I'm *not* leaving him behind,' I insisted, shouting. 'And if you're not going to help me just give me a gun and drop me off. I'll do it by myself.'

Rico sighed. 'All right, take your position.' He spoke into his pick-up. 'Raider Command to all raiders. There's been a change of plan. We're going after Narville.'

'This is a bad idea, sir,' came the reply.

'Copy that, Raider One, but we're doing it. Everybody, buckle up.'

I grinned thankfully at him and hefted the minigun, feeling a surge of something I hadn't felt in a long time.

We were taking the fight to them now, and it felt good.

Chapter Sixteen

We flew on, across the frozen shores, with the white-crested sea below us and gleaming bergs to our left and right, weaving between the great glittering canyons hewn from ice. The wind lashed at me and particles of ice in the air tore at my face, but I didn't care. We were going back into action at last. No more running. No more hiding. We were bringing it.

'So what's the target?' I shouted to Rico.

He turned to look at me, his beard and eyebrows speckled white with ice and snow. 'Stahl Arms,' he yelled back, pointing, 'in that direction. That's where they've taken Narville, plus a load of other guys too.'

I thought of Gedge. They'd wanted him alive. Bandit Four, too. And what about the rest of Bandit Recon? Had they been taken to Stahl Arms — alive? If so, why?

'How do you know all this?' I bawled at him.

'Arrogant pricks were a little too proud when they caught you,' shouted Rico. 'They got careless with what they were transmitting. This Stahl guy is bad business.'

That figured, I thought. The one recurring feature of this whole shitstorm was Stahl.

We flew on. I was in Raider Command with Rico manning a cannon by my side and De Castro flying. There were six or seven more Intruders behind us, but along with Raiders Two and Three we were the spearhead. Going fast. Hoping to catch up with the Overlord containing Narville.

Instead we met the first of the rigs, where AA guns and RPGs opened up on us, and suddenly the sky that had been almost peaceful was alive with warfare.

'All right, people,' yelled Rico above the noise. 'Watch your fire, check your targets, Narville's drop-ship is in here somewhere.'

Infantry stood on the deck of the rig, raking us with small arms fire, bullets spanging off the hull of the Intruder. I saw the vapour trail of an RPG. Thankfully De Castro saw it too and pulled off an evasive, our Intruder dipping and the RPG passing safely beneath us.

'Raiders,' commanded Rico. 'You are weapons free. Take it to them.'

Like we needed telling.

I saw the grenadier on the deck and found him in the sights of the minigun, squeezed the trigger, reduced him to screaming bloody hamburger. Then

I swept the rest of the gantry, taking out more infantry. Albini piloting Raider Three was urging us to shoot out the fuel pipes and I re-targeted, finding them on the belly of the rig, blue petrusite glowing in inspection windows.

The minigun chattered. Ripped them apart. And suddenly the rig was leaning, stricken, as explosions tore along that side.

'*Aroohah*,' yelped Albini from Raider Three as De Castro expertly banked away from the fire and to the other side of the rig where the hostiles were torn between shooting at us and diving to safety as yet more explosions obliterated their position.

'Area is clean,' announced Rico. 'All Raiders proceed to the harbour. This isn't done yet. Raider Two, lead the way.'

Pulling up at our side came Raider Two and I just had time to see Jammer in the pilot's seat as she gave us a wink. Then she was nosing ahead, leading us towards the harbour.

'Hey,' I shouted to Rico, 'she's cute.'

He nodded and grinned, yelling above the roaring sound of that rushing wind, 'Yeah, she's cute, and she's a bad-ass too – so take my advice and don't go letting her hear you say she's cute.'

I laughed then turned my attention to the next set of rigs. Like the first they looked as though they were used for mining petrusite but doubled as defensive outposts for the harbour and the main facility of Stahl Arms.

'Multiple targets, we have RPGs coming in,' said Jammer over the comlink. Now the sky was a tapestry of explosions, more RPG trails crisscrossing one another, the flare of muzzle flash as infantry opened up on us too. De Castro brought us low so that Rico and I could target fuel pipes again, and once more they buckled and exploded as we strafed them with miniguns, the rig instantly rocked by a series of explosions. Then Jammer had visual on dropships on the rigs deck and Rico was demanding ID.

My heart sank as Albini came over the comlink, 'Not our bird, sir. Narville is long gone. We're wasting our time here.'

'You let me decide that, Albini,' snapped Rico – and I knew then, if I hadn't known it before, that I'd missed the hell out of Rico Velasquez.

We raced on. The Higs would have air support soon, but for the time being we were penetrating their defences peachy keen. Was this all they had? We sailed on by as the rig blew up at our six, next chasing an Overlord that couldn't accelerate quickly enough and fell exploding into an iceberg under the onslaught of our guns.

'Command,' reported Albini, 'we're approaching Stahl Arms Deep South.'

Now I saw the huge facility in the distance. It occupied a mountain, a sprawling collection of buildings with one central edifice that towered over the entire complex, the whole thing looking less like a factory and more like a city – but a black and malevolent city that stained the mountaintop like a giant oil spill. Below it in the sea were more rigs. And now I discovered why they hadn't deployed air support . . .

'Command, we got major AA resistance on this one,' shouted Jammer, just as the AA cannons started booming and the three Intruders were in a world of shit.

'*Heavy missile fire incoming,*' yelled Albini. And there was a thump and my world spun crazily out of control as our Intruder spun on its axis.

'Command's been hit,' yelled either Albini or Jammer over the comlink. I wasn't sure which. We were going down.

We hit the edge of the harbour, the Intruder cartwheeling into the ice. For a moment I was aware of being thrown from the gunner's seat, like I'd been plucked from it and flung. Then everything went black, my hearing went, my head was full of stars and I was dizzy with concussion.

All around me was the wreckage of the Intruder. I turned on my side and vomited onto the ice, still fighting dizziness and disorientation. I could hear the bang and thump of gunfire. Then from above me the rushing sound of boosters, and looking up I saw the dark shadow of an Intruder. At the same time I became aware of Rico, yelling something . . .

I saw a body. It was De Castro, and I strained to see whether or not he was breathing. He was lying on one side, an arm outflung and his legs at strange, odd angles. Then I saw the blood spreading from beneath his head. Another one, I thought. Another good man down.

There was a chatter of gunfire from somewhere and a dotted line of tracer fire split my vision and sent the Intruder above us skittering away, dipping violently as it went. But where was Rico? Suddenly I had a lurch of pure terror at the thought of losing him a second time.

'Hey,' I shouted. '*Rico.*'

I almost didn't hear the reply through the noise of gunfire, the roar of the Intruder engines from above. But then I caught a groaning from my left and I did the check: arms, legs, ears, nose, then scrambled to my feet and scuttled over to where he was pinned beneath a piece of Intruder wreckage.

I heaved it off him and he lay there, grinning

grimly at me. 'Now you see why I didn't want to come in here?' he croaked.

'Can you walk?' I said, and held out a hand as he got to his feet. He saw De Castro and now I got a better look at him too. Poor guy had come through the cockpit of the Intruder by the looks of things; his face and head had been lacerated. Thankfully it had been quick. Rico confirmed it by feeling for a pulse, then nodding sadly.

Now I saw where we were – on an outcrop of the ice. Behind us was the sea and the smoking wrecks of the rigs we'd already passed. Ahead of us the two AA rigs, the harbour serving Stahl Arms and some kind of tanker anchored in the water. Our two Intruders hovered to try and pick us up, but they were already taking small-arms fire and the AA cannons would lock on soon too.

'Stop trying to land,' I yelled. 'Pick us up at the end of that tanker.'

I indicated across what seemed like an endless expanse of icy sea to the forbidding grey hulk of the tanker. At the far end was a deck just sheltered enough from the AA guns to allow an Intruder to land. Getting there – now that was another matter. But at least if we made it we could be sure of a ride.

'Hang tight,' yelled Albini, giving me thumbs-up, 'we'll see you there.'

He peeled away, Jammer too, and I watched as they flew out of range of the AA guns, ready to swoop in from the other side.

Rico and I looked at each other like it was old times. And I had to admit I liked this a whole lot more than sheltering in the hot and humid jungle, hiding from the Higs and waiting hopelessly for Earth to honour her promises. This way – this felt less like hiding and more like hunting.

With gunfire sluicing down around us we dashed across a gangplank to the tanker. Already Hig infantry were swarming on to the deck and opening fire. And it had begun to snow. It was icy cold and my fingers barely worked as I grabbed the minigun and we moved through the ship, a vast graveyard. Infantry came at us screaming, but we cut them down, a cascade of hot, spent shells pouring from the minigun. They sent a dropship to deploy some poor sap in a jet pack and we took him out. Then guys came at us with RPGs and we took cover and picked them off. All the time we moved forward, firing short, controlled bursts, with Rico scouting ahead then backtracking, till at last we reached the far deck where Rico set off a green smoke signal and we allowed ourselves to believe that we might get picked up.

'This is Raider Command,' he hollered into the

pick-up. 'LZ is clear. Get us off this boat. I want all Raiders to move into attack formation.'

'Copy that, Command. We are inbound on your smoke. How you guys holding up?' replied Jammer over the comlink. I liked hearing her voice. Found I wanted to hear a lot more of it.

Rico scowled. 'How we holding up? Nothing that won't improve if we could take out those AA guns. Right, Sev?'

'Right.'

I was looking to the far side of the deck and a dead Helghast, half his skull missing where it had been sheared off by one of my bullets. He was still strapped into his jet pack and seeing it was giving me a cast-iron eureka moment. I walked over to him, through the green signal smoke that parted like drapes for me, my feet clanging on the metal. Bent down to him.

The guns were silent for once. The gunners on the rigs near the harbour no longer had visual so they were saving ammo, but it wouldn't take long before they sent more troops over to the tanker. It wasn't like I had time for much training on this thing, but, inspecting it, I thought I could give it a go. Looked like it worked on similar principles to an Exoskeleton. Once again I recalled Dorweiler's words: think of it like an extension to your limbs. Plus I liked the weaponry: an SR3-88 submachine gun. Nice. Very nice. Yet again I found myself marvelling at the Helghast tech.

I looked over at Rico. 'What are our chances with so few Intruders?' I asked him.

'What?'

He looked over and saw what I was doing: relieving the dead Helghast of his jet pack and then kneeling, as I hoisted the heavy apparatus onto my back.

'You said yourself,' I grunted, taking the weight and getting to my feet, 'if we're going to save Narville, we need to take out those AA guns.'

'Yeah, but not . . .' He stopped, mouth dropping open, 'Oh, you're out of your mind.'

I stood there getting used to the feel of the pack. And you know what? It wasn't at all heavy when you became accustomed to it.

'Look, Rico,' I said, 'if I stay low and under their fire, then I think I can get close enough to take them out with charges.'

The Intruder arrived. Rico knew how stubborn I could be and we didn't have the time to argue. He climbed aboard, shaking his head, then retrieved a set of demo charges, which he tossed to me. I caught them and stowed them, grinning at him gratefully.

'Call us when it is clear,' he said. 'We'll be right behind you.'

The Intruder sped off and I stood there with the jet pack on my back. Okay, just me and you now, I told it. We're going to bag ourselves some AA guns.

Chapter Seventeen

The jet pack was a metallic embrace from behind and it seemed to thrum on my back as though it knew it was being called into action and was impatient to begin. I located the throttle and boosters on my left, the cannon on my right, took a deep breath – and toggled the twist grip. A set of gyroscopic stabilizers unfurled around me. The boosters engaged.

I was right. It was like flying an Exoskeleton – and remember what a sorry excuse I was for an Exo pilot? Two aborted attempts to get off the ground later and I was airborne at last. I was right about something else too. The AA cannons weren't able to target me and I reached the first rig in one piece, not even having to dodge a single RPG round.

There on the deck of the rig were infantry to meet me, but I had surprise on my side. These grunts, I almost felt sorry for them; they were stationed in one of the most heavily fortified defence positions I've ever seen and they weren't expecting a full frontal assault, especially not from a guy by himself. I doubt these troops ever saw action and no way were they elite. Why put your best soldiers where they weren't needed? They were cold, bored and out of shape, and I tore into them, making my way along the route to the AA cannon turret. I got there to find the place guarded by two operators who wheeled, cursing and reaching for their sidearms. I put them down, then went to the ammo store. The best place to set the explosives.

With freezing fingers I set the demo charges, then took off, heading up to meet Rico.

'That's it. Raiders – Raiders evasive,' hollered Rico, and moments later came the first explosion as my charge ignited the ammo. Then a second series of reports as the ammo began cooking off and discharging, beginning a long chain of explosions that tore the insides out of the rig. There was a scream and screech of tortured, rupturing metal and the gun platform, crippled, seemed to sink to its knees on the rig as the metal struts of its legs buckled. I engaged boosters to move further away from the explosion, just as Rico arrived on an Intruder.

'I stand corrected,' he said, 'nice work.'

I looked across at the next rig, a stretch of choppy sea and a causeway of icebergs between us. 'Looks different,' I shouted to him over the roar of the dropship's engines.

'I was just thinking that. I'll do some recon, then

meet you over there. There's a route across those ice-bergs.'

I made it across the bergs to the second rig where there were more infantry to meet me and – worse – more grunts wearing jet packs.

Now I discovered something. You could say good news and bad news. The good news? If I hit an enemy jet pack in the right spot the whole pack would explode, taking the grunt with it. A messy, painful death, but effective. The bad news? I was wearing an enemy jet pack and just as vulnerable.

I tried not to think about it. I tried not to think that I was facing guys who probably had hours of hands-on training using these things whereas I'd been wearing one for a matter of minutes. I tried to remind myself that these troops were probably Stahl's most expendable men. Now I reached the second rig and Rico came online.

'Yo, Sev, there's no way up. You're going to have to go down to the bottom of the rig and take out the support pillars. Two timed charges should do it.'

Away he went, leaving me to leap from pillar to pillar, setting the charges and fending off Hig infantry at the same time.

Two bozos from a platform opposite sprayed bullets at me and for a second I tried to remain behind cover as the metal around me rang with the sound of bullet strikes and ricochets. The thing with this jet pack, there was no cover to find. Usually your cover was the air. And trying to manoeuvre it beneath the support struts of the rig was proving increasingly difficult. For the first time I began wondering if I'd taken on more than I could handle. Just two charges, I thought. That's all I need. Then we can hit the harbour.

I came out from behind cover, used the jet pack to boost myself into the air and surprise my two snipers opposite, strafing shots across the platform where they stood. One screamed and fell into the ocean below; the other disappeared from view, just his leg visible, twitching as he died. I set the first charge, then made my way across to the next pillar, returning fire as I went, the stabilizers narrowly missing uprights on either side of me – one clip and I'd be sent off balance, probably hurtling towards the sea. Set the charge, and then set the second charge.

Now I had two minutes to make my way to the top, the only place there was enough altitude to get off the rig before it blew.

I headed through the main cargo hold, boosting up levels then flinching as bullets rang off the metal. I looked up to see Higs on platforms at my twelve, raining bullets on me. The stabilizers were hit and I staggered, targeting the infantry and returning fire.

They took cover, soaked it up then came back with a salvo that sent me hiding behind a crate in the hold. I was losing time. A voice in my headset told me. 'You have – one minute – and – thirty seconds – remaining.'

Of all the settings, I liked her the best. She sounded softer, more calming than the other pre-sets.

'You have – one minute – and – twenty seconds – remaining.'

I stepped out from behind the crate and engaged the boosters, shooting up a level and finding one of the grunts in my sights, taking him out with a short burst. On this deck I turned and ran towards some metal steps. Shit. Out of commission.

'You have – one minute – remaining,' she whispered in my ear, like she was counting down the time to bed, not a bomb.

I ducked as from behind me came the rattle of an assault rifle, and bullets pinged off my pack. Christ. If they hit the main power supply, I was dead. Like those grunts before. A messy and painful death. I turned and fired wildly behind, seeing sparks fly off metalwork and sending the gunners scattering.

'Come on, Sev,' urged Rico, 'get out of there.'

'You have – fifty – seconds – remaining,' she breathed.

I was sweating now. I wondered if the countdown woman would be the last voice I ever heard.

From somewhere else came more Higs, more infantry, opening fire on me. I returned it, using the boosters to get to the next level, Rico in my ear telling me to get the hell out, countdown woman sighing, 'You have – thirty-four – seconds – remaining.'

Thirty-four seconds till I die.

I saw a set of steps and made for them, boosting up through the hatch and twisting at the same time, taking out two enemy troops there – more by luck than judgement.

'You have – twenty-four – seconds – remaining.'

Ahead of me I saw a gantry that led to another set of steps, these taking me –surely – to the top deck. I made my way towards it just as two more grunts came running across my sight line, one of them screaming at the other, 'There he is. Kill the Vektan dog.'

Christ.

'You have – fourteen – seconds – remaining.'

The first one crouched, shouldered his rifle and opened fire, a burst that if I hadn't twisted in time would have ripped into my neck. I staggered as the bullets slammed into the jet pack, pulling me back-wards. I heard the hiss of something from behind me – the jet pack hit. That didn't sound good. Desperately I pulled the trigger, more to force them into cover than in hope of hitting them.

'You have – ten – seconds – remaining.'

The second one opened fire too and I took cover behind a large metal box, cursing. And this was it. So close. So fucking close. They had me pinned down and I patted myself down looking for – *yes* – a frag grenade.

'You have eight – seconds – remaining.'

I cooked it and threw. Ducked back behind the metal box and heard the screams at the same time as the explosion. Then I hurtled out from behind cover to see one of them, his face hanging in shreds, slowly folding to the deck, while the other stood, dazed, concussed, and I took him out with a shot as I thundered up the gantry, pushing past him as he fell and, reaching the steps, engaging the boosters.

Except . . .

'You have – two seconds – remaining.'

The boosters failed to engage. Instead came a warning alarm, a low klaxon sound that said something was wrong – something was terribly, terribly wrong.

And I wasn't getting up these steps in a hurry.

'You have – *zero* – seconds – remaining.'

I ran up the stairs, feeling more than hearing the thunder from the rig below as my demo charges activated and started a chain of explosions that would cripple the rig and me with it if I didn't get off.

And even as I reached the top of the steps bits of the shuddering, exploding structure were beginning to hive off while below me I could see Helghast troops throwing themselves from platforms into the sea below, hoping to avoid the explosion. Behind me there was the ripple of another blast and I felt a wave of heat that made my mind up once and for all, and rather than burn to death on the rig I hurled myself off it.

Now I've done some dumb things in my time. But leaping off a rig wearing a jet pack with a bleeping warning alarm has to rank among the best of them. Still, what was the alternative? Stay behind and die in the fire? I'll take my chances with the water any time, thanks.

And they engaged. The boosters engaged. For a second I allowed myself to believe that I'd made it when a piece of shrapnel from the explosions behind me punched into my jet pack, and suddenly it was on fire.

I had an image of the grunts I'd dispatched earlier screaming, unable to claw the furnace from their back before it exploded, and desperately didn't want to go like that. Frantically I grabbed at the buckle. Fingers slick with blood clawing at it.

Snick.

It came off.

Whoomp.

The pack exploded midair, and buffeted by the explosion I fell, hit the deck. Not the soft landing I'd hoped for, but no bones broken far as I could tell, so I lay there for a second to luxuriate in the feeling of being alive. I scrambled to my feet to watch as with a great grinding of metal the huge rig sank into the sea, which roiled and seethed at the sudden rude introduction of thousands of tons of platform. Before I knew it – just as I was thinking that I was home and dry – a huge tidal wave of water was rolling towards me. I was too late to avoid it. It hit me, knocking me off my feet, taking me underwater.

Then, above me, grinning at me from the deck of an Intruder as I surfaced, was Rico. 'Hey, look who decided to go for a swim.' He indicated the harbour. 'You ready to do this?'

Chapter Eighteen

The harbour was a freezing stretch of metal with glinting ice coating every surface, and icicles like rows of fangs along handrails that lined the seafront. We were at full strength now. Behind us we'd left the smoking piles of the rigs, neutralized, and our blood was up, ready for the fight as our Intruders approached the harbour. We watched Helghast troops scurrying to their positions, their breath clouding, frantically gesturing to one another as we came closer and closer.

And they couldn't believe it. A breach of their outer defences was unthinkable for them yet here it was, almost imminent. Watching them, it was difficult not to gloat. They thought they were impregnable. If you'd shown them some tattered Intruder dropships and just a few handfuls of exhausted ISA troops and said that these are the guys to make you look like chumps, they would have laughed in your face. But here we were, making them look like chumps.

But don't get cocky, Sev. It ain't over till it's over. The Helghast still had greater numbers and vast fire-power – and they were ready to prove it right now. As we attempted to land, the machine guns on the lower deck of the harbour opened up and suddenly all was noise: the roar of the dropships' retro thrusters, the relentless crash of the machine guns, bullets slamming into the ships and ricocheting from the deck, the air alive with sparks and splinters. Jumping from our Intruder, Rico and I dived for cover in time to see Helghast infantry moving into position on the top of a heavily fortified bunker at our twelve. Among them I saw a WASP trooper, but before I had a chance to pin him down he'd fired, a cluster of missiles that fizzed through the glacial dusk and into Intruder Three, just as the last of our guys leapt from it.

'*Albini*,' screamed Rico into his pick-up. 'Albini, are you okay?'

'Affirmative, Raider Command,' replied Albini through a cloud of static. We breathed a sigh of relief. 'Got out of there just in time.'

I looked around the deck. The next Intruder had landed and ISA guys were piling off, but the machine-gun nests had found their range and at least half of them were cut down. I shouldered the assault rifle and fired volley after volley, Rico doing the same, screaming into his comlink, 'Find cover, goddamnit. *Find cover.*'

Now there were enough of us to lay down cover fire as the rest of the Intruders docked and the men dispersed, but we were pinned down, the remorse-less clatter of the machine-gun nests keeping us crouched behind the crates. I peeked and saw a WASP trooper taking aim and took some shots at him. Enough to send him back behind cover.

'We're not going anywhere until we take out those machine-gun nests,' hollered Rico, his assault rifle jumping in his hands as he too returned fire.

The WASP trooper took aim again. I saw him too late and he fired, the missile battery twisting as it came exploding into crates in front of us, one of our guys blown apart in an explosion of blood and uniform.

I blinked away the image, instead firing wildly at the WASP trooper so that he ducked down, cannon unmanned for a moment.

'We need one of those,' I said, pointing, and Rico nodded.

'Got it,' he said. 'Let's get to the top of that bunker.'

'You got it. Give me cover,' I yelled back as Rico slammed in another clip then leaned from the side of his crate, his assault rifle barking, and I left the safety of my hiding place and scrambled up the har-bour to the next crate, three grunts pinned down behind it. Bullets thudded into the titanium, rebound-ing from the metal walkway, the noise deafening. Only a crazy person would leave cover now.

A crazy person or me. And I took off for the next

set of crates. Kept low. Into the storm of hot death sent from above. Then to the next one. Rico followed suit as we made our way to a set of frozen steps, thundering up them to surprise a group of hostiles on the upper deck.

We dealt with them and Rico pointed me in the direction of another set of stairs. I went for them, was in the bunker now and racing through, taking out unwary Helghast as I moved forward.

On the roof a set of WASP troopers thought they were immune from attack and were manning a pair of floor-mounted cannons. They didn't hear or see me coming – not until I opened fire on the first one who spun, screaming, blood arcing through the air as he hit the floor. The second was reaching for his pistol, but I got to him first, dug my thumbs through his mask and into his eyes, twisting and breaking his neck at the same time. He screamed, gurgled and collapsed at my feet and I pulled my fingers free of his skull with a squelch. For a moment I looked down at him, disgusted with myself. Sick with what war had made me do.

Secure that shit, Sev, I thought, and I took hold of a WASP launcher, squinting down the sights. Down a level were the machine-gun nests dug into bunkers, keeping up a relentless barrage, orange muzzle flash bright against the grey concrete of their surround.

Below them along the harbour, pinned down behind crates, were my guys, so I took aim at the first nest, took it out, heard Rico cheering over the comlink, then shifted my aim to the second. As it went up, I heard the Raiders urging each other forward and they began to swarm up the harbour.

Their artillery gone, the remaining Higs couldn't deal with us and within minutes we'd worked our way over to the facility side of the harbour and were regrouping. Rico, Jammer and a few others made it first, reaching a storehouse where we found ourselves looking at a huge steel door. On the other side of it was a hill that led up to the cable-car station, the cable car leading to the main complex – to Stahl Arms. That was where we needed to be. One problem. The Higs knew we were coming. And how.

Rico moved over to me, keeping his voice low. 'If we move in now, they'll throw everything they have at us.'

'Copy that,' I said.

'Think we can make it up the hill. Just us and a couple of other guys?'

'What's on your mind?'

'Let the Higs think we've moved out. Let them reduce the alert status, then push forward, take the cable-car station.'

'And then what? Attack? Four of us?'

'No, not attack . . .' He grinned. 'Infiltrate.'

I nodded as Rico thumbed his headset. 'All Raiders, listen up,' he barked over the comlink. 'We're about to unleash a shitstorm of Helghast activity here. I need all of you to clear out.'

They bitched and moaned as Rico explained that he wanted them to hook up with Narville's men. And he was right; they should. Somewhere out there the guys who had escaped the jungle base were under the leadership of Doc Hanley. Now, I liked the doc well enough and he was a fine medic – even if his bedside manner left a lot to be desired. But he was no military leader. The men needed guidance.

As Rico convinced the men, Jammer worked on the control panel for the door. At last she stepped away as it opened; beyond it, the hill.

'Good luck, Rico,' she said. Then turned to me. For a moment I let myself swim in her gaze – in the biggest brownest eyes I ever saw. 'Sev,' she said, acknowledging me with a smile that was slightly crooked. It was like God had created the perfect mouth so he just had to add an imperfect smile to even things up.

Then she turned and went, and Rico was watching me watching her, shaking his head and smiling. Paavola and Schofield remained behind with us and we waited for the dust to settle, then began to make our way up the hill.

Rico was right. We met resistance, but with nothing like the ferocity of before. Possibly they were scrambling an aerial assault on our retreating Intruders (let them try – Jammer and Co. would be ghosts before the first pilot strapped on his helmet) or maybe sending infantry after them along the harbour (let them try . . .), but we got no more than the usual guards, and we moved quickly enough to take them, the firefight short and sweet, before occupying the cable-car station – just as a car descended. Paavola and Schofield stayed outside as me and Rico took up position either side of the door, and I controlled my breathing, which clouded in the freezing air. How many would they send?

The cable car clanked to a halt, swinging for a moment before the door sighed open and I got to find out how many men we were worth.

Assholes. They sent just two of them. Either comms were down between here and the main facility or they were seriously undermanned. Either way I wasn't bitching. We took them down the minute they stepped out of the cable car. One each. Quick and ruthless.

I was standing over my guy – dealing with that same sickening feeling – when his comlink crackled, his command wanting a status report.

'Vigilant Base to Argus Two. Vigilant to Argus Two. Come in. Over.'

I looked at Rico. He looked at me.

'Argus Two,' came the call, more insistent this time. 'I repeat, this is Vigilant. Do you copy? Over.'

I reached for his mask and pulled it to me, suddenly aware of the dead man who had worn it, the last of his warmth ebbing away.

I cleared my throat and, doing my best impersonation of a Hig grunt, replied, 'Area secure, Vigilant. All enemies eliminated.'

Rico raised an eyebrow, amused at my sudden transformation to Helghast.

'Copy that,' came the reply. 'Return to base, Argus.'

'Roger on your last transmission,' I responded, and the comlink closed.

Now I reached for the dead grunt's uniform, pulling on his helmet.

'What are you doing?' started Rico, not smirking any more.

I turned to look at him, staring at him through the mask, hearing my own breathing through the respirator. 'I'm getting us inside,' I said, finding the Helghast growl easier to manage behind the respirator. 'What are you doing?'

Chapter Nineteen

Like I said a while back, the day of the Helghast invasion on Vekta was when war stopped becoming something we trained for and became something real. For me at least. The first time I ever saw combat was hot, burning chaos, a bullet-riddled hell, and all I could do was hope to make it out of there alive. That's what I thought war was all about right then: survival.

But you know what? I was a rookie. I had no experience of death. No combat experience at all – plenty of simulations, for sure, but nothing actual. Suddenly to be thrust into that obscenity, it does something to your mind. How you deal with it, that's what makes you a soldier. And I guess I was one of the lucky ones. Because what I realized – and I realized it pretty quickly – was that, yes, war *is* survival. But not just your own. You're not there for yourself. You're there for the man next to you.

Which is how come I found myself dressed up as a Helghast trooper, sitting beside Rico who was dressed the same way – like a couple of third-graders going trick or treating – taking a cable car right into the heart of enemy territory. Because you fight for your comrades and because no one gets left behind.

As we were hoisted higher and higher, I stared out of the window. Dusk was coming in. The brilliant white of the ice cliffs had been shaded grey. I saw thick, oily columns of smoke rising into the sky from the rigs we had destroyed, and below us the harbour, getting more distant now. On it were scattered fires, red-orange against the gunmetal of the walkways. Bodies were dotted along its length, but as we ascended higher and higher in the cable car they became barely visible pinpricks. We were leaving a battlefield behind us.

And going up to – what? Something about this whole incursion felt wrong. Here we were taking the car up to the main Stahl Arms facility – a base that had been under assault not two hours ago, and it felt like they didn't give a damn.

Now, even if the Higs had fallen for it and thought our main force had retreated and the rest of us were dead, well, hell, the place should *still* have been on high alert. Any similar facility on Vekta would have gone into instant lockdown at the first blip of an enemy dropship. These guys? They'd sent two guards down in a cable car. And I wasn't hearing warning klaxons. I wasn't seeing air support or a massive deployment of infantry. Seemed like it was just another day at the office to them. They were either dumb as a box of sand, way over-confident, or . . . there was something else.

But what?

If Rico was as bothered as me by the lack of a welcome committee, then he didn't show it. And once he'd pulled on the Helghast combat helmet and respirator I couldn't even see his eyes, let alone tell what was going through his mind. He was probably thinking the same as me: that the mask was uncomfortable and unwieldy and that the goggles gave everything the same reddish tinge; that he felt protected by it, but also like it took something from him. Looking at him and seeing him looking at me, I saw the masks were just another way the Helghast robbed the people of their identity. Anything human, like a face, they tried to rub it out. This was an entire race of people with seriously fucked up priorities.

Which was another reason we were going to rescue Narville and Bandit Recon. Because our refusal to give our buddies up to monsters made us human.

Suddenly the car stopped, shuddering to a halt and swinging wildly on its cable. Outside was a lower platform serving what looked like an observation deck, and once the car had stopped swinging the doors juddered open and in came a blast of freezing air, followed by two troopers. They grunted at us. I looked at them and nodded my head, grunting back. Christ, what if they wanted to start up a conversation? What did Helghast soldiers gas about when they weren't busy trying to kill ISA guys? The game last night? Where to buy respirators that didn't chafe? Maybe they were good, loyal Helghast and expected to start talking about how they were an ass-kicking race of super-humans, and soon the whole universe would bow down before them, *mwah ha ha ha*.

I swallowed fear, looked out of the window. What I saw were the peaks of the mountains, dusted with snow, and I realized that we were now at the foot of the main Stahl Arms complex, a vast monolithic series of buildings. Around it were defensive arc towers, blue electric light crackling at their tips. From sentry positions searchlights probed the darkening sky, while huge strips of window were stark white against the black of its shell, and landing lights twinkled on a deck at the far side. As I watched, an Overlord was coming in to land. Did this contain Narville? I wondered. It was possible. Especially if the Overlord hadn't made its way directly back to base.

From opposite one of the Hig grunts cleared his throat and my attention went back to our guests. Shit. They were staring intensely at us. For all I know they could have been flashing us friendly smiles from beneath those respirators, but I didn't think so – something about the body language, the way they shifted, looked at each other, then back at us.

Now we were being drawn up into the base of the main facility and towards a platform situated below the landing deck. Suddenly I could no longer see the tops of the mountain, the searchlights and the smoking rigs. Now as the car was hauled into the depths of Stahl Arms, what I saw were the steel and titanium supports in the belly of the compound; gantries, walkways and aisles. Now I saw the docking bay and a metal platform where a bunch of guards stood awaiting our arrival and my heart was hammering. There were more guards here than usual, surely?

One of them approached the car as the doors opened, his hand at his sidearm, and he swept his gaze around the interior, looking first at Rico and me, then at the other troops. Satisfied, he ushered us out and the two other grunts stood first, filing out of the door and onto the platform, their boots ringing on the metal. Rico stood too, and moved in front of me – which is when I saw the blood on the back of his uniform. A big stain; it looked like it had come from a neck wound sustained by the previous occupant. It was still wet.

Jesus. I glanced out onto the platform. All those guards. One of them was bound to see the blood. My mind raced. Should I create a diversion? For a moment I pictured myself starting a snowball fight. Anything to take the Higs' attention off Rico's bloodstained back. But somehow I didn't think a snowball fight was quite the Hig style and, anyway, Rico was on the platform and moving up behind the other two riders when there came a shout from the first guard. *'Stop.'*

All three of them turned round.

'You,' said the guard, but he was pointing at the other two. 'You go ahead, report to the desk sergeant and get your orders.'

The two looked at each other, then at Rico, and then with an obvious sense of relief, went on their way.

The head guard now turned his attention to Rico. 'And, *you* –' his pointing finger swivelled. His other hand went to the butt of his pistol again – 'approach me.'

Like all Higs he sounded like he was talking from within a deep abyss.

Slowly, Rico walked back along the platform towards him. Now the other guards had started to take an interest and were coming over, moving closer. Maybe we could take them out. But then . . . what if we did? We couldn't operate the cable car to escape. As soon as gunfire was heard in the docking station, more guards would be called.

I tried to control my breathing. Control my fear. Maybe this was it. End of the road. Okay, if I was going down I was taking as many of them with me as I could. Surreptitiously I moved my hand to the front of the assault rifle, feeling for the safety under my gloved finger and sliding it off. Maybe we could take these guys out, make a dash into the main facility, damage as much equipment as we could before they put us down . . . Go out in a blaze of glory. Maybe one day the kids in modern history would learn about Sev and Rico along with Jan Templar.

'What have you got on your back?' said the head guard.

Rico looked at me. I realized that one of us was going to have to say something before we raised their suspicions simply by being a pair of say-nothing assholes, and I was about to speak when Rico piped up.

I don't think I'd ever heard Rico talk like anybody but Rico before. He wasn't one for doing impersonations of other officers. When Rico spoke, it was in a Rico voice, so I guess I almost died when he opened his mouth and began to talk – in a perfect approximation of Helghast.

'I don't know, sir,' he rasped. 'What do I have on my back, sir?'

The other guards chuckled and moved closer.

Playing to the crowd a little, the chief guard said, 'Turn round, soldier.'

Rico turned and the guard placed a fingertip to the uniform, bringing it back with a blot of red on the grey glove and showing it to us. 'Why do you have blood on your uniform?' he asked.

Rico turned back. 'I don't know, sir,' he croaked.

Shit, Rico, don't lose it now, I thought.

'You. Don't. *Know*?'

'From an ISA dog,' I said quickly, my voice not as authentic as Rico's, but seeming to have the desired effect.

Now the chief guard turned his attention on me; red glowing eyes seemed to burn into me. 'But you reported the ISA intruders neutralized,' he said accusingly.

'One of the intruders was wounded and playing at being dead, sir,' I said, coming to attention a little, 'and following my report launched an attack. This must be his blood. I pulled him off and cut his throat.'

There was laughter from the Helghast around us. Just the thought of an ISA guy getting his throat cut was enough to have these guys busting a gut.

'Cut his throat, did you?' the chief guard snickered.

'I did, sir, yes.'

'Very good, very good. Unlucky for you that it

wasn't one of the king killers. Chairman Stahl has made it known that he will be most grateful to any who slaughter those dogs.'

'A king killer, sir?' I queried.

'One of the men responsible for the death of our beloved autarch, idiot. One of them is being brought in now and taken to Chairman Stahl.'

Narville, I thought.

'It would have been my honour to kill any one of them, sir,' I rasped, 'and I wish I could report that I had. But the man I killed was merely a lowly dog named Tomas Sevchenko.'

'Really?' said the chief guard. 'That name ... Interesting. Wait there.'

We stood on the platform, shuffling. Rico looked at me and was probably thinking, What the fuck are you up to, Sev? But to get to Narville we needed to get close to Stahl, and maybe this was a way of achieving that. Around us the other guards had relaxed and were moving back to their stations. I saw the head honcho with his hand at his ear, reporting. Then he nodded, finished the communication and returned to us.

'Right, you two. I can verify that Tomas Sevchenko was one of those that Stahl hunts. It appears that you may be in line for a commendation. You are to report to the main desk for your next instruction. Is that clear?'

'Yes,' sir,' we growled in unison.

'Excellent,' he said. 'Now go.'

He pointed us in the direction of a set of steps at the other end of the platform and we were just about to make our way towards them when suddenly, 'Halt,' he called, and once again we stopped, hearts sinking. I turned to see him striding down the platform towards us and as he did so he reached to the top of the cable car and scooped a handful of snow from its roof. For a nuts moment I thought there really was going to be a snowball fight, until he reached us, took hold of Rico's shoulder, spun him round and rubbed the snow into his back until the bloodstain was all but invisible.

'Can't have you meeting Chairman Stahl with blood on your uniform, can we?' he said. 'Even if it is the king killer's blood.'

'Thank you, sir,' croaked Rico, inclining his head, and at last we turned and made our way off the platform, feeling his red eyes boring into our backs as we ascended the steps to the deck above, both breathing a sigh of relief.

The next level was like a different world. Back down the steps was the bare guts of the complex: unfinished raw metal, old neglected consoles and discordant clanging; here, just one level above, were huge glass panels and panoramic views, holographic displays and brushed, burnished metallic surfaces. Footsteps no longer echoed. We trod silently on the soft-coated, shining floor as we made our way along a short corridor and to a security point, suddenly feeling too big and coarse for this pristine, high-tech world. To my left, I saw the landing deck through reinforced glass, an Overlord on it, its doors opening as I watched. Hig troops dragged two men in yellow prisoner jumpsuits from the hold. One, an ISA guy I knew, a member of Bandit Recon called Scanlon, who looked pretty badly beaten-up; the other, Narville. That made sense. The Overlord had made a detour to pick up Scanlon, which was how come they were only just arriving.

I tapped Rico and pointed him in the direction of what was happening. In reply he nodded imperceptibly. Both of us watched as Scanlon and Narville were frogmarched to a checkpoint.

Now, ahead of us, we saw the two grunts from the cable car passing through security at the end of the corridor and into a vast hall beyond. We moved up behind them trying to look like we knew what we were doing – like this was something we did every day. A guard looked up as we arrived, assault rifle slung across his shoulder.

'Unit?' he demanded.

'Argus Two,' replied Rico.

The guard nodded, checked a screen in front of him and seeing the name nodded approvingly. 'Ah, the king killers,' he said. 'Docking bay informed us that you were on your way.' He looked at us carefully, from one to the other. 'The information has been relayed to Chairman Stahl,' he said.

I held my breath.

'And the chairman wishes to see you,' he continued.

Game on.

'First you are to report to the factory floor in order to collect something . . .' He checked his screen again. 'Doesn't say what. But you're to go directly there before proceeding to the broadcast room. They're due to begin presently, so I wouldn't hang around if I were you.'

Rico and I both nodded.

'You may go,' he said, and motioned us through the gate so that now we were entering what looked like the main hub for the whole facility, an expanse of floor surrounded by sets of double doors, stairways and clear-glass elevators. Scores of workers were hurrying to and fro. Some, like us, wore military uniform with full masks; others in long white lab coats or the uniforms of technicians, wearing half-face respirators that showed their eyes. Coming into the same hall was Narville, Scanlon and their two guards, the prisoners in particular looking incongruous in their surroundings, and we found ourselves falling in behind them as they crossed the polished floor. Everything here was clean and sparkling. An air of quiet industry reigned, until the peace was suddenly broken by a shout from Narville, who pitched to the floor. At once the party stopped. His guards laughed. Those around sniggered, stopping to watch for a moment as Narville was dragged roughly to his feet.

'Don't try anything like that again,' snapped one of the guards, but Rico and I both knew that Narville had done nothing. There was to be no humane treatment here. Narville was no prisoner of war. He was a plaything. One of his guards saw us watching.

'Yes?' he said, almost threateningly.

'We're for the factory,' I replied.

'Better get there, then,' he said crossly, waving us in the direction of a set of double doors. They slid noiselessly open as we approached, then closed behind us, admitting us to yet another new world.

Ahead of us stretched a metal walkway, and once again our boots were ringing as we made our way along its length, peering left and right into glass-fronted development labs that lined the way. At the end of the walkway was a second set of doors and these opened to admit us to a balcony.

Here the first thing to hit us was the noise. The reception area had been an oasis of calm, quiet as a morgue, clean as an operating theatre, serene as a Zen garden. In contrast this was a bombardment of the senses, like having a jackhammer inside your skull.

The second thing to hit us was the sheer space of it, and for a moment we stood, taking it all in – or trying to. Directly in front of us was a wall of grey metal panelling, so close that it felt as though we could lean over the balcony to touch it. It stretched down to the floor and then up almost as far as the eye could see, so that both of us stood with our heads tilted right back, trying to see the top of what, I eventually realized, was a brand-new, just-being-built battleship.

Stretching away from us like a giant black knife blade, it occupied what was a gargantuan hangar space and was about the same length as an ISA cruiser turned on its side, though more squat. Around it swarmed hundreds of technicians and engineers, all moving with the purpose of workers whose job is almost complete. They rushed this way and that on the factory floor, buggies with trailers weaving in and out. I watched a team of men working on something along the flank of the colossal ship and saw that they were spraying on the logo of Stahl Arms.

I wondered if the Helghast military knew about this ship. I guessed not.

I looked at Rico just as he was looking at me and

we had a mind-meet moment. What we were seeing here, this was new. This was important somehow.

'You.'

The shout tore into my thoughts and I started, looking down at the factory floor to find its source. Staring up at us with the clean lines of the battleship hull, behind him was a technician in a long coat, wearing a respirator.

'What are you doing there?' he demanded loudly.

'We were told to report to the factory floor,' I shouted back.

He looked us over and frowned. I realized that it was odd to be able to see his eyes and I found myself looking down into them as if hoping somehow to solve the mystery of what it was that made his people tick. He gazed back disinterestedly before raising a finger and pointing vaguely over to the other side of the cavernous hangar. 'Go through to Workshop Four, to Factory Control,' he said.

I indicated thanks and we turned to continue along the walkway, passing along what was no doubt the stern of the battleship, coming next to a huge computer room.

'This looks like some kind of mainframe,' said Rico, amazed, as we passed. 'What sort of a computer is this?'

I shook my head and we moved along, finally

passing through doors in the next workshop and then – at last – into Number Four where we descended steps to the factory, crossing a highly polished floor to Factory Control. From behind a counter, a bored-looking clerk glanced up at us with barely interested eyes.

'Who are you?' he demanded, reaching to scratch beneath his respirator.

'We're Argus Two,' replied Rico.

This seemed to take him by surprise. Suddenly he was looking at us with new, interested eyes.

'The king killers?' he said, suddenly alert. 'Chairman Stahl's personal assistant has notified me about you.' It was beginning to dawn on me that killing Tomas Sevchenko made us quite the celebrities around here.

'Yeah,' continued the clerk, his eyes darting from me to Rico, 'Chairman Stahl's assistant has instructed me to hand you an important component that you are to take to the broadcast room.'

'The broadcast room?' I asked, careful not to let my voice change, despite my surprise. 'What's happening in the broadcast room?'

The clerk laughed and settled back in his seat, putting his hands behind his head. 'Well,' he said, looking very pleased with himself, 'there is to be an execution. The first king killer, the captain they brought in earlier, name of Narville. Chairman Stahl plans to execute him live on air.'

I caught my breath.

'Here.' The clerk reached beneath the brushed metal counter for something, a box that he brought out and slapped down on the top between us. A small, white plastic box. 'You'll be needing this,' he smirked.

'Why us?' asked Rico.

'Why you?' grinned the clerk. 'Because Chairman Stahl wishes to reward you for your bravery in killing one of the autarch's assassins, a dog by the name of Tomas Sevchenko, I believe.'

I felt rather than saw Rico bristling with anger beside me. *Please don't lose it now, Rico*, I thought. *Please don't lose it now.* Instead Rico spoke and when he did his voice sounded measured and composed – and he was still in a perfect approximation of Helghast, asking, 'And how does he wish to reward us?'

'You're going to be Narville's executioners,' sniggered the clerk.

Chapter Twenty

We trudged back the way we'd come, carrying the component and trying to have a hushed conversation at the same time.

'They're going to kill Narville,' said Rico under his breath, like I might have missed that bit.

'They expect us to do it,' I said, like Rico might have missed that bit.

Our minds were racing. How were we going to get out of this? Okay, I thought, pull yourself together, Sev. You wanted to be near Narville – you got your wish.

We walked back along the walkway, past the mainframe and the battleship construction and to the corridor that led to the landing-deck level. There we found ourselves in the antiseptic hub once more, where soldiers and clerks, technicians, engineers and pilots all made their way from one place to the next. Where before I had detected a sense of purpose in the air, now there was something more. What I could feel as we made our way into the hub was a sense of expectation, of excitement: Stahl Arms was preparing itself to hear from its leader.

In front of us a door slid open and we found ourselves in yet another corridor, walking in the direction of the broadcast room. Now we saw the first of the guards. They lined the glass and steel walls of the corridor, silent sentinels forming an avenue that led towards our destination. At the door a guard glanced down at the white plastic box I held.

'Argus Two?' he asked.

'Yeah,' I said.

He stepped aside to allow us through. The doors opened. We walked in.

'Are you the executioners?' asked a guard by the door. We nodded and he collected our rifles then motioned us forward – into a room whose occupants were awaiting our arrival.

One wall of the broadcast room was a mosaic of screens showing closed-circuit footage from around the complex, Pyrrhus and even what looked like the senate room of Visari Palace. They showed Helghast gathering around screens, ready for the broadcast, while senators were filing into their grand chamber, taking their seats. The whole city it seemed – maybe even the whole planet – was preparing for Stahl's broadcast.

It would be relayed to them via a camera on a tripod, set up close by. Two grunts stood beside it and one of them indicated the white box I held now, impatiently beckoning me forward to hand it to him.

'Take your positions by the gun,' said the camera operator and we did as we were told.

I counted five other grunts in the room as well as Narville and Scanlon who knelt with their hands secured behind their back and their heads bent. And Stahl, of course, in the centre of the room, facing the camera. He stood with his arms folded, holding a pistol, an StA-18, and wearing a calm, almost beatific smile in contrast to the air of tension around him. I'd seen photographs of him before, of course, in military briefings, but that was years ago and he had aged since then. He was greying, even more gaunt. He looked more like his father now, Khage Stahl, the great Helghast industrialist, founder of Stahl Arms. As we moved across to the cannon, he opened his eyes and gave us a theatrical bow. A deep bow, intended to acknowledge us not just as executioners but as specially chosen executioners.

Yeah, what an honour. I felt a droplet of sweat make its way down the inside of my mask. That was the kind of honoured I felt right now.

His acknowledgement was the extent of his gratitude, though, for Stahl was almost ready to begin. The camera operators were busy finishing making adjustments, whatever was in the box having provided the final piece. And now Stahl turned in the direction of his two prisoners.

'Captain Narville,' he said, 'do you know who I am?'

Narville raised his head to look at Stahl, watching him as he walked towards them and then behind them. Narville stayed silent.

'I said, "Do you know who I am?"' repeated Stahl. Narville turned his head away.

Stahl snorted. 'Typical,' he said, then put his StA-18 to the back of Scanlon's head and pulled the trigger.

The report echoed around the room, bouncing off the walls at the same time as Scanlon's brains slapped to the floor and he pitched forward, blood already spreading from a ragged hole at the front of his skull.

There was a moment of shocked quiet, the only sound the sticky spread of blood on the floor and the death rattle of Scanlon's boots scuffing the floor.

'*We are prisoners of war,*' shouted Narville suddenly, his face drained of blood. 'We have rights. You just violated the Stockholm treaty.'

'Stockholm?' Stahl sneered. 'What planet do you think you're on?'

Just then the camera operators completed set-up and motioned Stahl, who looked delighted, clapping his hands together and stepping over the still-twitching corpse of Scanlon to take centre stage.

'Showtime,' he said, grinning.

Now the camera operator began counting down. On the screens the people of Helghan gathered around their monitors and Stahl watched them from the corner of his eye, a satisfied smile on his face. A smile like things were going his way. Like nothing could stop him now.

We'd see about that. I looked down at the arc cannon. People were about to die in this room. Just a question of who.

'Broadcast is now planet-wide,' confirmed the camera operator. 'We are live in five. Four. Three. Two. One . . .'

Helghan stopped as the logo of Stahl Arms appeared on their monitors. The seated senators leaned forward.

And Stahl began.

'Goodday, my fellow Helghast, I am Jorhan Stahl,' he said, with a self-deprecating smile. 'This is something of a rarity from me because speeches are not my forte – but honesty is . . .'

I looked at Scanlon on the floor, Narville kneeling next to him, his shoulders slumped. Surreptitiously I reached to the arc cannon and very gently tried to swivel it one way or the other, instantly glad I'd checked because it was fixed in place, pointing forward, for display only.

Meanwhile, Stahl continued. 'I believe that what I have to say today you will find very refreshing,' he said. 'My father and Visari, both great men, built this country from nothing using sharp minds committed to our future. Together they built a nation: Visari gave us purpose and hope, my father's factories gave us the most powerful army the universe has ever known.'

He reached a crescendo, sounding like a true fanatic, the colour rising in his face and spittle flying from his mouth.

All the grunts in the room were watching Stahl, rapt. They were off-guard. My eyes went to the release mechanism of the arc cannon. They wouldn't be off guard by the time I got that puppy free, though.

'But that army has failed us.' Stahl was shouting now. 'They have allowed themselves to become fat, lazy and careless.'

On the screen I saw great uproar at the senate. Stahl saw it too, revelled in it. 'But that changes today,' he continued, and it was almost as though he were addressing just them now. 'The time has come for some new fucking management,' he said, threateningly. 'I know what this nation needs and I will cut out this disease of compliance and subjugation. So to honour Visari tomorrow we launch the greatest military campaign in our nation's history . . .'

The greatest military campaign in our nation's history? What the fuck? My mind raced. I thought of the battleship, the mainframe. I thought of the irradiated petrusite and the weapons we'd seen. *Tomorrow?* Now it began to make sense. How come we'd met so little resistance. They were too busy preparing for something major.

But now Stahl was indicating us and I opened the release on the cannon stand, pulling the weapon free and hefting it. Christ, this thing was heavy. Holding it, I crossed the room.

'. . . and to celebrate that I will give you justice, revenge and the death of his killers,' finished Stahl.

The camera swung to see Narville kneeling on the floor and for a second I had a weird, dislocated feeling as I watched myself on TV dressed in a Helghast uniform, holding a huge arc cannon to the head of my captain.

I released the safety. The cannon thrummed and streaks of energy began escaping from the main housing. It was green, I saw, just like I'd seen used on Bandit Four back in the jungle. Now sparks flecked the barrel as I brought it close to Narville's forehead, thinking, Sorry, sir, but it's got to look convincing.

And Narville could feel the electricity building, the charge increasing. He could feel his death seconds away and he closed his eyes, ready for it to come. Now the weapon was virtually jumping in my hands, desperate to discharge.

So I put it out of its misery.

I swivelled and the look on Stahl's face made everything worthwhile as I ripped off my helmet and mask and grinned at him: Tomas Sevchenko, king killer, at your service.

Stahl's eyes widened as he recognized me.

'*You*,' he started, but you're dead . . .'

'Wrong,' I said, and pulled the trigger.

But Stahl was suddenly fast and though the arc cannon was powerful – the most powerful weapon I'd ever fired – it sure wasn't quick, and as the tendrils of electricity reached from the barrel Stahl grabbed one of the unsuspecting grunts and dragged the man in front of himself, using him as a shield. The greedy emerald bolt found its target, instantly enveloping the grunt, who rose into the air, seeming to expand within the shining, oily bubble of light, then bursting, splattering the room with bloodied meat.

I glanced at the screens to see a scene of complete panic as I swivelled towards another of the guards, one who'd recovered enough presence of mind to reach for his assault rifle. He never got to pull the trigger before I unleashed more green death on him and like the first guy he dissolved into a scarlet shower of body parts. Too late I saw a pair of guards bundle Stahl out of the door, just as the sentries from outside began pouring in. At the same time, Rico was grabbing an assault rifle and opening fire on the other guards, two of them going down instantly as I took out the next one, leaving him to rush to Narville. I saw him grab a combat knife from one of the fallen Higs and was just about to use it to release Narville when one of the guards was upon him and he was twisting, slashing at his attacker's respirator and sending him tumbling to a wall, where he lay writhing, not quite dead. Next Rico slid on his knees to Narville, slicing his hand restraints and pulling him roughly up by the shoulder.

'Rico,' exclaimed Narville, 'you're alive.'

'Yeah, no thanks to you,' snapped Rico in reply. One thing about Rico, he really held a grudge.

Now Narville rushed to my side, snatching up an assault rifle and opening fire on the sentries as they came hurtling through the door. Only a couple even made it across the threshold. Between me with the arc cannon and Rico and Narville with assault rifles we took out the entire squad, and as the last of them fell the room was suddenly quiet, settling in the wake of the short battle. For a moment or so Narville and I stood catching our breath and he clapped a hand to my shoulder, looking at me.

'Thank you, Sev,' he said

'No one gets left behind, Captain,' I replied. Gradually we became aware of low conversation followed by an agonized squeal at the far wall where Rico was bending over the grunt he'd wounded with the knife.

And it looked like he was finishing the job.

'What are they doing to them?' he was saying through gritted teeth, and the Hig managed something in reply, a single word, before he lost consciousness – probably blacked out with the pain – and his body went limp.

Narville went to move over there, but I stopped him with an outstretched hand, shaking my head no. I guess I didn't like what Rico was doing any more than the captain did, but . . . I don't know – I'd just seen Scanlon get his brains blown out and we needed to find the rest of our men. I wasn't about to stand around debating ethics. Rico turned to face us, wiping the bloodied blade on the leg of his pants, his face grim.

'Hig tells me that they got some of Bandit Recon in the holding cells below,' he said. 'Got some down in their labs too. Let's go. He told me the way.'

'In the labs?' said Narville. 'What are they doing to them there?'

Rico looked back at the body on the floor, leaking blood. 'Scumbag just said "tests".'

Narville looked at Rico and Rico returned his gaze defiantly.

'You realize you just violated the Stockholm treaty?' said Narville.

'Yeah, and what of it?' said Rico.

There was a pause.

'Nothing of it,' said Narville. 'Good work, soldier. Let's rescue our boys.'

Klaxons began sounding, alarms going off. We made our way up the corridors, taking down Higs who tried to stop us. Civilians cowered as we ran, the entire place in uproar. Now we moved out into the hub, firing indiscriminately and panicking civilian workers, Rico shooting the hell out of an operations desk, hoping to disable their surveillance, before we headed towards a set of doors and from there worked our way down to the labs – and there were greeted by a scene straight out of hell.

Higs in lab coats scattered and ran as we entered, leaving behind inspection tables with corpses of ISA laid out on them. The bodies were in various states of mutilation. Some almost recognizable as humans. Others missing limbs. Others who looked as though they had exploded from the inside, their torsos caved in. They'd been doing tests on our boys. Or that's how it looked. Tests similar to those I'd seen in the jungle. I recognized one of Bandit Recon, his mouth

open in a final scream, his hands formed into agonized claws.

Moving through we found a section of toughened
glass cells, and three of our guys imprisoned there –
three guys who had been waiting to die, and who
wept with relief when we turned up to let them out.
Breathlessly they explained that the rest of the team
was in the holding cells. Seven men, the last of Bandit Recon.

'Stay sharp,' said Narville. 'They're not going to
give up the other prisoners without a fight.'

Klaxons continued to howl around us.

'Sir,' I said to him, 'that speech Stahl was making . . .
it didn't sound like they're going to honour our white
flag?'

Just as I said it I realized this was one vital bit of
intel I'd so far withheld from Rico – you can guess
his reaction.

'Our *what?*' He started, looking like he'd just been
slapped.

I ignored him for the moment. 'They're up to
something, sir. We saw this computer mainframe.
They're constructing a –'

'*Sevchenko,*' interrupted Narville, 'this isn't the time
or the place.'

'Wait a second,' said Rico, not about to be put off.
'A white what?'

I turned to him. 'Vekta capitulated last night.'

'The general ordered the immediate surrender of all ISA forces,' confirmed Narville.

'*Surrender?* And I guess you were just going to follow those orders?' barked Rico.

Narville rounded on him. 'If it meant saving the lives of my men and getting them home . . . yes, Sergeant, I would have.'

I butted in. 'Respectfully, sir, but depending on their plan . . . there might not even be a home to go back to.'

Narville looked at me like I was someone with a hunch. And that my hunch was about as welcome as a fart in an Exoskeleton right now. He was right, of course. I was just a guy with a hunch, it was about as welcome as a fart in an Exoskeleton and just as much use – unless I could get something more concrete.

'I only need a couple of minutes,' I pressed. There had to be a data centre around here somewhere – in the vicinity of the labs was the most likely position for it. If I could find it, who knows what I might be able to discover.

'Okay,' agreed Narville, although he didn't look happy about it. 'Make sure it's only a couple of minutes. Take Velasquez with you.'

Rico didn't need telling twice. He stayed behind with me as Narville and the three Bandit Recon moved off, heading for the holding cells. They'd find the complex in disarray and with any luck the Higs would assume that the invaders were making their escape right now, not fighting our way more deeply into the facility. What kind of dumb-ass would do that, huh?

Rico and I moved off in search of a data centre, Rico giving me an aggrieved look.

'I'm sorry, man,' I shrugged. 'It slipped my mind.'

Chapter Twenty-one

I was half right about the defence we met. And we made it to the data centre with minimum resistance. Rico tried to figure out a console by the door as I stood guard, the warning alarms still wailing over-head, but there was no sign of more guards and it felt as though we had this section of the facility to ourselves – for the time being at least.

With a satisfied grunt Rico stood back, the doors to the room slid open and cautiously we walked inside, expecting to meet guards or computer operators, but finding none. Around us hummed machinery. Graphs and figures danced on screens along the walls. Stand-ing there I realized that the screens reminded me of my father's office, and it was enough to throw me back in time and hit me with a sudden sense of long-ing and loss that was almost painful.

But as quickly as it came it went, and Rico was moving across the floor to a console that dwarfed the others, undoubtedly the main control terminal. A screensaver of the Stahl Arms logo rotated lazily above a keyboard and it flicked off as we approached, sensing us, and was replaced by a holo-image of a spinning globe.

I felt a slither of worry in the pit of my stomach, Stahl's words running through my head. *The greatest military campaign in our nation's history*. What bigger target than our mother planet? Earth.

In front of us was a heliodisplay, on it a list of folders represented by icons. I jabbed randomly at them, opening files containing lists of figures, graphs showing profit and loss – lots of profit, not much loss, I noted – opening folders to find something – anything – of interest. At my shoulder Rico pointed out a folder on the screen.

'Try that one,' he said.

I did. It opened and a new image unfurled just to the left of the still-revolving Earth. This picture showed a room – a room I recognized; we'd passed through it in their labs. It had been empty, its distinguishing feature the grotesque splatters of blood all over the walls, a charnel house. It was empty in the video we watched too, but as the video rolled a Hig lab technician dressed head to toe in a hazmat suit appeared, looking up to the camera. Next the door opened and a grunt entered, dragging one of our guys with him, one of Bandit Recon – Poulou, his name. He looked half dead, exhausted. The Hig scientist gave him a cursory glance, appeared to be saying something to someone off-camera and then walked out of shot, just as Poulou scrambled to his feet, looking scared and wary.

'Test subject two-twelve,' came a disembodied voice. I could hardly bear to watch.

Next a panel in the ceiling of the room slid open and a small silver sphere dropped to the floor beside Poulou. He stared at it, eyes widening as it seemed to shudder and vibrate, then began to glow green. It was the same green Rico and I had seen collected from the pit outside Pyrrhus. The same green that had leapt from the barrel of the executioner's gun in the broadcast room. The most powerful weapon I had ever used and here it was in the hands of the enemy, being tested and developed. I barely needed to watch to know what happened next. I was getting used to seeing how petrusite behaved.

Tendrils of evil green light untangled themselves from the sphere and engulfed Poulou and, sure enough, he began shaking as though gripped by an invisible giant hand – until blood began to pour from first his nose, then, sickeningly, his eyes. His screams became gurgles as he was torn apart. Rico and I watched open-mouthed.

Then the test image flicked off, and the files must have been chained because another one opened automatically, this one showing drawings and schematics of something that turned out to be familiar. It was the battleship we'd seen being constructed in Workshop One. Three-dimensional wire models of it rotated before our eyes, pivoting up and down from prow to stern. Gracefully the image shifted to show the top of the ship, which bristled with cannon emplacements, the dark slits of observation ports and a cloaking cone.

Even as a model the ship inspired fear and awe in equal measure. Data showing its capabilities flashed up on the screen as the camera crawled over the hull and swung to below the ship, zooming in on a large cannon turret constructed on its bow, and again I barely needed the read-out to inform me what it was. A petrusite cannon. A devastatingly large petrusite cannon by the looks of things. The file showing the ship's stats was chained to another and suddenly the revolving globe image of Earth flicked on and off as the animation was woken from sleep. What we were now seeing was a simulation – showing a fleet entering Earth's orbit. A fleet led by Stahl's behemoth. The cannon on the bow glowed green then opened fire and what looked like hundreds of bolts of petrusite leapt from it onto the Earth's surface.

It took me a second to work out the targets. Earth's major cities. As we watched, the green impact dots spread, creating a large emerald amorphous cloud that slid, covering all in its path. Pretty soon the green seemed to cover the Earth's entire surface. I thought back to Poulou, how the petrusite had seemed to contain him within a globe before he disintegrated. Next to me Rico echoed my thoughts.

'Jesus Christ,' he said simply.

Spinning figures showing the expected death toll appeared on the screen, passing the hundred millions. Then the words – PROJECTED SURRENDER: FIVE DAYS – flashing triumphantly before the simulation ended and cleared. The globe flicked on and off again and went back into sleep mode. Around us the room hummed.

So that was it. Suddenly everything made sense. The irradiated petrusite. The kidnapping back in the jungle . . . everything.

Stahl had been using us as pawns in a plan to not only wrest control of Helghast for himself, but to expand his empire – to Earth, causing the death of millions upon millions of people. The whole show due to start – *Christ* – tomorrow.

'We've got to tell Narville,' I said.

Chapter Twenty-two

Jorhan Stahl was no longer feeling quite so pleased with himself.

Quite the opposite: he was most displeased. Not with himself, of course, but with the hapless incompetents surrounding him. Those bumbling fools who had allowed *two* ISA men – oh, and not just any old two ISA men, but the two king killers, Sevchenko and Velasquez – first into the facility and then into the broadcast room itself, where they had begun an assault from which he had only just escaped with his life intact.

Not so his dignity, of course. He had humiliated himself on planet-wide television. The entire Helghast race had seen he, Jorhan Stahl, made to look foolish. And, what's more, a cowardly leader. The kind of leader who would use his men as shields without a second thought; the kind of leader he purported to renounce. The idea had been to increase the people's respect for him. Not to lose it altogether.

Around him, the base was in pandemonium because, having rescued their captain, the rogue ISA men had set about freeing their comrades, starting a battle that continued to rage. Stahl's factory remained under his control, but only just, and more by luck than great planning.

He found his hands gripping into fists as he made his way quickly to the data centre, two very alert troopers with him, one ahead, one behind. They tensed as Stahl's personal assistant came hurrying down the corridor towards them, his eyes wide above his mask.

'Sir, Chairman, sir . . .' the assistant began.

'You told me the assault was at an end,' barked Stahl. He pulled his pistol from his coat as he walked.

The assistant, half-running to keep up with him, looked down at it and swallowed. 'That was the information we were given, Chairman,' he pleaded.

'Where was my security?' barked Stahl.

'I'm sorry, sir,' babbled the assistant, 'we are at full strength. Preparations for the attack on Earth have –'

Stahl stopped. His guard stopped. The assistant stopped. Stahl raised his pistol and put it to the assistant's eyeball.

'Can you think of one good reason why I shouldn't kill you?' he asked, pleasantly enough considering the circumstances.

The assistant squeezed his eyes tight shut, his legs bending as the barrel of the gun pressed into his face. 'No, sir, I can't.'

'I thought not,' said Stahl, and his finger went white on the trigger.

'Sir,' screeched the assistant, now on his knees, 'I've thought of a reason.'

'Yes?' said Stahl, interested.

'It would be a waste of bullets, sir.'

Stahl sighed. 'I'm a weapons manufacturer, you idiot. One thing I'm not short of is bullets.'

He brought his other hand forward to prevent splashback and pulled the trigger. The back of the assistant's head hit a glass lab wall and he crumpled to the floor as Stahl continued on his way, wiping his bloodstained hand on his trouser leg.

Now he reached the data room and his two guards moved forward, announcing the room as clear before Stahl strode in.

'Chairman,' insisted one of the men, 'we have to get you out of here.'

'Not yet,' snapped Stahl. 'I have to upload the battle plans to my cruiser. Orlock is going to jump all over . . .'

As though summoned, the image of Orlock flicked on in front of Stahl, who stopped, frowned, then continued running his hands over the heliodisplay in search of the right files, not stopping as Orlock glared at him over the relay.

'I don't really have time to listen to you gloat,' said Stahl, acknowledging Orlock at last. But he continued working, files and folders zipping around the display under his fingers, which moved as though he was conducting an orchestra.

Orlock continued regarding him silently and Stahl felt himself wither a little under the admiral's gaze. Damn the man.

'*What?*' he demanded, at last.

Orlock allowed himself the ghost of a smile, and when he spoke it was with an extra authority that Stahl could hardly miss.

'You are to turn in your petrusite weapons, hardware, personnel and yourself to my control.'

Stahl froze. In front of him on the heliodisplay icons hung in the air mid-transfer. Very deliberately he looked at Orlock.

'Don't be absurd.'

Now he saw Senator Gunsteling sitting there too. That toady. That sick, snivelling ... *bootlicker*. And where the fuck was Senator Kuisma when he was needed? What the hell was the point of Stahl blackmailing him? Well, Stahl knew what the next broadcast on the Stahl Broadcasting Network would be. *The Kuisma Show.*

Senator Gunsteling interrupted his thoughts. 'Chairman Stahl, not only have you failed to execute Visari's killers, you managed to humiliate yourself in front of the entire nation.'

Yes, Stahl had to admit, there was a measure of truth in that. And, that being the case, perhaps his best defence was one not of defiance but of contrition. He calibrated his response accordingly, saying, 'Gentlemen, I understand you're upset. I've made you look bad. But the people won't give a damn about today the instant Earth becomes our territory. If you change my invasion plan, you risk all of that.'

'Chairman, this is not a negotiation,' replied Gunsteling. 'You will do what your autarch commands.'

Stahl was forming words to come back on that, having no intention whatsoever of doing what was commanded by the . . . and then the word hit home.

'*Autarch*,' he spat. 'Who – you mean Orlock? You made him Visari's heir?'

In his voice both contempt and despair.

'Chairman, if you refuse to do as commanded you will be considered an enemy of the state,' said Senator Gunsteling. 'Your assets will be frozen. We will hunt you down, drag you through the streets and execute you over your own broadcast channels. Do you accept the autarch's rule?'

Stahl thought. He looked at the screen for long moments, his mind racing. Then, at last, he nodded his head yes.

'Good,' said Admiral Orlock – no, *Autarch* Orlock – adding, 'The invasion fleet is gathering in orbit around the space elevator. Deliver the weapons in person. Immediately.'

And with that Orlock ended the link and Stahl was left to seethe and lash out, cracking the glass of a screen.

'Prepare my fleet,' he barked at a trooper. And, when the man did not immediately move away, screamed, '*Now*, you idiot.'

Yes, thought Stahl. He would deliver the weapons. He would deliver them in person. And plenty more besides.

Meanwhile, in the Senate Room of Visari Palace the new Helghast autarch leaned back in his chair, feeling very pleased with himself indeed.

He turned his gaze on Senator Gunsteling. 'The moment I have the weapons, I want Stahl killed. Is that understood?'

Gunsteling nodded and wheezed, 'As you command.'

Chapter Twenty-three

The Higs had got their shit together by now and we met heavier resistance this time: Hello, Higs using blue arc cannons. Pleased to meetcha, Higs in jet packs. And finally, in the vehicle compound, well, how you doin', ATAC?

It came at us just as we escaped into the yard, which was a vast asphalt expanse of storage hangars, repair bays and supply stores lit by harsh fluorescent white floodlights and coated with a layer of ice. And today, at least, it also contained an Agile Tactical Air Component. It rose from the horizon with an ear-splitting sound that was half buzz, half hum.

My heart sank. I hated these things. Single-pilot flying combat machines, they were armed with a missile launcher and dual LMGs, were lightning-fast and just as nimble. They looked like flying black bugs and even sounded like them – like all good war machines they were designed to strike fear into the heart of the enemy and I got to say it worked. Worked on me, at least. It hung there, a colossal black moth, regarding us across the vehicle yard, hovering, tilting slightly as though to inspect us from different angles, like a creature observing its prey, ready to strike.

Hearts hammering, we dived for cover, making it to a long repair bay just as the LMG of the ATAC began to whirr, and suddenly shells were slamming into the ground around us. For a moment we caught our breath in the repair shed, white striplights overhead bleaching us out, then heard the noise of the ATAC suddenly increasing and turned to see it behind us, hovering in the open doorway at the other end. *Shit*. Once again it opened fire. Once again we were scrambling for cover.

Inside the repair bay an Ice Saw and an out-of-commission APC were ripped apart by thousands of machine-gun bullets, one of them bursting into flames, and as we dived back into the icy night, the bay exploded behind us, the Ice Saw tossed into the air and thunking down, flaming on the asphalt. With a shriek of boosters, the ATAC rose and panned left, ready to finish us off, but suddenly finding the flaming Ice Saw blocking its view and needing to bank further left for a clear shot.

It gave us just the chance we needed. Rico and I nodded to one another and took off in opposite directions – Rico towards a hangar, me making a dash towards what I hoped was a supply store.

What I *really* hoped was a supply store, because behind me I heard the roar of the ATAC swinging round, and then the whoosh-screech of a missile that only just missed me, making a flaming crater of the asphalt, showering me with debris, searing my skin and, probably, stopping the pilot getting a good visual. I had the door to the supply store in sight now. Without stopping I brought my assault rifle to my shoulder and rattled off a clip at a panel to the side of the door, praying it was the old-style doorcon – the Circumnavigator is what grunts used to call it back in the day.

It was. I saw a green entry light flicker on for a second as the circuits sizzled and died and a little plume of smoke escaped. Machine-gun bullets tore into the asphalt as I hit the doors with my fingertips, already prising them open, pulling them apart with a shout then diving into the store. Denied, the ATAC angrily buzzed around the building, raking it with gunfire, and I spent longer than was comfortable tucked into a wall until the barrage eased off.

Good move, Sev. You're in a room full of high explosives being riddled with bullets. I scrambled to my knees and found a gun rack. Not what I was looking for. But by its side was a long crate and now we were talking because this was a VC9. Good of Stahl to stock it, I thought, snatching it from the box, then filling my pouches with ammo. I slung my assault rifle over my shoulder, loaded the grenade launcher, then flew out of the store to face the ATAC.

The pilot was angry, frustrated. That had made him sloppy. Good. Maybe he didn't know that what I'd entered was a weapons storeroom and that I was likely to be packing some serious heat. Maybe he just didn't care. Either way he swung round the front of the building to find me waiting for him, kneeling, with the rocket launcher at my shoulder snug against my cheek. I had him in my sights.

'Gotcha, motherfucker,' I said, and pulled the trigger. There was a screech. Air billowed. The rocket found its target and an explosion bloomed on the side of the ATAC, which spun away, wounded. Again I took cover, reloaded the rocket launcher and waited for it to come round. I took another shot and missed. Shit. Snatched at it.

Now it targeted me with missiles and I found myself running again as the ground erupted behind me. The ATAC hesitated then gained altitude as I disappeared between two bunkers, but I doubled back and instead of appearing at the other end like he expected I came round to his rear. Suddenly I found myself with all the time in the world. Crouched. Brought the VC9 up. Got the ATAC in my sights and squeezed. The launcher jumped and the ATAC was hit by a rocket it never saw coming.

And now it was badly damaged. The bug's engines had developed a knocking sound and one of its LMGs was no longer functional.

Still it came after me. I saw Rico on the other side of the compound loosing off shots that ricocheted from the shielding of the ATAC, which was enraged enough to turn and launch an attack on Rico, opening up with its remaining LMG and firing a missile that sent him darting back into the safety of a repair bay. But the assault gave me just the momentum I needed and once again I sprang from cover and just as the ATAC spun round I brought the rocket launcher to my cheek. For a millisecond we faced each other, the ATAC hanging in the air, me on the ground below. Like two duellists. Just a matter of who fired first.

It was me. My rocket slammed into the damaged ATAC, which exploded into a ball of flame midair, and even as I was celebrating its demise I was shielding myself from the shrapnel raining down upon me.

In the aftermath was silence. Just the sounds of the klaxon from the main complex. Me and Rico were high-fiving, enjoying the sudden lull in the action as Narville arrived with ten of Bandit Recon in tow. These guys had reverted to being proper grunts, dispersing by the numbers, and looked like a force to be reckoned. Bandit Four was among them and I looked for Gedge, hoping against hope that he'd made it, my heart sinking until I caught the eye of a grunt who raised his hand in a salute, giving me a lopsided smile. It was him.

'Shoulda let me take the shot,' he called.

Grinning, I waved him away, turning my attention to Narville who I took to one side.

'Captain,' I started, 'we've got a problem.'

And I was just about to tell him what we'd seen in the data centre when there came a great clanging sound from the main complex and a series of beacons on the roof of the main building burst into life, painting the night orange. Next a rumbling sound and now I saw it – the roof of what must have been Workshop One retracting, exposing a block of blinding white light that expanded as the doors pulled back. Then came thunder, the unmistakable noise of boosters engaging, and Stahl's ship began to rise from its cradle, a behemoth gleaming black in the night. It sent a dark shadow over us all, buffeting us as it rose clear of the facility then turned and began to move overhead, lights winking on its underside, the mammoth petrusite cannon squatting there, petrusite crackling along the barrel.

It had started.

Chapter Twenty-four

We watched the ship draw off, all sickeningly aware that we were seeing a battleship bound for Earth and there wasn't a damn thing we could do to stop it. The most powerful weapon we had available was the VC9 and we might as well have blown the ship a kiss for all the good that would have done.

Narville's mouth was working like he was trying to form words that refused to come. In his eyes was the same helplessness we all felt. And now we saw two more ships bearing the Stahl Arms logo rising from elsewhere in the facility, and the only thing between them and Earth's occupation was us – a few harried, exhausted ISA guys. We'd been sold out by our own people and were hunted by the enemy, and when you looked at it that way, maybe we should have just looked the other way and let them get on with kicking the shit out of each other. Fuckers deserved each other. But, no, that isn't the ISA way. You know our code that says no one gets left behind? We have another one too: never let Earth get invaded. Just that we don't use that one so often.

'Okay,' said Narville, trying to pull it together, finding the words at last. 'I'm betting that cruiser will dock at a space port . . .'

Of course. Fresh out of the workshop they wouldn't be battle-ready. Chances are they'd RV with other ships, probably in geo-stationary orbit outside the planet's atmosphere – in other words, at some kind of space station. It made sense, but even so it was just a hunch and, to be sure, we had to follow it. I saw Rico looking from me to an Ice Saw nearby – both of us having the same idea at the same time.

Then there was the roar of engines and an uprush of retro thrusters, the unmistakable sound of Intruders descending and I looked up to see two of them dropping from the sky towards us. Crouched on the deck of one was Jammer, and for a moment I let myself swim in those eyes. Did I imagine it or did she reserve a smile for me? Sure could get used to that, I thought.

Now she turned to Rico as he said, 'Didn't I order you to get back to camp?'

'Never follow a bullshit order,' she came back, sardonically, then indicated the captain.

'You must be Narville,' she said, in a tone that suggested she had been told all about Narville by Rico – and that the report hadn't been glowing. Narville frowned, his displeasure deepening as

Rico took over and began giving the Raiders orders.

'Jammer, get Narville back to his men. We'll stay in radio contact as long as we can.'

Me and him had a cruiser to catch; we'd be faster without the rest of the team tagging along and, besides, Rico was right: the men needed Narville. We could be an army again. The thought was enough to give us a renewed sense of purpose as Rico and I jumped into the Ice Saw, ready to take off and kick some –

Shit, it was cold. I looked in vain for any heating. Christ, these guys had the best weapons in the known universe and they couldn't even install a heater? Figured, I guess. If it didn't kill things, the Helghast weren't interested. My breath plumed thickly in front of me, and the windscreen was a mass of ice squiggles. From up front Rico turned round and made a face at me, like he, too, was freezing his balls off.

With a growl the Ice Saw engine engaged, and I took hold of the joysticks, easing them forward and letting the Ice Saw roll gently across the asphalt towards a linked fence at the far end of the compound where a carpet of shining-white snow stretched off to infinity. Its two huge, toothed tracks moved slowly on the surface, crunching on the frost. The engine purred like a contented big cat. It was twenty tons of traction, this thing; there wasn't a snow- or ice-covered terrain that could slow it down, let alone stop it.

Other surfaces it wasn't so hot on, but snow and ice? It ate them up. And if anything got in its way — whether animal, human, superhuman or just some pesky bit of landscape needed shifting — well, there was a driver-operated chain gun to take care of that. A forward-facing gun only, though, I noted, hoping that wouldn't matter. The cruisers were moving away from us now, so as we got to the perimeter of the vehicle compound I opened the throttle and the Ice Saw took a grateful leap forward, tracks pulling on the snow surface, engine thrumming happily as we took off, gaining speed, tearing along the mountainside.

Soon we were chewing up the miles, surrounded by a cloud of ice and snow, with Rico using the chain gun to destroy obstacles in our way as he weaved between clumps of dead blackened trees and steered us through deep, icy gullies.

We were descending, I realized. It was hardly noticeable, but we were. We'd come up the mountain in a cable car dressed as Higs, with rescuing our men the only thing on our minds. We were coming down trying to stop an attack on Earth. You couldn't make this shit up.

All the time I was keeping a close eye on the cruisers at our twelve . . .

Then — like some cat in a cartoon — I was doing a double-take as I saw more ships appearing.

'You see those?'

'I see them,' said Rico.

Now the sky was a patchwork of ships. The fleet was beginning to gather. And not just the larger crafts but smaller Overlord dropships flying at a lower altitude, probably on recon duty. Who should they find tracking the mother ships but an Ice Saw bouncing along below. An ant on the mountainside. Enough to warrant another look, obviously, because two of the dropships banked to come round and check us out. One of them hung in the air ahead of us, and the main doors of the hold slid open. I saw a grunt inside staring out at us, then gesturing. I twisted in my seat to see another Overlord at our rear.

'Rico, they're onto us,' I yelled.

'Copy that,' he shouted back.

The barrel of the mounted chain gun swung as Rico adjusted the targeting. On the screen I watched the sighting move to locate the Overlord in front of us. The ship was just about to peel away when Rico opened fire, raking a blast across its hull and sending the Hig inside sprawling.

The pilot panicked. Pulled away too sharply. With a scream the grunt in the hold fell forward and pitched out of the cabin to the snow beneath, landing in a tangle of arms and legs.

He was lucky: the snow broke his fall.

Then again he was unlucky. Because just as he was scrambling to his knees and pulling his rifle towards him, our Ice Saw was bearing down upon him and I was tweaking the steering to take him under the tracks. He howled as he disappeared beneath the sharp teeth, his body instant mush, blood streaking the windows of the Ice Saw. I saw a clawed hand lodged in the front axle and it took me a moment to realize that it was a dismembered hand. Then it was gone and I twisted my head to see red mess on the snow behind us.

And another Overlord.

We'd riled them now. Overlord One pulled away and banked hard, coming up on us for a missile strike. The chain gun pounded. The cockpit filled with the stink of cordite and we left a trail of spent shells in our wake. Sparks flashed across the Overlord and suddenly it exploded into an orange-black globe, and we were lashed by debris.

One down. Now the other came up on our flank, then was out of sight as I took us down a gulley with steep ice walls either side.

'Snow's getting finer,' Rico shouted back over his shoulder.

We came out of the other side of the gulley onto a plain and there was the Overlord again, swinging round to our front. Rico chased it away with a blast from the chain gun. It fired a brace of missiles, but missed, and there was a fountain of snow, flame and mountain in front of us, me steering away from the blast zone.

We thumped over uneven ground. I held on tight and gritted my teeth as we were buffeted by another explosion, the dropship staying to the side and rear of us. Clever boy. Out of the chain gun's range. Already it trailed a ribbon of smoke, damaged from our first blast.

'I need him at our twelve to finish him,' shouted Rico.

We raced across the plain, out of cover now. Ahead of us the ground dropped away into a shallow canyon and if we could make that then we had cover again and we'd be safe for the time being.

If we could make it.

The Overlord swung into position behind us, riding the sky, getting its aim. There was no way it could miss unless its targeting systems were damaged or the pilot was blind. And somehow I didn't think the Helghast used blind pilots.

Nope – there was no way we were going to make the canyon.

'Grab your nuts,' I shouted, and yanked on the joysticks so that the front tracks of the Ice Saw locked and it swung round in a plume of ice shards, coming to a stop with a screech of outraged metal. Facing the Overlord.

Man, I'd have loved to have seen the pilot's face right then.

Rico opened up with the chain gun, perforating the bow of the Overlord. Fire bubbled from its cockpit and straight away it lost altitude. For a second I thought it was going to hit us then it sailed over, getting as far as the canyon where it flopped to the ground and exploded.

I realized I'd been holding my breath and let it out in a rush, Rico doing the same. We looked at each other, and both began laughing with relief. Then we glanced up at the sky and we stopped. It looked like the Overlords had lost interest at least, as the fleet moved away.

We had to keep following. We got the Ice Saw going and we took off after it, both of us trying to ignore the clunking sound from the engine.

Pretty soon the ride had got even rougher. We'd come down the side of the mountain, I realized, and looking up and behind me saw the huge edifice of Stahl Arms in the distance, forty klicks away at least. Next we ran out of ice altogether; the Ice Saw was meeting hard rock and not liking it. Then it was juddering, the tracks screeching, sending a cascade of sparks above our heads, and I realized we were on a stony surface just as there was an unhealthy grinding sound and the Ice Saw stopped, unable to continue any further – because what good was an Ice Saw without any ice?

We pulled ourselves from the cockpit, the fleet still above our heads. Ahead of us was desert interrupted by a mountainside. Behind that we saw four pillars of light stretching from the ground upwards, going out of sight into the roof of the sky.

Space elevators. They were space elevators. Anchored on the ground and rising to above the atmosphere, where – I'd lay money on it – they serviced a space station. That was it. That was where the Higs were massing, ready for the attack. They would have been servicing the space station with the elevators, sending up personnel and supplies. But that operation was over. Their main fleet would be moving out of orbit soon.

Which made the elevator station vulnerable. And there had to be ships there, surely?

I looked back the way we'd come. Smoke rose in the distance from the carcasses of the two fallen dropships. Then I looked forward, to the mountainside and the four columns of the space elevators.

'How far do you think it is?' I asked Rico.

'It's far,' he sighed, and we slung our assault rifles on our backs and began to run.

'You know the direction we're headed?' I said.

'No. Do you?'

'If I'm right then about thirty klicks in that direction,' I pointed ahead of me, 'is Pyrrhus.'

'You think the space elevators are in Pyrrhus? They cleared the city and built them in six months?'

'Could be,' I said.

Thinking it through, it made sense: the irradiated petrusite created by Red Dust would make the perfect power source, probably the only one on the planet capable of juicing the elevators.

'Man,' said Rico. 'That must have been a helluva clear-up.'

Chapter Twenty-five

What felt like hours later we found ourselves at the bottom of the mountain. At its base was soft, brown and sticky soil that I crumbled in my fingers, seeing it cling to my gloves.

'Fancy a climb?' said Rico, looking up.

'Let's go,' I said.

I'm not sure what I expected when we reached the top, but what I saw when I scrambled to my feet, brushing the strange, clinging dirt from my ACU and then looking around myself, made me catch my breath.

Directly below us was a scrap yard. A vast scrap yard stretching as far as the eye could see on either side of us and maybe seven klicks deep, forming a giant strip of land like nothing I'd ever seen before – an endless river of garbage.

This was it – this was the Pyrrhus City clear-up. Here was where they'd taken the trash.

Past the scrap yard was an expanse of desert and then the outskirts of what had once been Pyrrhus, but which had now been virtually levelled – was just rubble, by the looks of things. And there, in the middle of the city, more or less exactly where we'd attempted the failed extraction six months ago, was the elevator station, made almost beautiful by the ropes of petrusite dancing above it.

'Jesus,' gasped Rico from by my side, 'look at them all.'

He was pointing above our heads, and my attention was jerked away from the scrap yard to the direction of the space elevators where the ships were gathering.

There were hundreds, maybe even thousands, of them, from battleships and cruisers to fighters and dropships. And not just the Stahl Arms war machine either. There were Helghast military ships approaching too, all of them vessels of war, making a mosaic of the sky. This was like watching the entire planet's military force moving out, and again I found myself awestruck by the sheer size of the operation. When we launched Operation Archangel against Helghan it was the biggest military operation in the history of mankind. But this – this was in a whole new ballpark. This made Operation Archangel look like a trip to buy groceries.

I heard a crackle of something in my ear and turned my head away from the great roaring of engines from above me.

'*Sergeant . . .*'

'This is Sevchenko,' I said, startled. 'Captain Narville, do you read?' If they were within comms range, he had to be near.

'Sergeant, finally,' he replied, voice full of gravity. 'I hope you're looking at the sky.'

I was. I swept my gaze left and right and all I saw was warships. At the same time I saw one of the cruisers seeming to blink and crackle, then light swept over the whole of the ship and it appeared to pulsate for a moment or so. Preparing, I knew, to warp. It did. With a pop and sizzle that left a shrinking white burst of light in the sky, the ship was gone.

'That was a warp launch,' I said.

Next to me Rico was nodding. 'A forward scout ship. That means the rest of the fleet launches within the hour. Sev, the invasion's started.'

'Captain,' I called into my pick-up.

Narville sounded grim in my ear. 'We saw it, Sergeant. Sev, if we're going to get the warning out, we need to find a ship as fast as we can.'

I looked ahead of me. The only way to it was through the junkyard, a ribbon of trash.

We made our way down. Everywhere were the carcasses of vehicles, huge mountains of waste metal of every sort: panels, turbines, wheels, cabins, barrels, piping, tubing, girders . . . Everywhere – everywhere we looked were the remains of machines, industrial, agricultural and military. Here in these machines was a history of the Helghast, layers of it, fossilized. It was as if an independent city had somehow sprung up in here too, because we soon found this world of garbage was intersected by roadways and walkways, creating a maze within the trash. As we made our way through it, canyons of junk metal rose on either side of us, creaking and clanking in a wind that blew dust and dirt into our eyes.

We passed through tunnels in the junk, through chains that clanked when disturbed. The place was almost ghostly quiet, I realized, the noise of the fleet a distant background rush.

All we had to guide us was the four pillars of the space elevators in the distance, but as we tried to make our way towards them we'd find ourselves stuck in blind alleys or doubling back on ourselves. Our only choice was to try to reach high ground, so we scrambled up some makeshift steps to get our bearings, with both of us feeling a bit shamefaced if I'm honest, a pair of grunts who couldn't negotiate a rubbish pile.

'Hey, how come you let Earth burn?'

'Ah, we got held up. Garbage was a bitch . . .'

At the top of the steps we cast our gaze around and the first thing we saw was our guys. Way off in the distance, moving across the desert in the direction of the Pyrrhus outskirts.

It was a raggle-taggle collection of vehicles, scavenged from the enemy by the looks of things, though I saw a few Archers in there as well. Looked like Doc Hanley had been putting his time leading the men to good use. Maybe I'd underestimated him.

Rico, seeing them, pointed. 'There they are.'

Meanwhile I was sniffing at the air. Below, in the scrap yard, there had been the oppressive smell of . . . I can only describe it as dead metal, festering rust. Up here I could smell something different. Something that smelled like . . .

'Ozone,' I said. 'I can smell ozone.'

'How can you smell anything?' said Rico disbelievingly.

Because it's so strong, I thought, my attention going now to a series of fence posts that lay outside the boundary of the space elevator complex – towards which Narville and his men were travelling, dirt billowing behind their speeding vehicles.

It was . . . it was a fence I realized, and what I could smell was petrusite. It was . . .

. . . switching on.

At the same time as an alarm sounded, the fence begun to sparkle and light up, activated by the first of Narville's vehicles, a tank and buggy that were instantly vaporized. We watched the explosion flower then die. Suddenly the posts were linked by a wall of luminescent green light, that same oily sheen that seemed to cast the world in a ghastly emerald hue.

And we stood on the top of the scrap pile and watched as our men walked into the trap. Watched, feeling helpless.

Chapter Twenty-six

'Nobody move. Everyone stand absolutely still.'

Narville looked around at his men. They were trapped. The fence, sensing an incursion, had engaged, destroying the first two vehicles that had triggered it. Many of the troops were caught outside the petrusite's reach and Narville saw Jammer in virtual safety, but those in the immediate vicinity of the posts – including himself – now found themselves enclosed by a bubble of it, with volatile tendrils of it reaching from the bubble canopy – reaching for them like fingers feeling blindly for food.

Now he looked to where an Intruder was similarly trapped by the seething bubble. On it were four Raiders looking carefully about themselves as the thick phosphorescent ropes of petrusite waved dangerously above them, every second threatening to bring death closer. One was less careful than the others, Narville saw – Badger his name – his movements were more jerky than the others, his eyes wider.

'Don't move,' repeated Narville.

Somehow these tendrils of petrusite sensed

movement. But Badger wasn't listening. Narville saw him doing the very opposite of staying still, instead cringing away from the dancing arcs of energy as they seemed to close in on him. He needed to stay still, goddamnit. He needed to stay still. The other Raiders on the Intruder saw the danger too, and were imploring Badger not to move. Now the entire unit was aware of it, a hush descending on the troop so that for moment the only immediate sound was Badger's frantic jabbering. 'Oh my God. Oh my God. What the hell . . . I can't do this . . .' Openly struggling with the urge to simply leap from the Intruder and run screaming over the desert.

'Badger, stop moving, man,' shouted Jammer.

'Do *not* move, soldier,' ordered Narville. Others were shouting too, their pleas having the opposite effect on Badger, as though he was panicked by the sudden urgency in their voices, his fight or flight instincts kicking in.

And suddenly everyone in the vicinity – Narville, Jammer, the other Raiders, everyone – knew that Badger was about to try to make a jump for it.

'*No*,' shouted Jammer. Everybody frozen in place like statues, nobody able to reach out and stop Badger.

'Don't,' shouted Narville uselessly.

Badger jumped.

He never reached the ground. Multiple petrusite creepers leapt towards him, greedily hoisting him above the deck of the Intruder where he was suspended for a moment, wriggling as though impaled on a hook, screaming in agony as his insides were liquefied before exploding, spraying his team with gore. But the petrusite hadn't finished, suddenly arcing further afield and this time catching the Intruder. On it the three raiders had no time to scream and simply disintegrated, their dropship exploding beneath them as the petrusite reached for another vehicle nearby, an Archer that went up with a *whump*.

For several moments afterwards the unit simply stood stock still, their eyes on the burning wrecks of the Intruder and the Archer, scraps of flaming flesh now dotted around the area.

Jammer's headset crackled. 'Jammer, what's going on?' demanded Rico.

'Sir,' replied Jammer, 'we just lost five guys.'

'So what's Narville's plan?' asked Rico.

'We're gonna hack the fence,' she said. 'Stand by.'

The comlink clicked off and she watched as Narville took Hooper by the shoulders, instructing him on how to penetrate the petrusite defences. The circuits were located in one of the fence posts nearby. But to get there Hooper and his touchscreen had to negotiate the petrusite tentacles. A minefield where the mines drifted around and were attracted by movement.

Encouraged by Narville, Hooper swallowed his fear and, carrying the keyboard, took his first step towards the unit. The petrusite around him became excited. He felt perspiration make its way down his cheek. Tried to control his breathing. He waited until the twitching bolts of petrusite had settled, then took another step.

He looked across the haze of green and estimated the steps between him and the circuits. Thirty or so, he thought.

He took another step. Twenty-nine.

Chapter Twenty-seven

Over in the scrap yard Rico and I watched, with Jammer filling us in. In the distance the fleet still hung in the air and I saw two of them warp. Like blips on a screen: one second there, the next not. Closer by, but still difficult to see, were our guys trapped by the petrusite, all of them depending on the progress of Hooper.

Who was moving very, very slowly.

Rico echoed my thoughts.

'This is taking forever,' he said. 'We need something faster than this.'

My attention had been taken by something to our right, further along the scrap yard – something that belched and rumbled as it moved lugubriously along the horizon. I tapped him on the shoulder and pointed him in the direction of what I was looking at, enjoying the look on his face as he turned and took in the sheer scale of it.

This thing was off-the-scale big. As big as an apartment block turned on its side, a huge warehouse on tracks, grinders at its front, cranes bristling along its back. It was a factory. A mobile factory. Commandeer it and nothing could stop us.

'. . . or bigger,' said Rico, his eyes lighting up. He keyed his headset. 'Jammer, we're making a move on the mobile factory. Can you fly?'

'Negative,' replied Jammer, 'but I can find something else.'

'Roger. Meet us at the factory,' finished Rico. We scrambled down the steps and back into the scrap yard, straight away finding ourselves right back where we'd started, ducking down blind alleys, taking wrong turns, lost in the metal labyrinth.

'There's no clear route to the factory. We going to have to go round,' directed Rico, and my heart sank. So far we'd managed to avoid any engagement with the enemy, but now, moving closer to the middle of the scrap yard, we were likely to encounter resistance, so it figured when two sentry bots then suddenly rose from the scrap and turned our world into bullets and sparks.

Christ, I hated them. This model wasn't fully operational during the Helghast invasion of Vekta, so we hadn't had the chance to see them in action until we responded with the attack on Helghan, and what we discovered was that they were tough little motherfuckers. Like the ATAC, they were styled to resemble flying bugs; they were equipped with two Sta3 LMGs, and they hated to lose.

We dived for cover. Through gaps in towering piles of junk I saw the two hovering metallic insects swoop and intersect as though jockeying for the better position, both of them trying to get closer, each wanting the kill. That was one of the things we'd been quick to learn – that sentry bots like to get up close and personal. An LMG when it was mounted on a flying machine like that, it lost its accuracy so they needed to get near to their target to finish the job. Pretty quickly we'd worked out that our best defence was to try to inflict maximum damage from range.

'Need to draw his fire,' said Rico. Like me he was watching the two bots through the scrap.

'Who goes?' I said.

He looked at me. 'Gotta be your turn, man.'

I shook my head. 'I took out the rigs.'

He sighed. 'Okay, I'll go.'

Sometimes it takes paper-scissors-stone to decide, but not right then. Rico leapt quickly from cover, crossing to a rusting turbine. Eagerly the two sentry bots followed and I pulled the rifle to my shoulder, finding myself with a clear shot at the rear of the first one – just as it opened fire on Rico. Shells pounded into the turbine and I could just see him sheltering beneath the onslaught as I filled the bot with a clip, straight away seeing smoke pour out of it and hearing the engine stutter. Gotcha.

Now. Where's the other . . .

Bullets rained around me. Bastard had outflanked me, come up on my side. My boots kicked in the dirt as I desperately scuttled out of the line of fire, reloading at the same time. My rifle jammed but Rico was there to save my ass, rising from cover and blasting the bot before it could unleash another assault. It was enough to send it off-balance and it went skittering away. At the same time I spotted a weapons rack and whaddaya know – they had a boltgun. I snatched it up, turning it over to inspect it. Man, I loved these puppies. We called them the Handyman. Weaponized industrial tools, they fired heavy explosive-tipped bolts that could pin a grunt to a wall before exploding. Messy. And as for sentry bots . . .

I listened for the sound of the sentry bot as it came back round. It was stuttering a little, already wounded. Okay, I thought, this should be short and sweet. Then I rose from cover, hoisting the boltgun, found the sentry bot in my sights and fired. It shuddered as the bolts found their target and I turned away as it exploded, raining hot metal on me. The other one was still out there, but it was damaged, and when Rico drew its attention with a short blast I was able to target it with my new best buddy, The Handyman, and he was the one getting a frag shower.

Both of the sentry bots were smoking ruins now, but Rico and I waited until the coast was clear before moving off, getting our bearings from the giant moving factory ahead of us and making off towards it. It was still our best chance to bust through the petrusite fence.

Across the desert, those ISA troops not trapped by the petrusite had remained close by – apart from Jammer, who'd taken off in a buggy – but all they could do was offer moral support to those who remained prisoners of it; who had now been standing for what felt like hours, stock still, not daring to move and reluctant even to talk. They were wondering how long they could stay this way. At what point would fatigue take over? Who would be the first to drop from sheer exhaustion and what would happen when they did? All focused their attention on Hooper, who was slowly – very slowly – making his way towards the circuit box. Each step he took disturbed the petrusite which would fizz and whip around him for a while – and during that moment he would stand and wait for death, praying that it would be quick and thinking of his two girls back on Vekta. He hoped they were doing well with their schoolwork and being good for Mommy while Daddy was away fighting the bad guys. And when death didn't come, he let his heart rate settle and then took another step, still counting, still waiting for death to come.

Chapter Twenty-eight

We'd worked our way round. Found a main route through the scrap yard then came into a clearing. Looking around we still had visual on the mobile factory. The top of it was just visible above the mounds of trash ahead of us, its rumbling even louder now. While to our left were the four columns of the space elevators in the distance, and there, I knew, were our men, trapped by the petrusite. Hold on, guys, I thought. We're almost there.

Then we saw the barricade. A huge sealed metal gate between us and the factory.

Frustrated I looked left and right, hunting for another way through to the factory that was slowly, inexorably making its way through the junkyard. Sure it was slow, but it would soon be out of range, and we had to reach it soon – especially as we were beginning to see more enemy activity now. The alarm had been raised and Hig grunts were taking up elevated positions on the other side of the barricade, snipers and infantry. Next they'd send dropships and then we'd be knee-deep in bloodthirsty Higs. We moved to cover and I peered around the side of a huge corrugated metal panel, scanning the area for something – anything – that might be of use.

'What about that?' I grabbed Rico and indicated a crane off to our left. It was on our side of the barrier and dangling from the arm was some kind of military vehicle. A big one, the remains of an AAPC, it looked like.

'What about it?' said Rico.

'You ever hear of a wrecking ball?' I asked him.

'Can't say I have.'

'Jesus, Rico, did you learn anything at school?' I laughed.

Rico grinned. 'I never *went* to school, asshole. You got a problem with that?'

'Only that it would help when I'm explaining my next half-assed plan, that's all. Okay, you see that crane? You see the personnel carrier? What's going to happen if we swing the APC into the barricade?'

'No more barricade?'

'That's right. Give yourself an – *argh.*'

Suddenly Rico was dragging me back into cover – just as a bullet thunked into a piece of scrap behind me, the sound of the shot a millisecond behind it. I'd have been inspecting my own brains right now if Rico hadn't seen the tattletale red of the sniper's laser-sight on my forehead.

'You give yourself an A,' he said sardonically, 'for asshole.'

I told him I owed him one and he told me he'd add it to the bill and then I took another peek round the side of our cover. So now they were taking shots at us. Peachy keen. Looked like it was going to be an interesting run to this crane.

Now we left cover, crouching and spraying bullets to give ourselves a bit of breathing space. I heard a loud humming and spun to see a sentry bot hanging there, mocking me, seconds before it opened fire, sending me scurrying back into cover and looking for Rico who was crouching in what looked like an old cruiser cabin, rifle perched on the window ledge. With one hand he gave me a thumbs-up, then opened fire on the bot. Taken by surprise, it was thrown back, already exploding as it hit a rusting tower and crashing to the ground, gushing thick black smoke. Fun wasn't over yet, though, and now bullets pinged to the metal around me. Their snipers had found their range. I risked a look from cover to see Hig snipers, their hoods pulled over their heads and the distinctive red strip at their eyes. They'd taken up position on scaffolding between me and the crane. Shit. These guys – they were deadly with the VC32. Not only that, but further along the scaffold on a platform I saw an emplaced Sta3 LMG, one with an armoured screen. They were powerful and they made a hell of a noise, but they overheated quickly. That might be a weak spot, I thought, especially if I could draw the gunner into opening fire for any sustained length of time.

On the other hand, no. I wasn't about to get that close. Not even I was dumb enough to take on a mounted LMG.

Okay, plan B. I opened a comlink to Rico. 'Cover me. I'm going to get myself a VC32.' And he gave me the nod as I very stealthily moved out of cover, praying not to be seen by the snipers.

Because here's the thing about snipers: they're patient, cool-headed, accurate and, man, they're dogged. They take up position, squint down their sights and wait for their prey to appear. And they'll wait and wait and wait. It's not a job for the attention deficient.

But what they don't have is good peripheral awareness, which is why a lot of snipers work in teams: one guy for the waiting and squinting, the other to watch his back. But these guys were just scrap-yard guards, they were not expecting sophisticated warfare, so they were working in teams of one – which made them vulnerable.

It meant I could outflank one. Not easily – let's not get cocky, kid – but it was possible to sneak up on one. This guy, for example; the guy I saw in front of me now, using a pair of barrels for cover, still as the night, a phantom waiting for me to appear so he could pop a cap in my ass. But – crucially – with a blind side.

Too bad for him. He and his buddies were still taking pot shots at Rico's position as I worked my way to the side of him, crouching there as he loosed off a couple of shots at Rico's cabin and taking my combat knife from its sheath. Now I was just an arm's length away from him, so close I could almost hear his breathing. I moved forward and reached with my knife hand, ready to bring it across the front of his respirator. He wouldn't see it coming. He wouldn't feel a thing. It would be instant.

He fired a couple more shots and I told myself he was trying to kill my buddy. Trying to make it easy on myself, hesitating as I did so.

Which was a rookie's error. Secure that shit. Make the kill. Worry about it later. That was how it went.

Sure enough. He went to reload and as he did so inclined his head a little so that he was looking behind himself – and saw me. With a shout he jerked as though electrocuted, swinging his rifle behind himself, the barrel connecting with my wrist, knocking my arm off even as I lurched forward to finish the job.

Messy. Christ, this was messy. Already he was casting aside the VC32 and reaching for his sidearm, an StA-18.

I recovered and came forward with the knife again, praying that I wasn't offering myself as a target for other snipers. He was quick. He'd pulled out the pistol and loosed off a shot, but he was shooting wild and shooting wide, the bullet getting nowhere near me. Then he was holding up a hand to ward me off as I struck, snarling, the gun no use to him now – not at such close quarters – and the blade of the knife slid into his neck at the jawbone so that he was writhing and gurgling, impaled by the blade, arms thrashing as he died on a piece of cold corrugated metal in the middle of a filthy scrap yard. As he did, he knocked off his own respirator mask and I caught my breath. He was young, just a kid. Hardly the first Helghast youth I'd killed and probably not the last, but even so. You don't get used to it; you never want to get used to it – not if you plan on staying human.

Now the other snipers had seen that something was wrong and turned their fire on my position, but I'd got what I wanted – a VC32 sniper rifle and I picked as much ammunition as I could from the kid's body before taking off with it to find cover of my own.

I'm good with a sniper rifle, comfortable with it. Perhaps it says something about me, but I don't want to see the whites of the enemy's eyes when they die. Not because I'm a coward, just because it's easier that way. War's easier that way. You can't let it get personal. So one by one I took them out, methodically working from one to the other, Rico providing cover fire. And that, gentlemen, I thought, as the final sniper folded to the deck, is how you work as a team.

The LMG gunner was the last to die. He saw me coming and panicked, stepping away from his mounted gun and yanking his assault rifle up to open fire on me. I was out of ammo but clubbed him with the stock until he went down, finished him off with a combat knife, made sure his respirator stayed on and tried not to think about it.

Now I was through to the crane, Rico at my heels, and we climbed a ladder to a high platform and a control deck, frantically trying to figure out how to work the arm of the crane. And failing. We ran from console to console, jabbing at buttons, but nothing we pressed or pulled had an effect and the arm remained immovable, console lights winking implacably at us.

Next thing we knew we were under attack from Hig shock troopers, and it got nasty. These were the guys who liked to bring the fight to you; who like to do it up close and personal, the elite of the Helghast forces. They came up to the control deck faster than we could pick them off, and came at us employing the usual shock-trooper tactics, rushing in armed with knives and small arms. I replied in kind, Rico too, bodies piling up around us. Now came another dropship, and as the doors in the hold slid open we let them have it, slaughtering enemy infantry before they could use the lines to deploy. Still they came, though, and for a moment it seemed like we would be overrun. I grabbed VC32 ammo off a Hig corpse and started picking off infantry as they took cover among the junk of the scrap yard below us. It was getting hot now. Christ, this was one well-protected scrap yard. I prayed that our guys in the desert were being left alone.

As I continued the battle, Rico worked on getting the crane arm working and at last, just as it seemed I had fought off the last of their guards, he cracked it, and in the next moment was controlling the crane. The APC swung overhead, hitting the barricade dead on and within seconds we'd shimmied down the ladder to ground level and were hurrying through the hole before more Hig reinforcements arrived.

Rico opened a comlink. 'Jammer, we're almost at the factory. What's your ETA?'

I could hear the engine of the buggy roaring in the background as she replied, 'Couple more minutes.'

Next we were climbing a fence and finding on the other side that we no longer had a visual on the mobile factory. I stood for a moment looking one way then the next. I could still hear the rumble of it.

'Where the fuck has it gone?' exclaimed Rico by my side, aiming a frustrated kick at a metal panel.

Which, as it turned out, was a dumb thing to do because the panel may have looked innocent enough, but it turned out to be performing the essential function of holding the whole shitpile together. The moment Rico kicked it away we suddenly found ourselves on our butts as what turned out to be a very precarious pile of metal gave way beneath our feet and before we knew it we were both sliding down a hillside of trash, landing on the ground at the bottom of a deep canyon of garbage, the steep sides of it rising on either side of us.

And still no sign of the mobile factory.

'Jesus,' exclaimed Rico, 'how the hell can something that big just disappear?'

We could still hear it, though, the sound of distant thunder. A rumbling that we couldn't quite place, and for a moment the two of us stood with our assault rifles raised, heads jerking this way and that like a couple of prairie dogs, trying to figure out where the noise was coming from.

The noise that was getting closer and closer. Until

I realized that the mountain of scrap metal towering above us on all sides was deflecting and rebounding the noise, fooling our ears, and that the factory could be anywhere. Bearing down on us right now, even.

'Jammer, we've lost visual on the factory,' barked Rico into his pick-up.

'You what?'

'You heard right. Fuckin' thing's disappeared.'

'Where are you?'

'We're at the bottom of the Grand Canyon of garbage here and we can hear it. Oh, we can hear it. Sure as shit can't see it, though.'

'Hang fire, I'll be with you any second.'

He closed the link and for a second or so we stood there like a couple of leftover turkeys, looking around ourselves, the ground vibrating beneath our feet.

Okay, this had stopped being funny now. Where in the name of Sam Hill was the mobile factory?

Suddenly a mound of trash to our rear began to shake as though caught in the first tremors of an earthquake. We wheeled to look at it, eyes travelling up and up as bits of scrap metal began crumbling from the huge pile and thunking to the ground around us. Just a few bits at first, nothing to worry about. Then large chunks of metal, most of an engine block, and next what looked like the partitions from the armoury of a cruiser came slicing

280

down to the ground, a sudden avalanche of parts, so that Rico and I were backing away with our hands over our heads to protect ourselves – and you can bet we were wishing that we were wearing regulation military headgear at that moment.

Then the mountain burst apart and all hell was let loose.

Chapter Twenty-nine

Hooper took another step forward and the petrusite hissed around him like snakes woken from sleep. He felt his fingers loosen with the fear and made a conscious effort to tighten his grip on the touchscreen. Not much further now. Five or six steps. He dared not look behind him to see how far he had come. All he knew was that the encouraging shouts of the men had become more distant. The circuit board was close now. Real close.

Suddenly the air was full of flying scrap metal as the mountain of junk appeared to explode from the inside, and we were hurled back, knocked off our feet. I found myself scrabbling in the dirt, my hands protecting my head as lethal lumps of trash stabbed into the ground around me. Then we heard an almighty grinding sound, and I had no time for a WTF moment because the next second I could see it for myself: the mobile factory.

It burst from the hillside and came with its huge grinders rolling, a nest of teeth at its bow. Scrap metal was being captured by the teeth, mauled by the grinders then drawn back into the body of the factory for processing, and what didn't get sucked inside was simply ploughed out of the way or catapulted forward. I had a second of thinking that at least we'd picked the right puppy for the job of knocking out the petrusite defences, because it destroyed everything in its path, before it struck me that we were in its path. It towered over us, casting our world in darkness and engulfing us with nightmarish sound of clanking metal. Behind the whirling wheels of the grinder – each tooth as big as a car – were its tracks, the height of two men, and on top of that the huge main section of the factory, made up of a kaleidoscopic patchwork of different metals, some sections new and shining, others rusting. Through windows I could see the crew and I knew that like everything else around here the factory was well guarded and getting up there was going to be a tough job, never mind controlling it. It was a monster machine, a behemoth, and I could only hope that it was easier to pilot than it looked from ground level.

But, hell, let's get our priorities straight, shall we? Right now piloting it was the least of our worries. Right now we needed to concentrate on not being eaten by it.

It hardly seemed possible, so slow and lugubrious was the factory, but with the bombardment of metal around us and the sudden surprise of its entry we were almost immediately pulled into it. We scrambled to our feet and ran, the knives and grinders at our heels. I stumbled. Rico caught me, yanking me to my feet, yelling into his pick-up at the same time, '*Jammer*.'

The two of us were running now, the earth quaking beneath our feet and mountains of garbage on either side of us avalanching trash into our path. Fall now and we were dead. If anything got in our way, we were dead. It felt like we were two specks of dirt around a plughole, gradually – slowly – being sucked in, that it was only a matter of time.

It struck me that I never expected to die this way. Always thought it would be a bullet or an explosion, or if I was really unlucky a knife. In the jungle there was the constant threat of fever, I guess. But one thing I never expected was that I was going to get crushed by a garbage factory.

Then – Jammer was there. An angel in the driving seat of a buggy with an ISA guy in the passenger seat, cresting a pile of trash ahead of us and skidding to a stop right in our path.

'Get in,' she screeched. No invite needed. Without breaking stride we both leapt straight into the rear seats of the buggy and she floored it, throwing us back. I twisted round to look behind us, taking in the factory again, my eyes going from the teeth and the revolving grinders right up to the main bridge where I saw two pilots at a windshield. All I caught was their red eyes and respirators, but I could have sworn that they were grinning at us. Laugh it up Higgleberry, I thought. We were in a buggy now and not stopping. And I turned to face the front just in time to realize that yet again I'd spoken too soon. Because in front of us the route came to an end – and we were speeding straight towards a mountainside of garbage rising up ahead of us.

'Shit,' said somebody, and it might have been me, or it might have been Rico, or it might have been the terrified ISA guy in the passenger seat.

Wasn't Jammer, though. Jammer was wearing an almost serene expression and despite the fact that we were all about to die I found myself simultaneously awestruck by her calm and stunned by her beauty. Maybe it wasn't so bad that hers would be the last face I ever saw, I thought, because we were definitely going to die, right? We were going to smash and explode onto the garbage or be chewed up by the mobile factory's grinders. They were the only two options, surely?

No.

Jammer stopped. Then reversed, the buggy's engine screeching a complaint. Building up speed now, she crunched the gears, danced on the foot pedals and spun the wheel, throwing her human cargo to one side as the buggy performed a 180-degree turn.

And by doing that she'd stopped us exploding on to the garbage. Which was good.

But now we were facing the oncoming mobile factory. Which wasn't so good.

The ISA guy was still jabbering like he was fit to wet his pants and even Rico was shouting in shock as we sped towards the factory. Just as we passed under sight of the control deck I caught a second glance at the two pilots and once again I could have sworn they were mocking us, but, hell, who could blame them? The buggy and the mobile factory were on a collision course and, in a collision between a mobile factory and a buggy, who was going to come off worst? Even I'd have put my money on the mobile factory, and I had more to lose than most. Then, just as it seemed the front bumper of the buggy was about to make contact with the foremost spikes of the grinder, Jammer was again pulling on the wheel and again she wore a look of complete contentment, as though in the eye of the storm, with her own and three other guys' lives at stake, she was at her happiest – like there was nowhere else in the universe she would rather be. And the buggy veered sharply to the right, as close to the blades and spinning grinders as it could get without being sucked in, garbage pissing down on us still, and Jammer slaloming through it with the grace of an expert.

Not that her expertise was doing much to comfort her passengers, all of us screaming, terrified we were going to be pulled into the jaws of the factory or crushed by the onslaught of flying waste pinging off it. There was no way we could make it, I thought.

No way.

Sure enough a huge chunk of junk knifed into the ground in front of us, blocking our path and we were certain to hit it. On one side of us an irregular pile of junk, impossible for the buggy to traverse at this speed, on the other side the factory, a cacophonous horror of blades and grinders and crushing tracks. Unless . . .

Unless Jammer saw a way. Which she did, and as the ISA guy in the front, sure of his own certain death, screamed and raised his arms over his face, Jammer stood on the pedals and wrenched the wheel to take us underneath the factory.

Yeah, that's right – underneath the factory.

Somehow she'd managed to negotiate a path

between the forward grinders and the tracks to take us beneath, where suddenly the ceiling was revolving gears and axle and there was hardly any room for a buggy stuffed full of screaming ISA guys and one beautiful, cool-as-ice ISA girl.

Controlling the rear of the buggy as it threatened to slide out, she steered us between the tracks of the factory and to the rear of the vehicle and the only exit. But suddenly there was no clearance and Jammer was screaming at us to get down as we crunched into the rear axle, which stripped off the buggy's rollbar with a savage screech of agonized metal, but with us intact – beat that – and we emerged at the other end of the factory with one less rollbar, but alive at least.

The buggy skidded to a halt and for a second or so we all looked at each other in complete silence, the enormity of our escape taking a while to sink in, before the ISA guy blurted at Jammer, *'Are you crazy?'* and she just grinned.

You know what? I hoped so. I hoped she was crazy because I was having an idea. We still needed to be on that mobile factory and now the crew would assume we'd been pulled into it. They were probably giving each other high fives right now, thinking of all the ISA burger they'd just cooked up below. That meant we could take them unawares – *if* we managed to board the factory that was. And to do that we needed our driver staying crazy because we needed to be up close and personal on that factory.

'Jammer,' I said, 'get behind it.'

She looked at me then looked at the mobile factory and saw what I meant. And with a smile that I packed away to enjoy again at a later date, she hit the gas and we took off in a cloud of dust, free, thankfully, of the flying barrage of trash, steering through the junk left behind by the factory and getting closer to the thundering tracks.

'Rico, are you with me on this?' I shouted over the roar of engines.

He gave me a look to say *You kidding?* and joined me as I climbed from the back seat to the hood of the buggy, Jammer keeping her nice and steady and steering a line towards the rear tracks. I crouched on the hood, holding on to what was left of the windshield with one hand and using the other to balance as Jammer brought us parallel to the factory. Seeing the juddering links of the factory getting closer, I knew that if I got this wrong I'd be hauled into the gears of the factory or pulled beneath the tracks, and either way I'd be decorating the scrap yard with my guts. Plus I had to get a move on or Rico wouldn't have time to make the jump as well.

I leapt. Made it on to the clanking links of the track and was dragged forward straight away. Quickly

I scrambled to my feet and just as the track was trying to take me down with it I jumped and managed to pull myself to a platform. As Rico joined me, I took my M82 from my back and checked my ammo. Time to meet the crew.

Chapter Thirty

We made our way to the first deck of the factory where the inside was just the way it looked on the outside: a cobbled-together patchwork of materials, a collection of repairs on repairs. I'd have liked time to admire the interior design, but two big grunts came to meet us and we dropped them, hardly able to hear the sound of our own gunshots it was so loud inside. We went down a level where we could see the grinders at work, pulling in the scrap to be processed. There we met more guards, but a short firefight later we had the deck to ourselves and we worked our way forward along rusting walkways – Christ, how old was this thing? – meeting the odd sentry and dealing with them one at a time. Now we moved up a level then again to another level, and we were up high now. Two grunts rushed us but we put them down then went to the handrails to look out over undulating hills of garbage, the height allowing us to see way over the scrap yard to the desert beyond where the ISA guys remained trapped by the petrusite fence. I could see Hooper. He was closer now.

We moved up a level where the fighting was still intense, but at last we found the door to the control room. Higs had locked it. I thought of the two pilots I'd seen – the gloating look I'd imagined them having. And I pictured the looks on their faces when we burst in.

Rico set the demo charges and we both stepped back to watch the doors blow, and we burst in.

Hooper had been wrong. It didn't take him thirty steps to reach the fence post. It took him twenty-seven.

'Hooper?' came Narville over the comlink. 'Looks to me like you're close. What's your status?'

'I'm here, sir,' whispered Hooper, as though the petrusite might hear him and come closer. As it was it hung nearby, fizzing and dancing.

'Take it nice and easy, Hooper,' warned Narville, and Hooper bit his tongue rather than reply, *What the hell else do you think I'm going to do?*

Instead he very, very slowly bent his legs until he was kneeling, level with the control panel. For a moment or so he basked in the feeling of no longer having to stand up, his muscles relieved at last, but then the green arcs seemed to rustle around him, animated by the movement and once again he found himself going . . .

dead . . .

still.

Droplets of sweat made their way down his face. He hardly dared swallow with the fear. And he waited. Until the tendrils of deadly energy appeared to calm and he reached to a pouch in his ACU and brought out a small countermand unit that with the gentlest *snick* leeched to the side of the control-panel door. He booted it up and watched numbers spin, a series of green lights flicking on until the lock was deactivated, and the door hissed open. Inside was the circuit board. A read-out showed Helghast symbols he didn't recognize, while bars he took to be energy indicators flickered beside it. He scanned the panel for any sign of an anti-tamper system. Saw none.

'I'm in,' he whispered into his pick-up.

'Perfect,' replied Narville. 'Just take it nice and easy.'

Yeah, yeah, he thought. *How about you come out here and take it nice and easy?*

Now he ran a line from the touchscreen to the console, holding his breath, half-expecting red warning lights to begin flashing. In return it registered the new hardware by doing nothing. Simply continuing to blink and flicker.

'What's your status, Hooper?' said Narville.

'About to start the hack, sir,' said Hooper. Very, very slowly he brought the touchscreen to his lap, and switched it on.

The control panel bleeped, not an especially angry bleep, the sort of bleep Hooper would have expected to hear in recognition of the touchscreen.

But then the read-out flashed and the Helghast symbols disappeared to be replaced by a timer and four empty fields awaiting the input of a code.

The override code. The one needed to disable the anti-tamper system, which had begun its countdown from sixty.

'Sir,' said Hooper, 'we have a problem.'

57 . . .

56 . . .

I pulled the dead Hig pilot from his seat at the windshield, Rico doing the same, both waving our arms to clear the smoke of the demo charges then seeing the desert to our left and pulling hard on the steering to get us moving towards it. Slowly the factory turned and began ploughing through a mountain of junk, pushing through to the desert where it began to trundle towards the petrusite fence. Jesus, I'd been right about it being a bitch to control. Rico and I struggled with the controls as though we were trying to pull it ourselves, realizing that we had almost zero control over it, just hoping we could somehow negotiate a line to the fence.

42 . . .

41 . . .

'Status, Hooper?' said Narville in his ear.

Hooper disconnected the touchscreen, trying to move fast without disturbing the ropes of petrusite. He ran a line to the countermand unit, fingers flitting about the touchscreen. He could hear his own breathing; a droplet of sweat fell from his forehead and splashed to the touchscreen. He set the countermand to search for an override code. Around him the petrusite fizzed and buzzed.

34 . . .

33 . . .

We were close to them now, and both of us saw it at the same time: our own men, still as statues beneath the canopy of petrusite, unable to move for fear of it striking them, but unable to move out of the path of the mobile factory – guys who couldn't even look round to see us coming.

'*Left, left, left*,' shouted Rico, and we both pulled to the left, faces screwed up with the effort, desperately trying to steer a path through our men.

'What's happening, Captain?' asked Hooper. His fingers didn't stop working on the touchscreen, eyes flitting from that to the countermand unit, then to the timer and back. All he could hear suddenly was the thunder of something at his rear – what sounded like a huge vehicle getting closer, and closer. Then the countermand bleeped happily, displaying the code, and Hooper looked at it for a second.

It was four zeros.

Those lazy fuckers, they had a four-zero override code.

As fast as he dared he disconnected from the countermand, ran the line to the fence control and began to input the code, eyes going to the timer. The noise of the vehicle behind was deafening, the ground shaking.

10 . . .

9 . . .

8 . . .

The read-out flashed gratefully. And paused. And then as if to say, *You didn't really think we'd use a four-zero override code, did you?* it started again.

4 . . .

3 . . .

2 . . .

Hooper squeezed his eyes shut and thought of home.

We hit the fence post full on and straight away the petrusite went down. I just had time to see Hooper diving out of the way as across the desert the fence flicked off and the world no longer had its green haze.

We'd taken damage, though. Nothing could withstand that kind of petrusite energy, and the factory was suddenly rocked by a series of explosions from below, even as it trundled on. In the control room we were thrown about as the factory began to go up around us; the only thing not affected was the tracks. Then the glass of the control room came in as the walkway outside went up, ripping a hole in the cabin through which we saw . . . Jammer. She was on an Intruder now.

'Get on,' she screamed. Again, no invite needed. We looked at each other then leapt – just as an explosion ripped through the cabin – landing in a heap on the Intruder, Jammer speeding away as the factory finally ground to a halt and burst into flames.

Jammer caught my eye. 'You guys ever think of leaving before the explosions start?' she said, with a half-smile.

I grinned. 'You can do that?'

PART THREE

Chapter Thirty-one

Narville's men pushed on, crossing the remaining stretch of desert and reaching the outskirts of the city. Meanwhile Rico regrouped with his Raiders to ready them for the final push towards Pyrrhus and the space elevators, giving his orders over the com-link. There was a sense of urgency in his voice. Like me, he was seeing the sky. Where before it had been full of enemy battleships, now it was emptying. They were going into orbit, probably heading for the space station, and from there they'd warp to Earth, taking the same path as the scout ship earlier.

Time was running out. For us. For Earth. We needed to move quickly, that much at least was clear.

Clear to everyone, it seemed, but Captain Jason Narville. Because Rico had barely finished barking, 'All right, people. Let's move out. Raiders, I want a full sweep, kilo protocol,' when Narville was breaking in and overruling him.

'Cancel that order, Raiders,' he snapped, sounding like he was ready to blow. 'This is the captain. Hold fire and stay in defensive positions.'

I was on the Intruder when it happened: me, Rico and Jammer on the deck. One of those moments when I knew things had just gone from bad to worse. I could tell from the set of Rico's jaw and the way his eyebrows knitted close together.

'Narville,' he came back, the whole unit able to hear him, 'that doesn't make any sense. We need to –'

But he was stopped by Narville going to a secure line, and next thing was holding his earpiece away from his ear as the captain came on, all guns blazing, loud enough for me and Jammer to hear him shouting, 'Sergeant, don't you *ever* question me on an open channel again.'

'You want to listen to what I have to say before you say no?' Rico shouted back, and I shared a look with Jammer, partly to acknowledge the shitstorm that was brewing. Partly because I just wanted to share a look with Jammer.

'*Velasquez,*' I heard Narville rage, 'apart from being ill-conceived and poorly executed, your plans cost more lives than they save. So no. I don't want to listen to what you have to say.'

'*My* plans cost lives?' retorted Rico, flaring, 'How many people did you . . .'

But he seemed to calm down before he said anything that might get him court-martialled, getting hold of himself before he continued, 'Look, all

I'm saying is we need to scout ahead, okay?'

Narville wasn't budging. 'You have your orders, Sergeant,' he said, like that was the end of the matter. 'This is not a discussion.'

From across the deck of the Intruder, I saw Rico go several shades of purple before exclaiming, '*Mother-fucker*,' and instinctively I reached to take his shoulder and calm him down.

'Let it go, man,' I said.

'Sergeant Sevchenko,' said Narville over the com-link, breaking off his secure line with Rico – something that would only enrage Rico further, I knew.

'Sir?' I replied.

'Report to my position immediately.'

'Yes, sir,' I said.

'Can you try and do what Narville's asking?' I said to Rico, thinking that yet again I was having to keep the peace between these two – just in case we didn't already have enough to contend with. You know, little things like reaching the space elevators, finding a ship, doing something about the impending attack on Earth.

Rico frowned at me. But he knew that the stakes were higher than any grudge he held against the captain.

'Sure,' said Rico as the Intruder landed and I dis-embarked. But as I jogged away I glanced back to see him and Jammer deep in conversation. Cooking up something? Maybe. Maybe not.

Or maybe I should just do what I was told and report to Captain Narville, even though I had a strong hunch I knew what he was going to say, and that it would be asking me – correction: *telling* me – to keep a tighter leash on Rico.

I jogged through the rubble, getting a good look at the remains of what had once been Pyrrhus, the Helghast capital city. Last time I'd seen it was through a snowstorm of ash and it had been ablaze, a world of debris strewn with bodies and wreckage. Then it felt as though the city would stay burning forever, and would remain in a permanent state of scorched horror.

The Helghast had been busy in the meantime, however, that much was clear. It was as though the ruins of the city had been turned upside down and emptied of debris then placed the right way again, leaving just the empty bomb-damaged buildings, the scarred streets and sunken roads.

I dropped down into a trench and jogged along it towards Narville's position, pulling myself out at the end and making my way towards where he stood, another grunt approaching him at the same time, who was catching his breath as he gasped, 'Sir, we've captured a bunker full of Helghast ordnance.'

'*Where?*' asked Narville, taken by surprise. You couldn't blame him for that. Good news had been in short supply these last six months or so.

The trooper pointed away. 'A couple of klicks that way.'

What Narville intended to do about that I never found out because he looked up to see me approaching and his face darkened. He was thinking, no doubt, of the argument he'd just had with Rico.

'You might want to keep your friend on a tighter leash, Sergeant,' he said tightly.

See? I was right about that.

Sucks being right sometimes.

'Sir, with all due respect,' I said, so only he could hear me, 'he saved both our lives. You and me – we're only here because of Rico.'

Narville looked doubtful, but only for the cameras. I could see that he knew I was right. He of all people. Narville would have died at the hands of Jorhan Stahl's executioners without Rico, not just a victim of the war, but a point scored in a propaganda battle. And that was no way to go at all.

He knew this, the captain did. Deep down he knew that even though he disliked some of Rico's methods, and even though some of Rico's methods could be wrong-headed and plain dumb, he got things done, and there was no better soldier to have at your back.

Narville opened his mouth to speak, but I never got to find out what he was going to say, because there was an enormous sound, like the entire world was splitting in two and we were both clapping our hands to our ears and wheeling round to see . . .

Oh no. A MAWLR.

As we watched, it rose from the crater, four spidery legs extending as it unfolded from the landscape, the huge main cabin swivelling and pivoting, looking for all the world as though it were an animal waking from sleep and stretching its neck.

It towered above the crater, Christ only knows how many tons of war machine bristling with weaponry: AA cannons, LMGs and, of course, a petrusite cannon. Located on one side of the main cabin, the cannon was almost half the size again, and it crackled and popped with deadly blue energy as though just beginning its charge.

Now the MAWLR moved. It crabbed like some bad-dream sea-creature looking around itself and seeking out its prey. And it didn't have to look far, because, below it, the ISA troops had been making their way across the rubble of the cityscape to the space elevators, and maybe a few of them had been remarking that things were quiet, but, hell, the Helghast were staging a major invasion of Earth so most likely there would be just a small unit left

behind to guard it – when suddenly the space elevators' defences had engaged. And it wasn't a small
unit. It was a MAWLR. And it had brought some
pals. Because at the same time as the gigantic mech
appeared on the skyline the comlink was alive with
our troops reporting hostile activity from within the
space-elevator station. They were mobilizing.

'All troops,' ordered Narville, the panic etched on
his face, 'do not engage. I repeat, *do not engage.*'

Do not engage? I thought. What the fuck?

'What are you doing?' I called to him, my voice
almost lost in the deafening blare of the MAWLR.

'We'll get to that weapons bunker,' he yelled back,
running for his tank, 'regroup there.'

I stood with my mouth working uselessly for a
second. Wow, Narville loved to regroup. And when
it came to *not* engaging he really was your boy.

Then the MAWLR's main cannon began to charge,
petrusite wrapping itself round the barrel in a loving embrace. The huge cabin swivelled to target us
and it softened us up with a WASP attack, a cluster
of eager missiles that made the ground erupt
around us, knocking infantry off their feet. Then it
hit us with a petrusite bolt and two Archers were
sent spinning and exploding. I saw a guy blown apart
in a red jumble of arms and legs; others burning,
screaming.

Narville was screaming orders into the comlink, but the troops had lost formation and were scattering. Ordered not to fight back they were doing the only other thing they could. They were running. Suddenly I was cut off from Narville. I keyed the headset and told him I'd meet him at the bunker, then grabbed the ISA guy from earlier.

'The weapons bunker,' I shouted at him, 'where is it?'

'Just follow the trench.' He pointed, and darted off.

I ran into the trench. The walls rising on either side of me were shaking, earth crumbling off as the ground seemed to quake under the force of the MAWLR's attack. As I ran, I heard Rico over the comlink, still arguing with the captain.

'Narville, *do* something,' he insisted. 'You *have* to attack,' he was still shouting as I reached the bunker, where the captain, Hooper and two other guys stood watching through observation slits in the concrete – watching the MAWLR turn our fighting men into fleeing livestock.

Again, I heard Rico come over the comlink, and I could hear it in his voice that he'd finally lost patience with Narville, and that he'd decided to force his hand. And that, I knew, was very bad indeed.

'All right, Raiders,' he announced now, 'this is

Raider Command. Form up on me. Get ready to go in. Armour Command, what are your orders?'

He'd batted it right at Narville: make your choice, man.

I knew what Rico would be thinking. That the Intruders had the best chance of taking the MAWLR out. I wasn't sure we had anything at ground level capable of even scratching its paintwork. And, since that MAWLR and its buddies were what lay between us and the space elevators, it had to be stopped.

I watched Narville carefully as he chewed over his reply, praying he'd make the right decision and wondering what I'd do if he didn't. I liked the captain. I'd risked my skin for him. And he was one of us. Most importantly, he was still our captain. But how many bad decisions did it take?

'Repeat. Armour Command — what you want to do?' pressed Rico.

'God help us,' said Narville, almost to himself, and then into the radio, 'this is Captain Narville. All units pull back immediately. I repeat, all units disengage and fall back to defensive positions.'

Shit.

Over the comlink I heard Rico telling the pilot, 'Take this down. *Now.*'

Great. He was on his way. That's all I needed. That's all *we* needed.

'Sir,' I said, rounding on Narville, hoping to talk some sense into him before Rico arrived. 'We're running out of time. You saw that scout ship going to warp. Forget about trying to get us home. We have to find a way to stop the fleet from launching.'

'This is not the time to question orders, Sergeant,' snarled Narville.

I could hear Rico's Intruder descending outside the bunker, the rush of the engines only just audible over the relentless sonic pummelling of the MAWLR. Any second now he was going to storm in here and all hell was going to break loose. And you know what? A bit of me thought, *The hell with it*. One of them wasn't fit to lead boy scouts, let alone command an ISA unit. The other one was a bull-headed liability with the anger-management skills of a frag grenade. What did I care? Let them kick shit out of each other.

'What the fuck you doing?' Rico was shouting, storming into the bunker and going right up to Narville's grill. 'We're out of time here and you want us to fall back and regroup? *For what?* So we can try again later when the Helghast invasion is over?'

'My priority is the lives of my men,' Narville came back, squaring up to Rico. 'Now, get back in position.'

Rico pushed his face close to Narville. Even closer.

'Or *what?*' he spat. 'Just order the attack, you fucking coward.'

Narville took a step back and swung at Rico, catching him full in the mouth and drawing blood. Rico was rocked on his heels then flew at Narville, the two of them about to tear each other to bits, when I rushed in, pulling them apart.

'Hey. Hey. Look, the both of you, just back off.' I pulled them apart, where they stood glowering at each other. 'Captain, there are more important things than our men. Billions of lives are at stake. We can't let the Helghast get to Earth with whatever weapons Stahl's been making.'

Narville and Rico still looked as though they wanted to murder each other, but now Narville turned his attention to me, indicating out of the observation slit at the same time. The MAWLR was still visible on the horizon; it was moving round the perimeter of the elevator.

'If we go out there, we can kiss our asses goodbye,' he insisted. 'We need to think. There *has* to be another way.'

I looked at him. I'd tried with Narville. Lord knows I'd tried. But looking back I couldn't remember him make a single good call during this entire wretched campaign. I'd thought maybe I could talk some sense into him. I'd thought the threat to Earth would be enough for him to see that withdrawing and regrouping were no longer options. But Narville's problem was that he was still trying to do everything by the handbook, without realizing that the time for the handbook was gone. I could see that he wanted to protect the men and nobody respected that more than me, but there weren't just a few lives at stake here, there were billions, and when Earth was overrun nobody was going to say, 'Well, at least Captain Narville followed established protocol.' They were going to say, 'Why didn't that asshole Narville do something?'

And then they'd say, 'And how come Tomas Sevchenko was standing around with his thumb up his ass the whole time, huh? What a loser.'

So, yeah, I'd tried with Narville. Matter of fact I'd tried with both of them: him and Rico. But now was the time to stop giving a shit about them and start taking some action.

I reached for my weapon, knowing I was going to have to go it alone and feeling a kind of peace all of a sudden, as though a great weight was being lifted from my shoulders. And my voice was calm as I told them, 'Fine. I'm going to outflank it.'

Rico rounded on me. '*On foot?* That's even worse

than his idea,' pointing at Narville, who looked as though he wasn't sure whether to praise Rico for his insight or reprimand him for his insubordination.

'You can either help me or get the hell out of my way,' I told them.

'Sevchenko, stand down,' ordered Narville, 'this gung-ho crap is going to get us all killed.'

'No, this . . .' I indicated Narville and Rico as I spoke, 'this is going to get us all killed.'

I looked hard at them both, wanting to make these two squabbling infants feel ashamed of their behaviour. Neither said anything. I slung my M82 across my shoulder and indicated to the other two grunts.

'You two are with me,' I told them, and they fell into line behind me as I left in search of the ordnance, hoping I could bag me one of those WASP launchers.

And I guess my words must have had some effect, because as I stormed out of the bunker and into the trench, I heard Narville over the comlink: 'Armoured division, this is Captain Narville. We need to draw its fire. Hit that MAWLR with everything you've got. *Everything*, you hear.' Sounding like a man with a sense of purpose for once.

And the next voice I heard was Rico: 'Raiders, this is Raider Command, listen up. We're going in hard.'

Well, I guess at least I'd made Rico a happy bunny. Narville? I'd worry about that later. For now I had a MAWLR to catch.

Chapter Thirty-two

Once again, Pyrrhus had been turned into a vision of hell. Above was the fleet, the boosters roaring as they continued moving off. On the ground was the MAWLR, its honking so loud and constant that it was almost overwhelming. Now there was small-arms fire too, as the guards engaged our troops, who were returning fire. They'd been ordered not to engage the MAWLR, but they sure as hell weren't going to stand around and be cut down by Hig grunts.

I let my two sidemen take down any opposition we met as I moved around beneath the MAWLR, searching out weak spots.

'Look,' called one of my sidemen, 'it's venting heat every time it shoots its main guns.'

That was it. This machine was using so much energy it had to vent, which meant . . .

I saw them: orange glowing cooling vents on the underside of the machine. Every now and then they would expose. They were the weak spots. I targeted one with the WASP launcher, squeezing the trigger and watching the missiles fizz to their target.

'Whatever you're doing, do it again,' yelled Narville in my earpiece as we all saw the MAWLR rock on its feet, seeming to falter so that for a second – a tiny exquisite moment – I thought it was going to topple over there and then.

I caught my breath. *Hallelujah, I'd hurt it* – the first sign that it could even be harmed let alone defeated.

It was just the encouragement our guys needed, and now our armoured divisions opened up on it, while Rico's Raiders began making passes, raking it with minigun fire, and suddenly it was as though we were a team again. Just that one hit was enough to do it. I reloaded the WASP cannon and moved around a foot of the MAWLR, hoping that its sensors weren't sophisticated enough to pick out one grunt on the ground below, because, if they were, I was about to get a petrusite bolt up my ass.

But no. The cabin continued swivelling, charging up its arc cannon again and blasting at an armoured division trying to make its way through the rubble. Armour Six, I think it was. Poor bastards.

But now, looking up at the MAWLR, I realized I might have injured it – I could see black smoke pouring from the panel I'd damaged with the WASP – but it was nowhere near neutralized and it was still inflicting heavy damage on our troops. Even so, now I felt like, 'It's me and you, buddy, me and you,' and

I reloaded the WASP cannon and fired again, at another panel, gratified to see flame flower and smoke pour from it immediately. Next I found myself diving for cover as a huge metallic foot crashed down into the stone by my side and I used the opportunity to catch my breath for a moment or so.

You might be big, I thought, lying in the rubble and staring up at the huge mech hulking over me, but I'm fast. And you can't see me.

I reloaded the WASP cannon and darted to my right, grateful for the covering fire coming from ground troops, finding a vantage point then locating another panel in my sights. The WASP launcher jumped in my arms and the missiles whooshed up, leaving trails behind them and smashing into the hull. Still overhead were the Intruders.

'That's it, you've done major damage,' screamed Rico, sounding elated. Then adding, 'you've got ground infantry heading your way.'

That figured. The Higs had finally worked out where the real danger was coming from and they'd sent a tank after me. I let my sidemen deal with the bulk of the unit, still desperately trying to finish off the MAWLR, which had now developed jerky, uncertain movements, like its systems were having difficulty coping. I could see multiple fires along the cabin too. I was starting to believe that this thing could come down. I was starting to realize that I didn't want to be around when it did.

Whoosh.

Another volley of missiles up into the panels. And then Narville was shouting about incoming mortars, the MAWLR's ground support desperate to protect Big Daddy. I crouched in the shelter of a ruined building and looked up into the sky, past the MAWLR to where the fleet had been.

It was no longer there. The fleet had left. They were on their way to the space station. And then to Earth.

Christ.

I took two more shots at the MAWLR and then, suddenly, Narville was screaming that it was coming down – and it was. As I watched, its legs bent at their knees as though it was a huge defeated animal, and with a monumental screeching of metal it folded to the ground, flames still billowing along its underside where I had targeted the cooling vents.

And the noise stopped. At last, the unending, deafening blaring of the MAWLR ceased.

Funny, I thought, looking at it. In the end it had come down almost gracefully.

Then I had an earful of appreciation. The com-link crackling with troops wanting to thank me, including our illustrious captain, who said, 'Sev, I don't know what the hell you were thinking about there, but it worked. Nice job.'

Yeah, no thanks to you, I thought, but accepted the praise. After all it's not every day you get to bring down something the size of a . . .

Suddenly there was a sound from behind me. It was the honking sound of the MAWLR, and I turned, knowing what I was about to see before I did.

Now I knew why it had folded so gracefully to the ground. It wasn't neutralized. It wasn't even disabled. It was simply reconfiguring. Getting ready to attack again.

'This thing isn't getting the message,' screamed Narville over the conmlink. 'Sev, get the hell out of there. All units. Open fire.'

He sounded as frantic as I felt, because we were in a world of shit now. Our troops had stood down and were doing all but cracking out the beer in celebration of the MAWLR's demise. Suddenly it was up and attacking again and they were caught unawares. An RPG unit sent up a volley of missiles, but the MAWLR didn't even notice. It was now up to full length, the cabin was swivelling to find fresh targets, the cannon charging at the same time – then it discharged towards the main tank column and suddenly Archers were exploding everywhere and I was thrown backwards, my head connecting with rubble.

I saw white. Then stars. My mind slowed, and I staggered when I got to my feet, doing the check: arms, legs, ears, nose. I could hear nothing but the sound of the MAWLR. I could see nothing because of the dirt and dust swirling around me. My world was reduced to just me and the fighting mech. Where was everybody?

'Narville,' I shouted groggily into my pick-up, 'do you copy? This is Sevchenko. Does *anybody* copy?'

I got Jammer. Heard the roaring sound of her Intruder thrusters over the comlink. She was flying close to the MAWLR, I could tell, and like the rest of us she was panicking, only just keeping it together.

'Sev, this is Jammer,' she yelled. 'We're still operational. If any Raiders can hear this, follow me in.'

Still fighting. She was still fighting. Then I heard the shrill screech of WASP missiles from the MAWLR and above me saw an Intruder explode – Jammer's Intruder, surely?

No, I thought. *Please no.*

The radio went dead. There was no response. Not from Narville or Jammer.

An ISA guy came jogging out of the smoke and I grabbed him, snatched his radio, barking into it, 'This is Sevchenko,' trying to keep the outright panic from my voice, but failing. 'Jammer? Rico? Do you read? Captain Narville?'

No answer. All I heard over the radio was static and the sound of screaming from far away – and of course the all-encompassing throb of the MAWLR. I looked around myself, suddenly feeling more alone than I ever had done in my life.

Then I grabbed the ISA guy.

'Where are we going?' he yelled.

'To finish what we started.'

Chapter Thirty-three

I'd seen a freight elevator. If I could make my way to that, then I could get up high and meet the MAWLR on its own terms.

I began to fight my way over to it, coming across the odd ISA grunt, most of them reeling around in confusion not knowing what their orders were or where to go. Knowing only that they had to escape the MAWLR.

I saw a minigun and picked it up. Then began working my way to what had once been some kind of factory. There, Hig infantry threw themselves at me, but I cut them down with the minigun, rushing headlong into battle, hardly concerned for my own safety now. Needing only to get to the freight elevator. When the minigun was empty, I tossed it aside and pulled my M82 from my back, and at last I reached the huge gantry that towered into the sky, a least as tall as the MAWLR was. And there I found a control panel. I called the elevator, watching it come down to meet me while keeping an eye out as the MAWLR made its way round the rear of the space elevator station.

At some point, I knew, I would need to entice it towards me. But for the time being I got my bearings, reaching the platform at the top of the elevator and running to the railing to look down.

There I saw a sight that made my heart sink. Below me lay the tank column, burning. Across the landscape were the carcasses of burning tanks, thick black smoke billowing from them, and I saw bodies dotted around too, all of them ISA by the looks of things, and then I saw the flaming wreck of an Intruder and recognized it as a Raider Two. Jammer's Intruder.

Suddenly my head seemed too heavy and I found it going down, the air coming out of me. I felt what I hadn't felt in a long time – I felt defeated, so that I almost didn't raise my head at the sound of rushing feet, but did, almost wearily. And I turned to see three capture troopers running along the walkway towards me.

'Where do all you guys keep coming from?' I sighed to myself as I braced myself to meet them.

They reached the entrance to the elevator platform, and stood there posing for a second so I could get a good look at them. Scare tactics. The red of their eyes glared within their sleek combat helmets; their shielding shone in the dark light at the top of the tower, the wind whipping around us. Their weapons were sword attachments to the right wrist. They would be experienced and highly skilled at using them, experts in hand-to-hand combat. These were the elite and like the guys we'd met in the scrap yard they liked to see the whites of your eyes when they put you down.

Thing was, they'd made a big mistake.

Big mistake.

See, there may well have been three of them, and in any other circumstances they weren't odds I cared for much, but these guys had a major disadvantage: they weren't armed with M82 assault rifles. And I was. And you had to be a chump to attack an angry grunt armed with an M82, especially if you were going to come armed with knife-hands.

So-called elite, I thought, raising my assault rifle. This would be short and sweet.

But I was wrong. Mistake was mine. Chump was me. They were fast – far more agile than I ever could have imagined. I had the chance to squeeze off just three shots, all of which ricocheted from the shielding of capture trooper one, who bounded across the platform, spun and sliced his sword across the assault rifle, dragging it from my hands.

It took me a second to comprehend this sudden and unwelcome turn of events. I was the grunt armed with an assault rifle, about to bag myself three capture troopers and laugh at the idea of them ever being considered elite. Suddenly I was the schmuck who had got overconfident and lost his weapon. The schmuck who was about to face three fast, highly trained and experienced elite capture troopers.

You can bet I was taking them seriously now. I ducked as number one sliced outward with his sword, and I came up lucky because the forward momentum took him towards the railing and I was able to slash back with my elbow and knock him over the railing. He screamed as he fell, a drop of about a hundred feet. Number two came at me, sword swinging, and again I ducked, smashing my fist into the shielding at his stomach, a blow that probably hurt my fist more than it hurt him, but at least it stopped him swinging the sword for a second, and I was able to grab his torso and ram his head into the railing so that he sprawled to the deck, temporarily dazed.

Number three was coming at me now and I only just had time to dive out of the way as he sliced forward with the knife. It brought me into the centre of the deck where I rolled onto my back just in time to meet him as he sprang at me, catching the side of my face with a swinging fist, then with his blade, about to finish the job.

Dimly, I became aware of two things. First, that there was a fourth capture trooper thundering along the walkway towards the decking and that meant I had no chance, not with three of them; me, dazed and unable to fight back.

The second thing I became aware of was the roar of an Intruder and weakly I raised my head to see the ship draw level with the deck of the platform. On it was Jammer, *alive*. She sat at the rear as though wounded. In front of her, facing towards my position, was Narville – again, a very much alive captain Narville – and he was holding a minigun. The two capture troopers screamed and went down in a welter of blood as he raked gunfire across the platform, saving my skin, and then I heard rather than saw the fourth capture trooper running onto the platform and found myself squeezing my eyes tightly closed, expecting him to ram the knives home as he reached me. But instead his target was Narville and without breaking stride he jumped to the hand rail and leapt off the elevator platform and on to the Intruder.

For a moment the capture trooper was dangling from the cockpit of the Intruder, then he brought back his blade and smashed through the glass of the cockpit and I caught sight of a shocked-looking Hooper within, the Intruder immediately beginning to lose altitude and spin as he grappled to steer and fend off his assailant at the same time. But the Hig wasn't interested in Hooper; he wanted Narville and Jammer, and even as the lurch sent them sprawling he was hauling himself up to the main deck.

I saw Narville pull himself to his feet to meet him, the minigun having gone over the edge. Bravely, he moved forward to protect Jammer who knelt injured at the rear of the Intruder. Face to face now. The capture trooper moved forward, his knife hand raised, ready to finish Narville, and I watched, helpless, from the freight elevator platform.

Then, suddenly, came the roar of another Intruder and rising level with us was Rico. He stood on the deck holding a grapple launcher, and for a second we all stared open-mouthed at him – including the capture trooper. It was just the distraction Narville needed, and he leaned back and kicked the Hig in the chest, shoving him backwards from the deck of the Intruder just as Rico opened fire with the grapple launcher.

The capture trooper was sent flying, speared by the grappling hook that slammed through his head and then plummeting to the ground below.

And somehow, against all the odds, we were all still alive.

We looked at each other: me, Rico, Jammer and Narville. We'd shared something, though nobody wanted to give it a name.

'Sev, are you okay?' called Rico. I put a hand to my forehead and checked out some blood there, but it was nothing.

'Yeah,' I grinned, 'I'm okay.'

Not that we had time to celebrate the fact that everybody was alive and ass-kicking, because the MAWLR chose that moment to open fire on our position. It was still some way off, but was making its way towards us. Sensors must have picked us up. And it still remained between us and the space elevators.

As though I'd suddenly remembered the threat to Earth, I looked up into the sky to see the empty space where the enemy fleet had been. Just us now.

Rico indicated the MAWLR. 'Dammit,' he exclaimed, 'it's blocking the elevator.'

'Rico, go,' said Narville to him, and as they looked at one another I could see them putting their differences behind them. 'I'll follow your lead. We'll do this together.'

Rico nodded then spoke to me, 'Sev, you're with me,' before barking orders into his pick-up. 'Raiders, this is Raider Command. All groups on my vector. Let's finish this.'

We looked over to where the MAWLR was beginning to lumber towards us.

Either we died or it did.

Chapter Thirty-four

The MAWLR must have been weakened. It didn't look to me as though it was at full strength. Even so, an under-strength MAWLR was more of a daunting prospect than a full-strength anything else, but we had four Intruders and we were swarming all over it, opening fire with the onboard miniguns, bullet strikes sparking on the cabin of the MAWLR as we raced around it.

'Proximity defences coming online,' warned Jammer. 'We got rockets inbound.'

The MAWLR was doing everything it could to protect itself from the onslaught. It was desperately trying to keep us away from its arc cannon. But Intruders are agile and fast. No, they may not be installed with a rappelling system, but they sure as hell can move quickly in the air.

Somebody screamed that the cooling panels were open and we raced round to the side, pummelling the open vent with bullets until fire began pouring from it. All the time the MAWLR blaring.

'What does it take to kill this thing?' shouted Rico.

More than we had? I wondered. Not for the first time. Because now came more inbound missiles, a salvo of them passing so close to us that Hooper had to execute an immediate evasive manoeuvre.

'We need to get that last panel,' shouted Rico now. The smoke billowing from the MAWLR was thicker than ever and we could hardly see the Intruders on the other side, keeping up their barrage of the cabin. For a moment we thought that we had finally defeated it when there was a great explosion, but then Jammer detected an auxiliary power supply kicking in and – for Christ's sake – it *still* would not die. I began to worry that we were going to run out of fuel or ammunition, that the MAWLR was simply impregnable, that it couldn't be beaten and we were going to have to retreat and find some other way through to the space elevators.

Then, at last, chains of explosions erupted along its hull. Then more. Until the MAWLR was finally crumpling to the ground and suddenly the comlink was alive, everybody celebrating the fact that it was finally dead.

Meanwhile, the ground troops finished clearing up the rest of the Higs, and we moved through to the space elevators. We were there, at last.

And disappointment doesn't cover it.

Because there we found that the set-up was not as

grand as it had looked from the distance. Sure, there were the four space elevators side by side, stretching up into a limitless sky, but at their base we had expected there to be at least the *remnants* of an operation: vehicles, some kind of operation centre, some comms equipment at least.

But there was nothing. Instead there were simply metal steps leading up to concrete bunkers in which were the huge pods used for the elevation.

We looked in vain for ships. What we needed most were ships, so that we could get off this rock and warn Earth of the invasion. But there were none and we were standing around struggling to process that information and somehow deal with the almost total crushing dismay of knowing that all our efforts had been for nothing when Rico arrived in his Intruder, the ship settling to the ground and dispensing one very happy grunt, who without picking up on the general mood, indicated the MAWLR behind him and announced, gleefully, 'Now *that's* what I'm talking about.'

Behind him, the MAWLR continued to flame and smoke, and every now and then a chain of small explosions fireworked across it. When I looked across the rubble of the city to see the crippled MAWLR, it felt good; when I remembered that we had pushed our way through here to find ships that did not exist, I didn't feel so good.

Now Rico picked up on the atmosphere and he looked around the yard, perhaps for the first time taking in that the elevator station was a bare-bones facility, and not brimming with the equipment we needed, and that standing around it was a threadbare unit of dejected grunts. The MAWLR had killed almost half our guys and I could see the reality of the situation hit home on Rico's face as he gazed at the remaining survivors.

Hooper stepped forward to explain. 'There are no ships down here,' he said, his voice flat and emotionless, drained of life and hope. 'Our only way off this planet are these space elevators,' and with that he signalled behind himself.

'There's just not enough of us left,' said Narville, shaking his head, staring at the ground, looking like the rest of us felt: defeated.

It wasn't like Rico to accept defeat easily, though. 'Look,' he said defiantly, 'if we're going down, then let's take as many of these bastards with us as we can. I want it to mean something.'

He was just venting, though. What bastards to take with us? Where? There wasn't an enemy to be seen. Where were the enemy right now? They were on their way to Earth. And once they had Earth that was it. They were on course to dominate the known universe.

Jammer stepped forward. You could almost see her mind working. She was another one who never gave up.

'They gotta have a communications room up in the station, right?' she said, waiting for someone to take her up on it.

Narville nodded. 'We could still warn Earth,' he agreed, and Jammer moved over to a primitive-looking console at the base of the nearest elevator and began poking around.

Rico still wasn't convinced. 'Is that *all* we can do?'

Heads went down. Narville moved over to Rico, and in a quiet voice said, 'You did your best, son. We all did.'

And now, for perhaps the first time since I'd known him, I saw Rico Velasquez's shoulders slump as he began to admit defeat.

I stepped forward, took a deep breath, knowing that next thing I said could change everything. My next word had to be the most important of my life.

'*Bullshit*,' I said.

They all looked my way. I swallowed. Okay, I'd hoped for something a bit more profound than 'bullshit' but, even so, I carried on. 'Do you know the odds against us still being here?' I added. 'Right here, right now? They're astronomical. That means something. Now maybe we can't stop the invasion.

But warning Earth? There's *nothing* more important. Jammer, get on that console. Pull up the layout of the station at the top of the elevator.'

Jammer flashed me a smile. 'I'm on it,' she said with renewed purpose.

I turned to the other survivors. 'Listen up. If I'm going down, I want to make sure all these bastards remember my name.'

As though to add a touch of drama to my speech, the crippled MAWLR behind me exploded, and I stood there as the shockwave rode past me.

Rico looked my way, grinning and pointing at me. 'And *that* is why you don't fuck with the ISA.' His announcement met with cheers from the other men, suddenly raring to go, spoiling for a fight.

'Jammer, Hooper, which elevator will get you closest to the communication centre?'

Jammer pointed. 'That one.'

'Take that one and get a warning out. We'll take the other one. Find a way to delay the launch.'

'How?' asked Hooper.

I looked at him. 'We'll de-orbit the space station,' I said.

Chapter Thirty-five

De-orbit the space station. Create a diversion for Jammer to reach the comms room.

Which meant reaching the space station. Which meant penetrating the heart of the biggest enemy force this side of Archangel.

It was a suicide mission, and we knew it. The mood? Well, it was no pity party. There was no wailing and gnashing of teeth and nobody had to be talked into going. We were ISA; we had a job to do; we were going to do it, and every man among us wanted to be a part of it.

On the other hand, we weren't exactly laughing and giggling either.

We took secondary elevators up to the main pods, most of us standing in one of them, with Jammer, Hooper and a smaller team in the other, each rattling to the uppermost portion of their respective elevator pod. Sixty exhausted guys trying a final roll of the dice to save an Earth that had sold us out.

If we succeeded, Earth owed us an apology, that much was sure.

A posthumous apology, it would have to be.

The main pod was the size of a small hotel – a hotel designed to blast off and shoot up the elevator cables to the space station. There were sections of it designated for supplies, weapons and goods, and we passed these as the elevator took us to the passenger section of the main caddie. They were empty, the other sections. Not long ago they would have been full of cargo destined for the space station, all helping to supply the Helghast for their invasion of Earth. But the time for preparation was over; as far as we knew, the invasion itself was imminent.

If you're one of those guys who likes to look for the silver lining, then you might say that with the invasion imminent at least the Helghast would be focusing their resources on that and hopefully not monitoring events back on their home planet nor on the space elevators. It also meant that the elevators themselves were empty and would travel more quickly, ultimately delivering us swiftly to the space station where every second would count when it came to the element of surprise.

And that would be your silver lining. That would be about the extent of it.

The secondary elevator stopped at the passenger caddie and metal gates slid aside to allow us out. We walked onto the main gantry, with boots clanging on the metal, and it struck me that after the fury of the battle with the MAWLR, the world was suddenly still. I could hear the whistling of the wind through the elevator structure, and from somewhere came a ringing sound as a loose cable was blown against the metal. Otherwise, there was silence, each man contemplating his end, thinking that maybe he wouldn't die, but most likely he would, because one thing we knew about this space station for sure was that whether it was Jorhan Stahl's personal army or the massed forces of the Helghast military it would be well manned. We had to expect some serious resistance, whether we caught them by surprise or not.

If we did get out of this alive – just on the off chance that we might get out alive – then I was going to buy that girl a beer.

We moved into the pod where there were racks for passengers and an operations centre. Narville took a seat, wheeling himself along the panels to get the measure of the control system, then beginning to flick switches. Initializing lights came on in the panel. Then bright white illumination flicked on along the whole of the length of the pod, and I knew how a bug feels trapped in a light unit. Looking across I saw the same thing happening in the elevator next door as Jammer flicked switches too, caught a glimpse of her before the lights flared on and her

pod was turned into a huge shining lantern, suspended in the sky.

We moved to the racks, sat down and reached for
overhead harnesses to secure us in, and for the first
time in what felt like hours, someone spoke.

'Hey, how come there's no cup holder?' said
Gedge, and we laughed at that, maybe longer and
louder than the gag deserved, but enough to remind
ourselves that we weren't dead yet.

The humming grew louder. Again I looked to the
side and now saw Jammer's elevator begin to vibrate.
I craned my neck to look down at the ground and
could see the boosters engaging, creating huge, billowing clouds of smoke at the base, then suddenly
the white, illuminated pod was away, racing up high-
tensile carbon nanotube cable towards the space station, and I felt as though I'd just seen an apartment
block blasting off into space.

Meanwhile, our pod was ready to go. Narville
wheeled himself into the centre of the console and
latched into the Frontier base, ready for launch,
checking the pilot's seat was secure then reached
behind to pull on his harness. He checked over his
shoulder that we were secure and we regarded him
balefully.

Satisfied he turned to the front. 'Prepare for laser
ignition,' he said.

Then flicked a switch.

And suddenly we were pinned to seats, immense G pressing down upon us. The feeling was like being in a drop, except in reverse, the speed seeming to increase, then increase further, until I began to wonder if we were going to be able to take it any more. After all, we were human and the elevator was designed for Helghast, and did they have superior physicality? I wasn't sure. I don't remember learning about that. I wish I'd paid more attention in sch– *argh*.

And then just as it felt as though the flesh of my face was about to pull away from my bones, and as though my entire body was about to be shoved through the floor of the space elevator, we broke free of the Helghast atmosphere and my next thought after the relief of being freed from the G was, At last. At last I'm off that godforsaken planet, and even if I do die up here on this space station the one good thing about that will be the fact that I didn't die on that shitty rock below.

Suddenly the pod began to slow and we went from being pummelled with G to experiencing a sudden, nauseating sense of drag. I looked to the aperture and saw space outside, immediately aware that we'd blasted our way right into the heart of enemy territory. Around us was the fleet: thousands of cruisers, battleships, dropships and fighters.

Supply ships moved between them. I saw smaller shuttles, not like anything I'd seen before. Strike ships. They were making runs between the fleet and the main space station, and now I got my first good look at that too, the sight making my jaw drop.

If Helghan on the ground was a planet of ruin and wreckage, uninhabitable ice flats and hostile jungle, a place where its naturally occurring features and its inhabitants had somehow colluded to make it the most hostile, dangerous and unwelcoming place in the entire universe, then here was its polar opposite.

Here was a man-made city in the sky. Here was the ultimate expression of the Helghast dedication to the war machine and to the expansion of their race. It began with the most advanced vehicles and cruisers and breathtakingly sophisticated weaponry, and it ended here with a city in space: a modular station with a huge main stem hanging in the air, its core unit surrounded by a series of further ring modules, all of which had their own docking station and all of which now buzzed with traffic, the whole thing hanging in geo-stationary orbit.

And now, looking out at the massed Helghast army, I had to pray they hadn't got their shit together enough to realize that we'd hijacked their space elevators. We were sitting targets if they decided to blow us out of the sky right now. I saw Jammer's elevator reaching a module above our heads and found I was holding my breath, half expecting to see it suddenly rupture and shatter as the Higs opened fire, either from space or within the space station itself. Nothing. Christ, the thing was bright enough. It was like a huge beacon shouting, '*Shoot me*,' up there.

'Jammer, do you read?' asked Rico over the comlink.

'Copy that,' she replied.

'You got company?'

'Couple of guards neutralized. Otherwise negative. I couldn't begin to guess why, but I'm not complaining.'

'Maybe because they know the main force is in this one,' I said, pointing to the aperture where we could see Hig infantry moving along the walkways of the lower ring. The ring at which we were about to dock. They were moving towards the docking station.

'Shit,' said Rico.

'Shit's about right,' I said, sighing, and now the men began to stand from the rack, reaching to grab overheard bars as the elevator shuddered to a halt.

We took up our rifles and checked ammo. Grim-faced, Narville joined us and the door to the pod slid open to reveal the walkway ahead of us. It led to the main ring, and there, we knew, they'd be waiting for us.

'All right, people,' said Narville, 'we're going to head for gravitational control. Let's buy Jammer some time.'

We moved forward, expecting to find the first of the Hig infantry we had seen mobilizing. Instead what came at us first were spidermines. They scuttled at us and we withdrew, knowing that the best method of dealing with one was to shoot it as it came towards you. You don't want to let it touch you; they have a nasty explosive radius. So we stayed clear and destroyed them before moving forward. We knew they'd been sent to soften us up, that was all – delay us while they got their asses in gear.

It looked as though we were in some kind of storage or engineering unit. As well as crates moving overhead on rails, there were chests and container boxes littering the walkway, and we used them for cover as we made our way further into the space station, every sense on high alert, expecting the first crack of gunfire any second now. Or maybe the attack would come another way. Gas, perhaps. Or vent all the air and let us suffocate to death? Obviously not, because the curve of the ring allowed us to see further along it and now we could make out multiple troops gathering.

Outside the window I could still see the fleet and it struck me that there must be thousands upon thousands of Helghast within feet of us, the thought spurring me on that if I was going to go I was going to take as many with me as I could. I was going to do things Rico Velasquez style.

Now we saw them around the curve of the ring, beginning to take up position. Like us, they were finding cover behind the supply boxes, as well as getting up high, taking elevated positions, waiting for us to get closer.

Then the first shots rang out. Sniper fire. So our heads went down and we took cover behind our position. Their infantry moved forward, the module suddenly full of the rattle of automatic gunfire.

And it was game on.

I crouched behind a crate, shouldered my M82 and fired off a clip at three Helghast infantry running headlong down the corridor towards us. One of them spun as a line of bullets ripped across his chest and into his face mask. A second tried diving for cover, but not before the back of his head exploded and he was crumbling to the floor with blood and brains sliding down the module wall behind him. More enemy infantry took up position ahead of us and for a moment or so we exchanged fire, neither groups making any ground. The M82 thumped into my shoulder as I finished a clip, hot empty shells raining to the metal walkway at my feet. Bullets ricocheted around us, off the metal of the module walls, off the toughened glass of the observation ports, and off the crates behind which we sheltered, and Christ it was hot.

Somehow we had to fight our way forward and do something about the gravitational control of the station. But for the moment they had us pinned down. I felt in the pouches of my ACU for frags and found none, screaming at Rico to toss me a couple. Pinned behind a box to my right he threw me the frags and I caught and began cooking them in the same movement, then called for him to provide cover fire, bobbed from cover and tossed them forward. Good shot. We heard screams then Gedge and Rico were moving forward, providing cover for each other, doing it by the numbers, textbook forward movement – I bet Narville was loving that.

And now we made our way quickly along the walkway, knowing that it wasn't over yet and, sure enough, it wasn't. Because next we found ourselves facing sentry bots and I was thinking, Shit, sentry bots. It would have to be sentry bots.

Chapter Thirty-six

'What is the name of Stahl's new ship?' enquired Autarch Orlock of one of his men. Orlock stood on one of the upper rings of the space station, in a corridor not far from the airlock to Pier Two.

'I believe he has called it the Khage, sir,' said the soldier.

Orlock nodded without replying. Of course. How very touching. Stahl had named his new toy after his father.

Well, a ship could easily be renamed, he thought as he continued to wait for Stahl, his hands clasped behind his back.

None could see, but he held them this way in order to hide the fact that they were shaking slightly, though even he himself did not know why they trembled. It was not fear that made them shake, of that at least he was certain, for there was nothing in this world or the next that frightened Orlock; from his days streetfighting in the dirt of Pyrrhus to his time fighting side by side with Scolar Visari in the military, and to facing down the Helghast senate, he had never known fear.

No, it was the anticipation perhaps, the thought of finally seeing the end of Jorhan Stahl, who had been a permanent thorn in his side and in that of the senate.

As he stood gazing out of the window, alternating between looking at the industry of his fleet and casting covetous glances at Stahl's gleaming new ship, another officer approached him, a nervous officer by the name of Zabiela, who cleared his throat to announce his presence.

'Sir,' said Zabiela timorously, 'the ISA army is here. They took out the MAWLR and came up in the space elevator.'

Zabiela delivered the news in a faltering voice, then waited to gauge the reaction of the autarch. He trembled, and unlike Orlock he knew exactly why it was he trembled, and it was nothing to do with anticipation and everything to do with outright terror.

He had good reason. Orlock was a man who showed his emotions more readily than his great opponent Stahl, and the hapless officer started to fret as his leader began to turn crimson and quiver with raw emotion.

'Enough with the ISA,' exploded Orlock at last. 'Either they die . . . or *you* do,' and he looked at Zabiela and smiled a thin, mirthless smile. A smile that made it very clear indeed that he would stay true to his word.

In response, Zabiela scuttled backwards, bowing his head in submission to his leader, then moved away, using his comlink to order that further defences be deployed against the invaders. 'Send sentry bots,' he commanded in an urgent, low voice. 'Send jet packs. Send everyone – *everyone*.'

Zabiela heard the sounds of gunshots and explosions over his comlink, swallowing hard as his second-in-command replied, 'Sir, we have reports of a further incursion close to the communications room. They've sent a small team. Your orders, sir?'

'Well, send a small squad to neutralize *their* small squad, but concentrate on the main attack, you idiot,' he hissed, and then added, 'either they die . . . or you do.'

'Yes, sir,' said the officer on the other end of the comlink, who ended the communication and turned to his subordinate officer, ordering him to increase the attack on the ISA intruders, adding, 'either they die . . . or you do.'

Orlock, meanwhile, had his attention arrested by the arrival of his nemesis Jorhan Stahl, who as usual came accompanied by his troopers, and who as usual wore an expression that Orlock did not especially care for: a rather self-satisfied expression. An expression Orlock very much looked forward to wiping from his face.

Stahl and his men stopped before him and Stahl did all but stifle a yawn, saying, his voice tinged with a rather contrived bored-sounding tone, 'By the order of the High Council, I, Jorhan Brimve Stahl, report for duty. I am willing to serve in whatever capacity the state wishes.'

His whole attitude indicated the exact opposite, and when he smiled it was the smile of a man merely *pretending* to be reasonable. At the same time he glanced at the autarch's personal guard and, though he tried, could not keep the grin from his face, adding with an audible sneer, '*This is it?* I thought you'd have more security.'

In reply Orlock said nothing for a moment. Instead he simply stared at Jorhan Stahl and for once he managed to keep his emotions in check, though behind his eyes his feelings churned. He reminded himself that all was going according to plan and that whatever confidence Stahl currently displayed was woefully misplaced – and that the fact would all too soon become readily apparent. In the end Stahl found himself unable to hold the man's gaze, and his eyes dropped away, leaving Orlock to enjoy a moment of small victory, and cap it with a further taunt.

'Like father, like son,' he said. 'It seems failure is the family business.'

He enjoyed watching his words strike home. The

way Stahl tightened and bristled in response. He noted Stahl's fist clench, and what a pathetic, impotent gesture that was.

Nevertheless, to his credit, Stahl once again held his gaze. And this time he came back to say, 'Ironic . . . that you needed both of us to help get you where you are.'

Now that was debatable, thought Orlock, though he let the matter rest, instead wishing to move on to the next order of business: the irradiated petrusite Stahl was due to deliver.

The *weaponized* irradiated petrusite.

And he turned to one of his officers, asking, 'Did he bring the weapons?'

The officer keyed his comlink, spoke into it and then listened. 'Station confirms electrostatic energy profile on the chairman's cruiser,' he reported. 'They are all there.'

Orlock nodded, satisfied. He turned his attention back to Stahl. 'You should be proud, Stahl. Your weapons are going to usher in a new era of Helghast dominance. I'll speak highly of you at your funeral . . .' He paused for impact, before indicating to the troops behind him and saying, 'Arrest the chairman.'

Arrest him, take him away and torture him. That's what Orlock had decided (and he thought he might well invent one or two new tortures just for Jorhan Stahl. There was something involving the introduction of a beetle into an internal cavity that he'd been rather looking forward to trying). But when he looked at Stahl afresh he realized that the chairman was looking rather unworried for someone about to submit to the custody of one of the planet's most sadistic men. He was not whimpering, crying or begging for his life – all of which were reactions Orlock might have anticipated, indeed hoped for. He did not even look unduly concerned.

In fact, he merely smiled.

Suddenly, with a sickening realization, Orlock spun to see his men behind him, and saw that two of them held their guns on the other two who, as he watched, dropped their weapons with a clatter on the metal floor and meekly raised their hands.

Betrayed!

'Ah, yes,' gloated Stahl, 'the men of our proud and painfully underpaid military. They are all so pathetically predictable.'

Orlock spun about, looking for his officers – *any* other men. But his soldiers were away seeing to it that the ISA were swiftly defeated (because either the ISA died or they did) while all other troops were similarly engaged. Apart from the two guards now held at gunpoint, he was alone. Outside, was his fleet. The entire Helghast military under his command, all within spitting distance. Yet he was a prisoner.

He turned back to face Stahl, who beamed as though having reached the end of the greatest banquet of his life. Then into his pick-up he said, 'Commodore, are you ready?'

The commodore was ready.

Stahl directed Orlock's attention to the huge observation window and Orlock knew that something very terrible was about to happen. His gaze went back to Stahl.

Who was smiling at him. An awful, triumphant smile that Orlock did not care for very much at all. As Orlock watched, Stahl said into the radio the single word, 'Fire.'

Orlock jerked his head to look out, his gaze going to Stahl's ship, the Khage, hanging in space like a malevolent black knife blade. On its underside the huge petrusite cannon was moving, targeting one of the battleships.

'You wouldn't dare,' said Orlock, though it was clear that Stahl dared.

The Khage opened fire. A bolt shot from the cannon to the ship, and for a second it seemed as though the shielding might thwart it. Orlock had a moment of hope. But then it pierced the entire hull, striking another ship hanging directly behind it, and Orlock was closing his eyes as his two battleships exploded into fire, breaking apart and spinning slowly away from the rest of the fleet, bodies falling from the cracked-open hulls into space.

Fire at will, thought Orlock. *Destroy it.*

And his officers did that. A salvo of missiles cut orange lines into the sky as the fleet returned fire. At least, thought Orlock, he would live to see Stahl's pride and joy destroyed.

But instead of exploding as the battleships had before it, Stahl's cruiser seemed to somehow absorb and disperse the missiles and Orlock wheeled to confront Stahl, unable to keep the surprise and even a hint of admiration from his voice as he said, 'You've developed energy shielding?'

Stahl simply smiled. Indeed he had developed energy shielding. In the laboratories of Stahl Arms on the frozen shores his men had worked not only to harness the power of radiated petrusite to use as the most deadly weapon the universe had ever seen, but also to utilize it in defence. Now he had the most powerful weapons ever created by man, and the most powerful defences too. He was, quite simply, unstoppable and how sweet the irony that the first to see it should be his arch-enemy Orlock.

And, still smiling, he told the soon-to-be-ex-autarch, 'You're not watching.'

Once again their gaze went through the observation port as a batch of bombers deployed from the underside of the Khage. They passed through the shielding – another innovation from Stahl's development labs – the shielding was one way. And launched missiles at the fleet.

Nuclear petrusite missiles.

Two ships were vapourized instantly. And in the next moment bombers and fighters were launching from both sets of ships, and there was full-scale warfare in the skies outside. A civil war. Chairman versus autarch.

Orlock watched. He took a measure of satisfaction from the fact that his fleet had responded quickly, but it was clear to him that Stahl had more powerful weaponry and that his fleet would soon be lost. Unless . . .

He turned to Stahl. 'This is how you'll get the senate to accept you?' he asked, trying to think fast. Trying to use any leverage he could.

And Stahl knew it. He knew that Orlock was desperately stalling because . . . the very idea of him wanting to be accepted by *the senate*. He had no need of those decrepit old men. He would see them slowly dying at the bottom of a toxic pit as soon as his current business was complete. He laughed. 'The senate will beg *me* to forgive *them*,' he jeered, 'right after you do.'

He drew his pistol, reflecting that the last time he

had used it was to punish an incompetent subordinate, and that this was a very similar situation.

'Get on your knees, Orlock,' he said. And he raised the pistol, pointing it at Orlock's head.

Now it was Stahl's turn to have things take an unexpected twist. Now it was he who was to be denied the pleasure of an eagerly anticipated reaction. For Orlock was not whimpering, crying or begging for his life. He did not even look unduly concerned.

Stahl took a step forward, bringing the barrel of the gun close to Orlock's forehead.

'I said get on your –'

But he never finished his sentence.

One thing Orlock had learned as a streetfighter was the value of a concealed weapon. In fact, he had long ago made it his policy never to leave home without a concealed weapon, and today was no exception, so that about his person he had a knife. It was, in fact, the very knife that he had confiscated from the dead fingers of the man who'd inflicted the wound to his face, a totemic knife in many ways, and he wore it in a wrist mechanism specially calibrated to deliver the knife into the palm of the wearer with a certain flick of the wrist.

Which is what Orlock did. With one tiny movement the knife was in his hand and he was stepping forward and ramming it into Stahl's guts at the same time as he knocked aside the pistol.

Stahl screamed, dropped his gun and reeled away. Orlock's two loyal men used the sudden confusion to reach for their weapons and in a moment the two traitors were falling as the air was full of bullets, men dropping around him as Orlock plunged the knife into the stomach of one of Stahl's guards. The years fell away from Orlock and he was back on the streets again: agile, powerful and ruthless.

Stahl, one hand at his stomach, with blood seeping through his fingers, aimed his pistol with his other hand, his arm shaking violently, but Orlock, his blood up and sensing victory, and using all his streetfighting instincts and his guttersnipe guile, drove his fist into Stahl's jaw. Stahl groaned and staggered, bent double. Orlock snatched an arc cannon from the floor and hefted it, distantly realizing that despite the turn of events he was enjoying himself more than he had done in years.

But it was short-lived.

As he moved forward to finish Stahl – already anticipating breaking the man's scrawny neck – a petrusite bolt flashed past him, taking a chunk of his flesh with it. He wheeled to see one of Stahl's guards looking at him with a mixture of fear and surprise. Surprised no doubt that his shot had hit its target. Fearful no doubt of reprisals. Indeed, Orlock's reply was swift and brutal. He raised the arc cannon and pulled the trigger, frying the guard, and then turned to look for the traitor Jorhan Stahl.

There was no sign of him.

Orlock hissed in frustration. He looked around himself and everywhere there were bodies. His own guards and Stahl's guards. But there was no sign of the chairman. The corridor yawned emptily at him. However, he knew that Stahl had not escaped out of the airlock, nor had he escaped past him. Which meant he was still here somewhere. Hiding. Like a cowardly dog.

'I know you're here,' growled Orlock. 'Come out, come out, wherever you are,' and he began to make his way along the corridor, to try to flush out his enemy.

Outside the battle still raged, the two fleets pummelling each other. No quarter asked and none given.

Chapter Thirty-seven

Jammer had moved through the ring with her men at her back. Finding a console she quickly hacked in and located the main comms room. At the same time she saw that men were being deployed in their direction and was just warning the team when the first shots rang out.

She ducked down. The ring was a series of platforms, most of which were lined with systems equipment, and there wasn't much room for cover. She fired a clip off then slammed in another mag, spraying wildly in front of her to discourage any capture troopers coming forward. Across the walkway were Hooper and the other men, firing forward and edging up the corridor.

So this was it, she thought. The Higs had sent a reception committee. Any hopes she had of reaching the comms centre easily were dashed. Might as well get on with it.

'You there, Jammer?' asked Rico over the comlink.

'Copy that,' she yelled.

'Do I hear shots?'

'Roger that also.'

'How hot are you?'

'I'm hot, Rico,' she yelled back, and neither of them bothered to make the obvious joke about that.

Bullets rang around the area. She was right. They had sent capture troopers after them, perhaps hoping to limit the damage to important equipment in the corridor. She hated capture troopers. She hadn't told anybody. She wasn't that dumb. But capture troopers – they scared the bejesus out of her.

One came forward now, screeching, with his sword raised. He appeared round the side of a partition behind which she was taking cover and she had no time to swing up her M82 and fire, instead snatching her pistol from its holster and firing blind, directly into his face. He screamed, splattering her with blood as he staggered back, most of the front of his face disintegrating. Now came another and Hooper dropped him with half a clip. Next she saw one of her men go down as two of them outflanked him, and before she could do anything about it the swords flashed and there was an arc of red blood, bright against the grey and silver of the walkway, and the man screamed.

Jaw set, she took down both of the capture troopers, then crouched and ran across the walkway to the dying soldier, checking for a pulse.

There was none. She closed her eyes and said

359

some silent words as around her the gunfire ceased at last. The unit sent to take them out had been small, more like a recon party than anything else. But soon they would send more men. And more determined men. And they would be less concerned about the damage caused.

Her team began making their way up the walkway again and she keyed to Sev on her headset, thinking that she could have chosen to link with Captain Narville if she was observing the proper chain of command, or to Rico who was after all Raider Command, and who had been checking on her, but she'd chosen to speak to Sev instead, and she allowed herself a smile as she spoke to him.

'Sev. Jammer. What's your status?' she asked. She hardly needed to ask. Over the line she heard the gunfire, and screaming.

'We've encountered heavy resistance, but otherwise everything is peachy keen. What's your status?'

'We've neutralized a unit they sent after us, now it's quiet,' she replied. 'Back-up will be along presently so I'm going it alone. I'm going to let the team take care of any reinforcements and see if I can make the communications room by myself.'

'Negative, Jammer.' She couldn't help but feel a thrill at the obvious note of worry in his voice. 'Stay with your team.'

'Why, Sergeant Sevchenko, are you worried about me?' she teased.

'Oh no,' he laughed. 'I'm worried about your team with you gone.'

'Well, they'll just have to manage,' she said. 'I'll move faster alone.'

'Copy that,' replied Sev, sounding reluctant. 'At least between us and them we should have enough of a distraction.'

She called Hooper over and pointed further along the corridor where the path diverged. 'I'm going left, you and the rest are going right,' she told him.

After the men had moved off, she was left alone in the corridor for a moment, and she looked around at the corpses littering the floor, including the one ISA trooper. She moved over to the body, took his dog tags and looked at his name. Jim Watts. She would make sure he was remembered.

Then her gaze went to the outside, where she saw Stahl's huge battleship. As she watched, a large turret on the underside of the ship was moving. A petrusite cannon, she knew, but bigger than any other cannon of that type she'd ever seen. Green energy flicked around it as it charged up, ready to fire, and she leaned to get a better look, wondering what it could be about to fire upon, when a bolt of petrusite shot from it and into two Helghast battleships.

Both cracked open and split, tumbling away, crippled, and for a moment she stood open-mouthed, unable to believe what she had seen because it looked like an enemy ship opening fire on another enemy ship, and how could that happen? She wondered if they had somehow infiltrated the enemy's structure to such a degree that they had people on board their command ships and that meant the day was won. But, no, that couldn't be. And, anyway, now she saw missiles being deployed and pretty soon a full-scale battle had commenced. And even though it looked almost too good to believe – as though her eyes must surely have been deceiving her – the fact was that the enemy were fighting. They had opened fire on each other and were fighting a civil war.

This was good. Properly good. At best it meant no attack on Earth. At worst an enemy that was more concerned with its own squabbles than with taking out the ISA. Either way she should move on to the comms room while they were still out there kicking the shit out of each other.

She put a hand to her earpiece, about to speak to Sev or Rico, just to check they were seeing the same thing as her, when suddenly there was a noise in the walkway and there in front of her was a Helghast infantryman.

She was unarmed.

She braced herself for the bullet. Oh, you stupid bitch, she thought. You dumb rookie. What kind of fresh-out-of-training recruit leaves their M82 *and* their sidearm lying on the deck? All she had in her hand was Digweed's dog tags, and the only weapon she had on her was her combat knife, which was strapped to her thigh.

The Hig stared at her but didn't open fire, and she thought she knew why he hadn't killed her yet, and that gave her a chance.

Then the trooper spoke. 'The knife,' he said simply. He indicated with the barrel of his assault rifle. His voice was gruff, betraying no emotion.

Okay, she thought. This was good too. He was underestimating her. She could use that. She nodded, pretending to look frightened. She needed him over-confident and careless. With over-emphatic movements she moved her hand to her thigh, which she brought forward a touch then slipped open the catch on the sheath of her combat knife.

'Very slowly, pretty lady,' said the soldier. 'Don't try anything fancy.'

She shook her head as though to say she wouldn't dream of it as she reached for the knife and withdrew it from its sheath.

'Drop it to the floor,' he commanded.

Now she had the knife clear of the sheath and in one fluid and highly practised movement, flicked it up, caught the blade between thumb and forefinger and threw it forward, directly at the soldier.

When Jammer had joined the ISA, all she'd wanted to do was be a pilot. Truth be told, she hadn't given much thought to doing much else when she got there. She just wanted to fly. Pretty soon, though, she'd worked out that things were tough for a woman in the ISA. She had to work harder to gain the respect of her comrades, and being their equal wasn't good enough. She needed to be *better* than them. And while being a pilot came naturally to her, the combat skills she needed to work at, so she'd taken to spending hours at the range. Hours of target practice with pistols, rifles and knives. Especially knives. When you were a woman in a man's army and, when you looked like Jammer, you perhaps had greater cause to be proficient with a close-quarters weapon, so Jammer had paid it special attention and she'd got real good with it.

There were some who said that she never missed. Which meant that as soon as the knife was in her fingers he was as good as dead.

But there was a minor difference between knife target practice on a range and on a space station being buffeted by war outside. The range wasn't in danger of suddenly lurching to one side. Which is what happened now. Whether it was an aftershock or shrapnel she didn't know, but just as she threw the knife the entire structure listed, throwing her off-balance.

The knife spun through the air, a flicker of silver steel, and instead of a slamming through the right eye-piece of the soldier's respirator mask, it speared him in the arm.

Shit, thought Jammer.

The Hig screamed in pain, reached and pulled the knife from his shoulder and in the next instant had leapt towards her, bearing down upon her, screaming that she was going to die.

Chapter Thirty-eight

'They're firing on each other,' said Rico, scarcely able to believe it.

We stared, all of us with our mouths hanging open. Because what we were seeing was the enemy tearing itself apart. What we were seeing was the enemy doing our job for us. And in that moment things changed.

Space was full of detonations, missiles and there was the constant *whump-whump* of explosions. Pieces of flying shrapnel and debris spattered gently against the observation windows so that it was almost as though we were all watching the grand finale of a blockbuster movie. Like it didn't involve us somehow. Then what we were seeing was ships belonging to Stahl, moving through the battle, heading towards the station.

'That's the same type of ship we saw earlier,' I said, putting two and two together all of a sudden. Stahl's strike ships were the only vessels capable of moving *through* the shield. If we wanted to get close to his cruiser then we needed to get hold of those ships – and they were coming our way.

'Did anyone see where they were going?' I asked.

Narville cottoned on. 'The second pier,' he said, our thoughts in sync. 'I like your thinking, Sevchenko.'

So did Rico. He opened a comlink. 'Jammer, forget the communications room. We need access to those strike ships.'

But Jammer was a little busy right then. There was the small matter of fending off her attacker who was coming at her with all of the strength and ferocity of a fighting dog. In this case a particularly angry and enraged fighting dog.

He grabbed her round the neck before she had a chance to duck under his grasp, and then was swinging her about the walkway, her legs kicking uselessly. Her hands went to his arms, and she tried to wrench free of his grip, but found she was unable to and choked, desperately gasping for air. Her vision clouded, becoming grey at the edges, and she realized that she was going to black out if she didn't find air.

And she didn't want to go like this.

Not like this.

Kicking legs found purchase on the edge of a console and she thrust backwards, enough to push the soldier off balance and send him flying, his head striking a panel as he fell. At last his grip relaxed and she was able to pull free, landing on her hands and knees for a second, choking and gulping down precious air.

The Hig was on his feet in seconds and lumbering towards her. She looked up to see him towering over her, and then saw black as he lashed out a foot that caught her on the head, a blow that would have knocked her unconscious, but was absorbed by the fabric of her hood. She spun away and scrambled to her feet as he came forward yet again. Throwing herself between two units, she lay there for a second desperately trying to regain her senses in order to fight back. There was a brief moment of respite as the Hig, grunting, could do nothing but aim useless kicks at her, unable to fit through the units himself. But she couldn't remain there for long. The unit was between him and the other weapons and he'd seen them, and was now rushing forward to pick one up. The fight was over in his mind. She could see that. He simply wanted to finish his victim now.

With a frustrated shout, Jammer pulled herself up and hurled herself from between the two units, grabbing the Hig as he tried to run past. Now it was her turn to have him by the neck, and at the very least she had managed to arrest his progress, stopping him from reaching the rifles. She squeezed. He gasped. But he was much stronger than her. He would easily shrug her off, and even now spun and thrust himself backwards, shoving her painfully against a row of cabinets.

She held on. Grimly, she held on. He did it again, propelling them both back with a crash against the cabinets, and again she saw stars, wondering how long she could hold on. She still held Digweed's dog tags and with a flash of sudden inspiration slipped them over the trooper's neck and began pulling, garrotting him.

Both of them in silent agony now. She, rammed against the cabinets; he with increasing pressure on the dog tags round his neck.

And then she could no longer hang on. The last of the strength finally left her body and she was forced to let go, crumpling to the floor, back against the cabinets, watching groggily as the soldier staggered, coughing, away. She still had Digweed's dog tags in her hand, she realized, and she gripped them tightly as the Hig made his way over to the rifles, and reached down to pick one up. Turning to face her, he raised it to his shoulder.

'You did good, pretty lady,' he rasped, still catching his breath, and squinted down the sights. She saw his finger tighten on the trigger. She closed her eyes.

Crack.

Jammer opened her eyes to see the Hig drop to

his knees, a smashed hole where the right eye of his goggles had been, blood pouring down his front. Standing close by was Hooper, his gun smoking. Smiling at her.

She managed to grin back, thanking him, and pulling herself painfully to her feet, wincing at the pain in her back, just as her comlink crackled.

'Jammer, forget the communications room. We need access to those strike ships,' said Rico.

'Way ahead of you, boss,' she croaked. Christ, nothing like a bit of time to recover. She went to the body of the Hig, searching through his ACU for . . . ah, keycards.

Next online came Narville, sounding revitalized: 'All right, troops, this is our chance. It won't be long before the Helghast know what we're up to and when they do they'll come at us with everything they've got. We'll regroup at Pier Two and take command of the strike ships. It's the only way we can prevent Stahl's cruiser from reaching Earth. Let's head out. This is it, boys.'

Jammer massaged her hurting back and smiled to herself. '*And girl*,' she thought.

Chapter Thirty-nine

The sentry bots came at us again as we made our way to the pier. I found an LS13 shotgun – great for sentry-killing duty – and made my way onto a raised platform, hoping the extra elevation would help. It did, and I took one out, relieved to watch it spin away and smash into the roof of the module.

That same moment, Narville was screaming over the comlink. A wrecked ship outside was about to hit the station. Next we were knocked off our feet at the same time as there was a great grinding sound, and the crippled ship collided with the space station. The gravity went offline and everything was floating, us included, as we continued to make our way up the corridor. I found a console and restored the gravity, then we moved on, still seeing the battle continuing outside the window.

We were looking for elevators to take us to the pier. In front of us it seemed as though the entire Hig army was approaching, while outside a civil war raged. The numbers were against us. The odds were against us. But then, it felt like they had been for the past six months, and now we were closer than we ever had been to warning Earth. We weren't slowing down now, not for nothing or nobody. None of us. We weren't stopping until the job was done or we lay dead, whichever came first.

We cleared the section of Hig troops and then opened a set of gates, storming through to the next section and raking gunfire across support troopers on walkways. A lift came down, more enemy troops on it, and suddenly the fight intensified, if that was possible. I glanced to my left and saw Rico behind cover ramming a clip into his M82, then standing and rattling off the entire mag. We cleared as many as we could, then a second lift came down and we were tossing frag grenades in to clear it, the infantry screaming as they died. I grabbed a rocket launcher to clear a knot of hostiles taking cover on a walkway behind us and the whole structure came down in a mess of twisted limbs, blood and fire, dead Hig snipers draped over misshapen metal.

'Everybody on the elevator,' commanded Narville, and Rico took out more enemies behind cover on another walkway above us, and then we were moving to the controls. I glanced behind me, my heart sinking. We'd lost a lot of guys on the way. I tried to do a head count and gave up at twenty or so, but it wasn't much more than that. Then, as the elevator rose, we got a good look at Stahl's cruiser – perhaps our first, and I found myself in awe of its sheer size. It was maintaining height in the middle of the battlefield, the petrusite shield still in place, and I could see bombers and the smaller strike ships flitting in and out of a docking section on its underside. Friendly ships could negotiate the shield either way, I noticed. Anything else just bounced off.

We climbed off the elevator to find a scene of devastation awaiting us. The space station was damaged now. Debris was everywhere: crates and boxes filled the corridors and were falling from the roof of the module. Still their infantry came at us and still we fought on. The strike ships had to be near now and their grunts were frightened and demoralized, their seemingly impregnable space station falling down around their ears. We reached an airlock, activated it and dived inside.

Chapter Forty

Outside, the battle continued to rage, while in the corridor it was still empty. Empty apart from the angry, stalking figure of Autarch Orlock, bleeding from where the arc cannon bolt had nicked his shoulder, but otherwise unharmed and thinking only of finding and then very painfully killing Jorhan Stahl. Unfortunately he wouldn't have the opportunity to torture him first. The time for the leisurely application of pain was over. He was going to have to satisfy himself with a simple kill. But at least there was that. Yes, at least there was that.

'You're bleeding to death, Stahl,' he taunted. 'You can't hide forever.'

He heard a sound and wheeled around, pointing with the cannon in the direction of the noise. Empty space yawned back at him. The silence pushed in, punctuated by the muffled explosions from the battle outside.

Where was he? That fucker. Where was he?

Meanwhile, Jorhan Stahl hid and he bided his time.

He had not spent his formative years streetfighting

and knew little about how to wield a knife effectively in combat. However, he was very good at hiding, a skill he was putting into practice at this very moment.

Watching Orlock pace the corridor looking for him brought a smile to his face even as he winced at the wound in his stomach.

Yes, the wound. Orlock was right about that. He was losing blood and would soon be too weak to move, let alone fight. He brought his hand away from the patch at his tunic and it came away red. When he looked down at himself, he saw the material darkening where the blood spread. He would need attention quickly. Couldn't hide from Orlock forever.

No, pleasing as it was to watch the autarch's frustration build, he was going to have to face him at some point. What he needed was a weapon. The floor was strewn with them. Assault rifles and arc cannons. None, sadly, in his near vicinity.

Something else then. Now his eye fell on a piece of coving that lay on the floor. Big enough and heavy enough to . . . he smiled, imagining it making contact with the autarch's ugly bald head.

Yes, that would do very nicely, thank you very much.

Grimacing slightly with the pain, he crouched and his fingers felt for the coving. Further up the corridor Orlock had his back to him, still trying to tempt him out of hiding. Now he turned, just as Stahl's fingers had closed round the piece of metal and he'd brought it to him, standing in his hiding place, waiting for Orlock to reach him. Stahl savoured the moment. The autarch was fat and slow and his arrogance made him careless; he expected no fight from Jorhan Stahl. He was to be disappointed.

Now, in fact. This very second. For Orlock was level with him and Stahl chose his moment to spring out, one hand at the wound in his stomach, the other swinging the piece of coving.

And, yes, it did make a highly satisfactory sound as it made contact with Orlock's head: a sound half-way between a crack and a squelch. Stahl had swung the coving as hard as possible. Hard enough to send Orlock flying to the deck.

Surely?

But no. Orlock turned, dazed. His movements were slow, and blood was already beginning to ooze down his head. Yet he was still raising the cannon, about to fire on Stahl, and his teeth were bared in a grimace. Amazed, Stahl swung again.

Then again.

And again.

Until Orlock was at last sent flying back, spitting blood and teeth, flesh hanging from his battered head in meaty flaps. He crashed into a console with his full weight and the huge thing tottered just as the space station also lurched, hit by yet another piece of debris, and Stahl was celebrating his good fortune as autarch and console both crashed to the floor and Orlock was pinned, helpless, beneath the unit.

Stahl dropped the coving and wiped blood from his face, breathing heavily. Now he picked up his pistol and aimed it at Orlock, about to finish the job.

'*Wait*,' gasped Orlock.

Stahl paused. He smiled superciliously and awaited Orlock's next words, enjoying the sight of him flailing about, desperately trying to come up with something that might save his skin.

'Stahl, think about what you're doing,' gabbled the injured autarch. 'You're going to leave Helghan defenceless.'

Stahl stood there for a moment, expecting something more from Orlock and when nothing came snorted derisively, '*That's it?* That's the best you've got?'

He raised the gun again. Time to get this over with, he thought. He felt a painful twinge in his belly.

'Listen,' shouted Orlock, the desperation plain in his voice, 'even if you win, do you really think Helghan's enemies will give you time to rebuild?'

Orlock had seen an arc cannon nearby. It was, he thought, close enough to reach with his fingertips.

All he needed to do was keep Stahl's attention away from what his hand was doing.

So he continued, 'Look around you, Stahl. You're destroying our people.'

Stahl knew that Orlock was merely playing for time, yet it was undeniable that he spoke the truth – whether intentionally or not. Stahl glanced outside the window where Helghast was locked in deadly combat with Helghast in space. Men were indeed dying. Men who would be loyal to him, Jorhan Stahl.

He thought about it for a moment. He let his gun arm drop and the pistol clattered to the floor. Orlock watched the internal conflict play out on his face.

'Unless . . .' said Stahl, the idea coming to him, everything seeming very straightforward all of a sudden, 'what if I had no enemies left to fight? What if I used my weapons to kill *everyone* on Earth? The colonies would be terrified. They would fall into line.'

He felt pleased with himself. Why invade and occupy Earth, creating a race of people united in their hatred of him, when it would be far easier to simply wipe them all out?

Thinking about it, he very much liked that idea, and he looked from the prone, trapped body of Orlock to the Khage outside, proving itself in battle, its shield flaring as missiles bounced harmlessly off the hull. Yes, he thought, he had the weapons and the defences to take over the entire universe. And as for the senate? He chuckled to himself.

'And I wouldn't need *your* help,' he said, pointing at Orlock who, in that moment, knew he was dead unless he acted straight away. And with a grunt of effort he twisted just enough to snatch at the gun by his side, sliding it towards himself as quickly as he could then half-rising to fire . . .

. . . where Stahl had been standing.

But was no longer there.

From the other side came a low, febrile chuckle and Orlock looked over to see Stahl holding an arc cannon on him.

Because Stahl had known exactly what it was that Orlock was doing with his pathetic creeping hand. Did he really think he could outwit Jorhan Stahl now? No, and as the autarch made his last hapless, feeble attempt to save his own greasy skin, Jorhan Stahl had skipped nimbly to one side and retrieved a much more powerful cannon, one loaded with irradiated petrusite – his baby – and brought it to bear on the autarch, enjoying the look of surprise on his face and snorting scornfully.

'Like I said,' he gloated, 'you're predictable.'

Orlock saw his death and his mouth formed an O

and in that second he at last knew fear as Jorhan Stahl chuckled and opened fire.

A bolt of petrusite leapt from the barrel of the gun and Orlock was engulfed by it. His body began to vibrate, his fingers formed claws. His mouth opened in a scream, but it was as though he was in too much agony to actually form a sound.

And then he simply exploded, leaving a Rorschach test of gore on the walkway floor around him.

Jorhan Stahl dropped the arc cannon and chuckled once more, coughing a little and wincing, but even his own pain was not going to spoil his enjoyment of the autarch's agony, and he looked over at the destroyed corpse of Orlock, slowly spreading across the metal walkway.

'Now *that* must have hurt,' he grinned.

At that moment his strike ships docked and the airlock hissed open, his men rushing into the corridor, and immediately to his aid, seeing the bloodstain at his stomach.

His commodore came to him. 'As per your orders, the weapons are primed for full deployment in Earth's atmosphere. We are ready to jump the moment you're back on board your cruiser,' he said.

Another troop urged him, 'Sir, ISA troops are approaching.'

Typical, thought Stahl. So much for Orlock's commands that they should be stopped at all costs. And he looked over at the remains of the autarch contemptuously.

'You couldn't even do that right, could you?' he spat. 'Utterly useless.'

Stahl went to move off, saying to one of his men, 'The moment we're off the station destroy it.'

'But, sir,' protested the grunt, 'the men.'

Stahl paused. 'Fuck 'em,' he said.

And with that, he left, moving towards his ship.

'We've lost gravity again,' called Rico.

'Forget it,' insisted Narville, 'the ships are dead ahead.'

We'd been taking short, shallow breaths because the atmosphere was being leeched from the space station. We didn't have much longer. Once again everything was floating: supplies, weapons, bodies, boxes, crates. It all hung in the air as we moved onward towards the strike ships. We came to some ladders and climbed up them, moving onto a different level. And finally we reached the strike ships, rushing into Pier Two just in time to see Stahl's personal ship detaching from the space station and leaving, bound, presumably, for his cruiser.

At the same time Jammer, Hooper and the rest of her team arrived, and I just had time to flash Jammer a grin before we were all boarding ships, a pair of bombers still docked. Jammer and Hooper took the cockpit of one, half the guys diving into the passenger racks; me and Rico went up front in the other, taking the rest of the guys – all that was left of us, about thirty ISA. The last few survivors.

Rico took the pilot's seat, using a keycard given to him by Jammer. I took the gunner's seat behind him and turned to check that passengers were secure. Receiving thumbs-up I faced front, getting the feel of the firing controls as Rico commenced launch checks, the cabin systems booting up and humming around us.

'Unlocking docking clamps,' said Rico.

Suddenly an alarm in the cockpit began sounding and I looked at a small radar display on my console, seeing a red blip moving towards our position. I looked up to see a strike ship moving towards us. Moving in for the kill.

The alarm became more frantic.

'*Move*,' I shouted, so loudly that Rico practically jumped as he reached and shoved the joystick forward. Any clamps still secure were taken with us as the boosters roared and the ship shot away from its moorings at the same time as the strike ship opened fire and I twisted in my seat to look out of the cockpit behind us, seeing the pier burst into flames.

Lucky escape.

I looked over to see Jammer's bomber moving away too. Over the comlink I heard a Helghast pilot shouting, 'Negative impact. Targets escaping in a stolen tactical. Firing.'

Negative impact. You better believe it, buddy. Now we're coming after your ass.

'There's the cruiser,' called Rico, pointing forward to where Stahl's huge ship hung in space. 'Plotting a course,' he added.

Next the sensors were going postal again as enemy ships – strike ships and bombers – began moving in towards our position. They were Stahl's ships *and* the Helghast military ships, I noticed. We seemed to have united the fighting Helghast factions – at least temporarily.

'The chairman is exposed,' called a Helghast pilot over the comlink.

Good, I thought, because we were after him now. I found myself grinning to hear Stahl next, scolding the pilot for talking over an open channel. I opened fire on enemy strike ships and bombers as they swooped in on us. Rico steered a path round the station and through enemy ships, using the confusion to find us a way through. Next we had visual on Stahl's cruiser. Easily the biggest thing in the sky, it dwarfed all the other vessels around it, a huge coil in the middle. Stahl's personal shuttle was heading towards it now and Rico brought us in behind it. Then the shuttle approached the green petrusite shield and passed through, and I swallowed.

We'd seen a ship's attempt to penetrate the shield and simply bounce off, and as our bomber and Jammer's ship approached it I wondered if we would suffer the same fate. Would we be repelled, bouncing off dangerously into space, or would we simply explode on the shield's surface?

We sped towards the shield.

'Rico, are you sure about this?' I said to him, leaning forward.

'No.'

'Jammer, are you sure about this?' I said over the comlink.

'Negative.'

I squeezed my eyes shut then – *whump* – we were through the shielding and opening fire on Stahl's shuttle as it manoeuvred towards the rear of the vast cruiser and into a strike-ship bay on the underside.

Jammer and Rico banked sharply, the engines humming happily as the two bombers nimbly diverted away from the main hull of the cruiser. Rico was looking at something on a read-out in front of him, frowning, and then said, 'The warp drive's online. He's going for Earth.'

Sure enough, the huge coil on the cruiser began to whirl, spooling up in order to power the FTL drive and creating a green vortex that was almost beautiful to look at. Rico was right. Stahl was heading for Earth. And if he reached it with that ship then it was sayonara Earth.

'Not going to let that happen,' I said. 'Jammer, target the guns and the engines. We'll take the other side.'

We swooped away to begin our attack run.

The Higs launched everything they could at us. But we were methodical, working on the ship's defences and banking around. Trying to target the coil to stop the ship warping away. The air around us was hot. We were buffeted by explosions, trying to move beneath their tracking to under the ship. Missile after missile went in. We heard 'hull breach on upper deck' over their comms and then Stahl ranting at his men: 'It's *two* fucking ships. *Get them*,' and that spurred us on.

'T minus fifty,' we heard. Warp launch imminent.

Still firing. The Helghast fighters were in disarray. Their pilots knew that the ship was due to warp without them and their efforts to take us out were half-hearted at best, while we took everything they could fire at us and more. Still pummelling the ship with missiles. And at last it seemed to go up. Explosions began on the underside of the ship and gradually moved along, chaining, until it seemed that the entire length of the vast cruiser was blossoms of fire.

It was a breathtaking sight: the cruiser, grey and monolithic, the green petrusite coil spinning madly out of control as around it the ship began to burn and then, very slowly, tilted forward and started to sink.

Chapter Forty-one

On the bridge of his ship Jorhan Stahl pulled himself to his feet. The FTL drive continued its countdown and as it reached the end he entertained the wild idea that the ship might simply warp, that the missile strikes had been less damaging than they'd first appeared. But then the countdown reached zero and nothing happened, and once again the Khage was shaken by a series of explosions. It lurched, everything on the bridge flying as it tipped. Ship-wide warning klaxons began sounding and the crew scrambled to emergency procedures, while on the bridge a second set of warning alarms bleeped, accompanied by the insistent blinking of lights across the displays as systems switched to cope with the power loss.

Stahl looked from one side of the bridge to the other, willing the auxiliaries to engage. The most powerful and advanced ship in the galaxy, the Khage was equipped with enough emergency protocol programming to cope. Only if the main core was disabled would the ship be in trouble. And . . . He checked. It wasn't. The main core remained online. The coil was still active.

But it was overloading, and with its circuits destroyed by the ISA missiles, was still attempting to power the FTL drive. Unsuccessfully – the FTL drive was fatally damaged – but it continued to do so, unaware of the power out across the rest of the ship.

He needed to disable the FTL drive, realized Stahl. Systems would revert to conventional combustion, and the coil would cool. They could pull out of the dive. He scrambled to the warp console, keying the override panel open.

'Chairman, you can't stop it,' shouted the commodore. 'It's too late.'

'Watch me,' snapped Stahl.

He wasn't going down, he'd decided. He was Jorhan Stahl and this was the Khage, and it was the most powerful weapon in the galaxy. It didn't get destroyed by a bunch of ISA grunts in stolen bombers. That would be just . . . *wrong*. It simply couldn't happen.

The commodore thought differently. He cast his gaze around the bridge and, seeing the hatch to Stahl's escape pod, considered simply taking it himself; it didn't look as if the chairman would be using it, after all. But then he decided against it and abandoned the bridge for escape pods elsewhere, leaving Stahl alone.

The Khage was re-entering the Helghan atmosphere now, listing at almost ninety degrees. Stahl hung on to the console. He initialized the override then raised his head to listen for the sound of the FTL drive spooling down. Still it screeched around him, and he swore and reached for a panel at the base of the console, yanking it open to reveal circuits beneath.

'Come on, come *on*,' he said, pulling at contacts desperately, taking it down the old-fashioned way, until suddenly the warp went offline and he was yelling in triumph as systems switched and the Khage began to right itself, the ground visible, moments away from impact with the space elevators and the crater on the planet face.

And he had done it. *Yes*. He had done it. *Fuck* the ISA.

Sensors bleeped, and he looked up to see incoming ordnance: a nuclear petrusite missile fired by one of the bombers stolen by . . . the ISA.

Fuck . . . the ISA.

Chapter Forty-two

I guess I fired because I couldn't let Stahl escape. Not with that kind of weaponry onboard. The question I ask myself now is that if I'd known what was going to happen to Helghan, would I still have fired?

My missile went straight into the main core and his ship exploded in a burst of green that burned our eyes. Space boiled. Everything went white and the bombers were pummelled with aftershock, Rico and Jammer suddenly forced to take evasive moves. We pulled away from the explosion, coming round in time to see tendrils of petrusite lifting from the planet surface as though sensing the presence of the great energy above and wanting to join with it.

And now the sky was torn by a great pillar of lithe petrusite that rose to join the billowing fiery shell of Stahl's destroyed cruiser. The two created an enormous secondary explosion that enveloped the space elevators and space station and at the same time engulfed the entire planet face, flooding over its surface. Taking it over.

And then the blast was heading towards us and

Rico was pulling us away in a steep climb to try to ride it out, surfing it out of danger. Around us the enemy fleet began to burn, our smaller craft staying just ahead of the bubbling death, and we saw other slower ships engulfed and exploding and then we were looking around desperately for Jammer's ship. She'd been there. Now she wasn't.

We craned our necks to look for her, Rico barking into the comlink, 'Jammer. *Jammer*,' getting more frantic, when suddenly she appeared at our side, so close we could see her grinning at us.

'Guys,' she said, 'what did I tell you about leaving before the explosions start?'

We grinned, relieved, and came back around to see Helghan – and what we saw was total devastation. The planet wore a death shroud of petrusite. Pools of it bubbled on the surface – pools that must have been hundreds of klicks wide at ground level, while the rest of the planet was cast in an oily green sheen.

'I'm not reading any comms traffic,' said Jammer, aghast.

'Yeah, we took out the whole fleet.' I don't think the enormity had sunk in for Rico yet. It was only just beginning to sink in for me and for Jammer.

'No, I mean *nothing*,' she insisted. 'The entire planet is silent.'

We looked down, wondering how many millions had just perished. The green shimmered back at us.

Death shimmered back at us.

I knew, as we banked away, that I'd be seeing Helghan burn in my nightmares for a long, long time to come. And I knew that I'd be waking up asking myself if I'd had to fire that missile. If I hadn't then Stahl would have made it to Earth, but even so . . . Yeah, I'd be thinking about that a lot, I knew.

As though Jammer was reading my thoughts, she drew up alongside me and flashed me a lopsided, reassuring smile that I returned. No doubt about it, she'd earned that beer.

Hell, I thought, as we turned and headed for home, I'd maybe even stretch to a burger too – if she was lucky.

Epilogue

There was silence. Just the low murmur of a wind that barely disturbed thick clouds of deadly petrusite hanging in layers over the ground. Through the dense fog were the barely discernible shapes of wrecked buildings, coated in green haze. Everywhere were bodies and the wrecks of vehicles, littering the entire landscape. This was Helghan now. Shrouded by green death.

Not everything was dead, though, for two hazmat troopers materialized from within the green mist. One of them was carrying a handheld sensor that had begun bleeping, and he directed it now towards an irregular shape that appeared from within the fog. In response it began bleeping more frantically.

'There,' he said simply, pointing, and the two walked over to what was lying on the ground. An escape pod.

The mist parted around them as they approached it, and as they did so there was a release of hydraulics, and the pod door slid open.

The two troopers looked inside. Both bowed their

heads; the trooper holding the sensor was the first to speak.

'Welcome home, sir,' he said.

Acknowledgements

Hermen Hulst
Arjan Brussee
Jan-Bart van Beek
Michiel van der Leeuw
Angie Smets
Brant Nicholas
Lambert Wolterbeek Muller
Paul-Jon Hughes
Mathijs de Jonge
Rob Heald
Victor Zuylen
Aryeh Loeb
Chris Weatherhead
Steven ter Heide
Andrew Holmes
Alice Shepherd